Cl[illegible]

Snee[illegible]g

Portraits of women by women

Lee Jackson, Editorial Director

FIRST EDITION

Melius Scripto Press International, Ltd

MELIUS SCRIPTO
PRESS INTERNATIONAL

Cover: Quirky Queen Illustrations by Gaynor Adkins

For more information, contact Melius Scripto Press International, Ltd., Kemp House, 160 City Road, London, EC1V 2NX, United Kingdom.

Visit: http://www.meliusscriptopress.com

Published 2026

ISBN: 978-1-9999258-3-3 Paperback

ISBN: 978-1-9999258-4-0 Ebook

Cloud Sneezing
Portraits of women by women
Melius Scripto Press International, Ltd

FOREWORD

This collection of stories, written by seven exceptional story tellers, is a mixture of fiction and memoir, with some poems too. *Cloud Sneezing*, which takes its title from the last story in the collection, the uplifting 'Sneezing in the Clouds' are written by women in full force of their voices.

In its pages you will find stories of the feminine, told by a sisterhood of women, about all the journeys along the road that women travel, journey through, and endure. An endurance of triumphs both big and small, in which they articulate what it is to be a woman. As Rose Campbell-Smith puts it in her aptly titled poem 'Waves of Sisterhood' these women have stories 'of healing, of sisterhood, of courage'.

At once triumphant, amusing, and uplifting, they don't shirk from the hard-hitting subjects that are also what it is to be a woman. Stories that include motherhood poignantly told, the suffering and cruelty caused by the sixteenth-century witch-hunts, and the suffragettes who chose to fight back and not to fear. In a rich variety of voices that encompass the compassionate, the seductive and the spirit of hope, the characters tell the stories that only women can, with their fearless, life-giving resilience.

The influence and the wisdom that form the backgrounds of these women writers is palpable. With generations of women that have gone before, mothers and grandmothers, they pay homage to the power, guidance and inspiration they have had, taking form in the craft of storytelling.

Mothers feature in varying guises. We have the secrets, loyalty, and familial discord portrayed in 'Red Suede Heels' by Laura Scott. The everyday demands of breast-feeding and the expectation of support from mothers and husbands in the ironic 'Mother's Day' by Michele Hinchliffe and, on another spectrum, the deeply visceral and heart-wrenching story 'The Dance' set in 1980s Arkansas by Robin Montgomery-Smith.

All facets of women are portrayed in the themes of this collection. Themes such as mental illness, amusingly yet sympathetically portrayed in Heather Grossart's 'Cuckoo' and the gently poignant story of dementia in Aimee McGowan's 'Beetroot'. The strange vernacular of a world set in the future in Charity Reed's 'In Search of Strawberries'. Rose Campell-Smith's evocative 'Untangling Time' portrays the weaver of time, who spins the thread of existence itself to 'untangle what was, what is, and what might yet be' who meets her reluctant apprentice.

I had the pleasure of teaching some of these women in The Open University's Advanced Creative Writing course, where all their hard work and determination has borne fruit. Often balancing jobs and domestic commitments, they are the outcome of what Mary Wollstonecraft advocated for all those centuries ago. Allowing for an educational system that included women, with the same advantages as men, would see women capable of anything they put their mind to, to the benefit of all society.

I commend this anthology to you. The courageous and uplifting variety of these women's voices, bear testament to the female, and all that she embodies, and all that she is capable of being.

Doctor Irene Hossack
Lecturer, The Open University
Great Britain

INTRODUCTION

SISTERS OF AUDACITY
By Charity Reed

We write of women in our wee stories
their lives, their deaths, their downfalls, their glories—
we write for those without a voice, who burned
as witches, and we write for those who turned

the tables, and we write for those who loved
and lost, and those who—when push came to shove—
fought back, plodded on, did all that they could
for children, husbands and the greater good.

We weep for the weak, we shout of the strong
of those who suffered, of those who were wronged,
those whose heads pushed above the parapet,
women whose stories have not been told yet.

Women with loyalty, hope, tenacity,
all women – the sisters of audacity.

The authors of this book met whilst studying creative writing at the Open University. We formed a group that met to critique each other's assignments and soon realised that we had an awful lot of stories about women, written by women. This seemed a good premise for an anthology, so along with another OU graduate of graphic design, we found a wonderful publishing company, Melius Scripto Press International who was willing to take a chance on us, and here we are.

Our WhatsApp group had the working title *Sisters of Audacity* so that's how we've come to describe ourselves—after all, we did have the audacity to imagine we could do this.

Our aim has never been to create female characters that are perfect—far from it—but women, just like men, have their own unique stories, and here we try to tell some of them.

This is a mixture of fiction and memoir, stories and vignettes, with a couple of poems thrown in. It's as diverse in content as the women who created it, and we hope you enjoy reading it as much as we've enjoyed writing it.

If you're wondering about the title, please refer to 'Sneezing in the Clouds' by Robin Montgomery-Smith—and remember to always lift up those around you.

CONTENTS

FOREWORD v
INTRODUCTION vii
CONTENTS ix
20lb. 13s. 4d. by Aimee McGowan 1
Five Find a Body by Charity Reed 8
The Glistening Man by Robin Montgomery-Smith 15
Launch Day by Laura Scott 25
Red Suede Heels by Laura Scott 28
A Perfect Arrangement by Charity Reed 39
Cuckoo by Heather Grossart 46
I Waited for You by Robin Montgomery-Smith 59
Beetroot by Aimee McGowan 76
A Rare Night In by Laura Scott 83
Phoenix Rising by Rose Campbell-Smith 89
In Search of Strawberries by Charity Reed 96
My Bridge to Nowhere by Rose Campbell-Smith 107
Mother's Day by Michele Hinchliffe 108
Reflections by Charity Reed 112
Josie's Secret by Robin Montgomery-Smith 119
Close to the Edge by Laura Scott 126
Untangling Time by Rose Campbell-Smith 133
It Only Took One by Aimee McGowan 139
Mary Mary by Michele Hinchliffe 144
A Chat with Pat by Rose Campbell-Smith 151

The Dance by Robin Montgomery-Smith 153
Life Is Sweet by Heather Grossart 160
This Is Where We Are Now by Michele Hinchliffe 168
Hope by Charity Reed 174
What We Remember by Aimee McGowan 181
A Moment of Grief by Laura Scott 188
The Witch That Never Burnt by Rose Campbell-Smith 191
A Grandmother's Love Is Forever and Always by Rose Campbell-Smith 198
Sneezing In the Clouds by Robin Montgomery-Smith 203
MEET THE SISTERS 209
- Rose Campbell-Smith 210
- Heather Grossart 211
- Michele Hinchliffe 212
- Aimee McGowan 213
- Robin Montgomery-Smith 214
- Charity Reed 215
- Laura Scott 216
- Gaynor Adkins 217
- Lee A. Jackson 218

AFTERWORD: The View from the Clouds 219
- WAVES OF SISTERHOOD by Rose Campbell-Smith . 220
- Scottish Women's Aid 221
- Acknowledgements 222

20lb. 13s. 4d.
by Aimee McGowan

Aberdeenshire, 1597

'Did ye hear, Isobel?' Willie came barrelling around the corner, puffing and panting.

'Hear what?' It was a small village, and news travelled fast, but I hadn't spoken to a soul all morning.

'They've took John!' He tried his best to whisper but it came out more like a shout as he doubled over, lungs desperately trying to pull air in.

'What dae ye mean, took?' I asked, letting my basket rest at my feet, its light weight was suddenly too heavy to hold.

'They've got him, Isobel! Si'd he helped the witches.' His face had turned wan, and the rouge from his haste to reach me was nowhere to be found.

'Surely no. John's harmless!' I could feel my stomach drop so it felt like it might land at my feet, alongside my basket. It was the smithy's family they'd taken just the month before last. I didn't expect more so soon.

'Aye. They've got him. A dinna ken what to do. Isobel, they canna kill John. He's done nothin' but try and keep his family goin'.' His chest heaved as his lungs tried desperately to fill. I touched his arm lightly, trying to calm him; upset would only get him into trouble too.

'Absolutely nothin' you kin do, Willie. No without drawin' them to you, tae. Where's Norma? And wee Elspet?' They didn't keep well, his family. That wouldn't count for anythin' though. Once they take ye, there's no way out, 'cept in a box. The best ye could hope was that you were already deid when they burnt you.

'Why don't ye go over tae the church and pray for them? They'll all need it.' I racked my brain to find something, anything to help him feel like he was helping. But it was true, there was no such thing as comfort for witches, or their accomplices.

'If it's aw the same, I'd rather stick 'round here. Eh. If it's OK with you, a mean?' he replied.

'It's ok wae me, but I've got broth tae finish, and tea to get made. If you're sticking round here, you kin make yoursel' useful.' I pushed open the door to my small cabin and set the basket on the table in the middle of the room, 'Here.' I handed him a bunch of lavender stalks, 'Shake these outside and get the beasties off.'

I watched him slowly make his way to the back of the garden, shaking the stalks back and forward like he was casting out the Devil himself.

'Willie! You'll knock all the flowers off doin' it like that! Need tae be gentle!'

I looked out to the field behind and saw the birds lifting, something about the way they flew caught my eye. It felt different; like they knew some poor sod would be meetin' their maker soon.

He was a decent man, oor John. Kept the inn going, which kept the village going. Poor Norma. There was no way she could cope without him. She was sickly—pale, weak and slow, if ye catch my meaning. I'd been dropping off broth and beetroots to her regularly to try and help, but I'm no healer. I do what I can, but that's no sayin' much. Though my lavender tea helped a bit with calming her when she took a turn.

'Here Isobel, this 'bout right?' said Willie, careful to catch any of the flowers he'd loosened off with his shakin' as he bent to fit in the doorway.

'Fine, Willie. Thanks. Give them here.' I took them and put a couple of handfuls into the pot of hot water, letting them steep for a bit. He watched my movements carefully, his face blank. I caught the slightest tear trying to escape his eye, but he swatted it away before I could say anything.

'It's no right, what they're doin'. We're decent folk here. Havna' done no harm tae nabdy. Go to church, live a prop'r Christian life, that's all we do.' He looked at his feet, which seemed to give him strength because when he looked back up, he had a wild look in his eye, 'Whits the world comin' tae where ye canna speak your mind without bein' 'cused a Devil's worship.' He spoke quietly, but his voice had an edge to it, one I wasn't sure I liked the sound of. Talk like that was never quiet enough.

'Hod your wheesht, Willie! Ye want them tae come for you too?' My eyes darted to the window, then the door. We were silent, two statues scared to move, scared to breathe. We waited—sure the door was goin' to burst open any second. There wasn't a sound outside, only the steady thud of my heart as it clattered its way up my throat to my ears. A few seconds slipped by before I could loose my breath.

'A ken what your sayin' Willie, but you cannae say things like that, no unless you want to bring the trouble tae your own door.' I strained the flowers out and put the tea in the pots. I tried to disguise the shakin' in my hands, but I was only foolin' myself. We were all uptight these days.

'I'm off to see Norma and Elspet, make sure they're alright, given the news. I wouldna' think it'd be a good idea for you to come,' I said, grabbing my shawl off the stool and pulling it tight around me, suddenly feeling a chill that I hadn't noticed earlier.

'Aye, you're probably right. They'll no be in the mood fir much comp'ny. I'll nip doon the courthouse, see if a cannae see John afore it happens. Might help; knowin' someone cares,' he said, handing me the pots off the table.

'Keep your chin up, Willie.' I tried to smile, but his eyes dimmed, and that tiny spark of hope he'd conjured with his last words vanished from them.

The village, usually bustling with activity, everyone goin' about their chores, was dead. Not a soul could be seen, not even the cats that lingered outside the bakers, meowing for crumbs. It was a ghost town. A mist had settled in, sucking up all the sounds, it scarcely seemed that anyone lived there at all. I pulled my shawl a little tighter, trying to keep the damp kiss of mist off my arms, and tried to keep to the side of the road.

I hadn't reached Norma's door yet when I heard voices—too low to make out who it was. I went to the window to check, make sure I wasn't burstin' in on prayers or the like, but it was just the girls in.

'Norma? Elspet? It's Isobel, I got some tea for you. I was hopin' it might help a bit.'

A second or two later the door opened and Elspet ushered me inside, silent all the while. Norma was sat at the table, like a spirit instead of a woman.

'Oh, Norma,' I couldn't help the pity in my voice, my heartstrings snapping at the sight of her. Shrugging off my shawl as I put the pots on the table, I made my way to her. She was utterly still, face blank and grey. Her ringed and puffy eyes stared on, a cloud covering them. Her pink nose was the only source of colour on her face. She didn't move when I hugged her. Didn't so much as blink. I looked at Elspet, the bairn had lines on her face that were usually reserved for those a bit older and wiser.

'Elspet, fetch a couple of mugs for me, lass.' I lit the fire, and she handed me the mugs, her fingers brushing mine lightly. She was stone-cold! I pulled my shawl off the stool, and wrapped her up, sitting her in front of the fire. She gave the smallest of smiles when I passed her the mug, hugging its warmth into her chest.

I turned back to Norma. She hadn't lifted her gaze off whatever she was staring at.

'Norma, kin you hear me?'

If she could, she didn't let on. No flicker of consciousness showed on her marble face. I touched her hand, and much like Elspet's, it was frozen. I rubbed them both gently, but she still made no move, no sound, the only sign she was alive was the slow, rasping sound of her breathing. She eventually moved her eyes, just the slightest, towards me. I'd never experienced being held in death's thrall until then. I inched back, my boot the loudest sound in the cabin. Forcing myself forward, I reached out to check her temperature. Her brow was cold, like her hands, but had a light sweat upon it.

'How long has she been like this?' I asked Elspet, who'd made short work of her tea.

'Since they took Pa,' she said, putting down her mug, 'I didna ken what to do.'

'OK. Pop over to Mrs Baxter's and see what she has left. If she's any oatcakes, they'd be grand. 'Think your ma just needs a little somethin' in her belly.' She nodded and ran off.

'Norma, I'm gonna need you to move your fingers for me. Can you do that?' I asked, my voice steady, though she was scaring the wits out of me.

'Norma,' I rubbed my hands over her arms, slowly, then propped her feet up. I'd seen people in states before after a shock, it helped to get the blood goin' again.

'Norma, I need to get you warmed up, can you drink some o' your tea for me?' Still, nothing. 'Come on, Norma. You cannae leave Elspet on her tod now. Get yourself warmed up.' This seemed to move her a little more and her eyes moved towards the mug.

'That's it. Nice and slow. Here, a'll hold it.' I grabbed my shawl back from Elspet's stool and wrapped her feet up in it, holding the mug under her nose. Sure enough, she dipped her head a little, ready for a sip. Elspet came back with a few oatcakes and put one on her ma's knee.

'Thanks, lass, just needs a bit of takin' care a', that's all.' She didn't look at me or reply, instead sitting with her back to me at the fire.

Suddenly Norma jumped up, spat out the oatcake and began to heave like she was going to be sick, but there was nothing in her stomach to bring up.

'No, no, no, no, no, no,' she wailed, over and over, crumping down on the floor, the tea spilling all over the table. I sat down beside her and tried to help her up, but she wouldnae be moved. Not an inch. It only made her wail louder, the closer I got, the worse she was. The door burst open.

'Whit in the Lord God's name is goin' on in here?' Members of the council flooded into the cabin, all in their official robes,

'She's had a shock, Laird, I think.' I jumped up from the floor, feeling like a bairn who'd been caught stealin' the honey.

'You! You've bewitched her!' The council's looks had turned to icy stares as the words raked down my skin.

'What?' The words slapped me in the face.

'Ye waited 'til she was vulnerable, then set about her wae your Devil's worship!' the council elder spat the words out, his face redder by the minute, cheeks bouncing as he cried, 'Witch!'

The villagers outside went still. They knew what that word meant. Elspet, who had been sitting on the stool near the fire hadn't moved, hadn't so much as turned in the commotion. They grabbed me and dragged me into the street, my legs fumbled uselessly behind me, the stones opening the skin on my ankles as they hauled me down towards the square. Their chants started again, slowly at first, just the elders, but it picked up, like a plague catching my neighbours, my friends, each drawn into the rising frenzy. When we reached the square, they dragged me to the well and bound my hands behind my back. I'd lost a shoe, and my dress had ripped open at the shoulder. My hands begged to be free to cover myself.

The crowd had whipped itself up by now, the shouts turning acrid.

'She cursed the Fowlers!'

'She cured the sheep wae her devilry!'

These were my friends, the people I'd tried to help, the ones who came to me when someone was ill or needed fixing and they couldn't afford to pay a healer. I'd helped almost everyone in the village. But none of that mattered anymore. My kindness had been taken and twisted, moulded into something horrid and unnatural. A couple of the older kids in the crowd hurled mud pats. One struck true, right across my brow. It must have had something inside because my head suddenly plummeted, wetness pouring down my face. My eyes stung, and it wasn't just from the tears, as my vision became blurred.

A shadow passed by, just out of view, though I couldn't be sure it wasn't just the blood, but when I turned, I saw John, limping away slowly from the court-house, Elspet helping to steady him. His face crumpled when he caught my stare, trying to shake Elspet off, but she held fast and manoeuvred him out of sight. My heart felt like it might break. Had Elspet done this to me?

'Isobel Skuddie, you have been accused. What say you?' The Laird mocked, stepping up onto the wall above me. We all knew there was nothing I could say.

'I am no witch. I am your neighbour, your friend.' I tried to instil my innocence into each word, but it was useless. My chin began to chatter uncontrollably, teeth knocking.

'You have been accused of using unholy magics to bewitch the village. You asked Elspet Mutray for a penny, which she gave, then you took the penny and placed it in a cloth. You enchanted that cloth and gave it to the said Elspet Mutray, bidding her to hang the same about her neck. Elspet understanding that the direction was plain witchcraft and devilry, cast the cloth in the fire. You cannot deny this love charm was Devil's magic!' he had worked himself up, his words becoming almost screamed by the end.

'No, I didn't, we were playing, Elspet was looking for comfort, I tried to help her. It was … not witchcraft. A game. I—I—' I couldn't think straight. Of course, it was silly, but she had been heartbroken that Thomas had rejected her, I just wanted to give her some hope.

'Guilty!' he growled, his smile showing his yellowed teeth.

The crowd went wild at his words, jeering, throwing mud pats and clambering over each other to scratch and pull at me. I was thrown into the courthouse, locked in a cage and left. It occurred to me that the world was a harsh place. They say God's love is all around, but all I saw was fear. It was fear that led to accusations. It was fear that made them round up whole families and kill them. Was it not Elspet's fear that led to my conviction? Of losing her father? I couldn't blame her, for he was all they could rely on. How many men and women would have to die before this madness came to an end? I was scared myself, I'd seen what they did to witches. They drowned them and burnt them, and those were ones who made it to their execution. The ones who didn't died from cold, starvation, or torture beforehand. I was terrified, but they would not see my fear. No matter how horrific my end would be, I would not choose fear.

Five Find a Body
by Charity Reed

'Eeew! What is that?' Jenny looked as shocked and disgusted as I felt.

We all stared at the turquoise cardigan and long ginger curls we'd uncovered.

'It looks like hair. Oh shit, I think it's a body.' I stopped scraping with my plastic spade, and we all went quiet for a moment.

'It can't be a body.'

'Well, what the hell is it then?'

'It's definitely hair.'

'Could be a wig?'

I was the eldest, and it was me that had discovered it—discovered her, so I felt responsible for the situation. 'It feels like real hair, and it's definitely a lady's cardi. We'll have to find out.' I continued digging, albeit with less enthusiasm, and some amount of reverence, until I felt the spade hit bone.

It's a strange experience when you realise, at 13 years old, that you have stumbled across a crime. Not just any crime, not the type of petty crime we were used to when Spug, Gareth and Tubby would break into the electricity metres on the estate, stealing the fifty pence pieces, or someone would spray 'School Is shit' or 'daran was ere' or 'All cops Are basteds' on the wall of the bottom café—we all knew that was Johnno by his inability to spell 'school' or 'Darren' or 'bastards' correctly. This was real. It was chilling. It was like something out of a book. We carefully scraped at the wet bank with our hands.

This had been my idea. I'd decided to see if it was true that if you dig deep enough, you'd hit water. My inherent laziness led to me experimenting by the river, as I concluded I wouldn't have to dig so deep if there was water nearby. Very resourceful thinking in my opinion. Anyway, that had been an hour before and so far, we'd failed to find water and come across the body instead.

We were on one of the many little bits of riverbank along the stretch of the Pennine Way that follows the South Tyne from Tynehead fell just a few miles up the valley, through the town where we lived, eventually joining the Tyne proper and ending up flowing into the North Sea at Newcastle. We spent every summer in that river, no matter if there was 'snow on the tops', despite a stark warning from Alice's mother that we should never enter the water if there was or we'd catch our deaths. If the sun was out, we would be in that water. We called it 'the sandy beach' locally despite the lack of real sand. In actual fact it's a bit stony, a bit grassy, and often muddy—but that's what we called it, and I suppose that particular mud is more sand than clay so maybe that's where we got it from. There are many swimming spots along the river, but the sandy beach was our usual choice back then—partly through accessibility, it was a two-minute walk for those of us that lived on the nearby housing estate—and partly because it only came up to our chests, so parents didn't bat an eyelid. A year or two later I'd be old enough to join the 'big kids' in the deep, dark, hitherto forbidden, depths of the Black Pool, but not yet.

We scrabbled at it carefully, fearing what we were disturbing, but having to make sure. I noticed that our voices had become hushed, and I could hear the warbling song of a dipper in the river as we worked in solemn contemplation. I'm not sure if we did that consciously or if it was just a natural fear, excitement, or veneration for the dead that drove it. I knew it was bone I'd hit, but something seemed wrong. 'This can't be a skull,' I said to the others as we uncovered the hard hairy sphere, still covered in cartilage and muscle.

'How comes?' asked Alice.

'It's too small. It feels like a knee-cap, but it's got the hair on.' I was as confused as I was mesmerised by our discovery. I'm weirdly squeamish about blood, but this dead thing didn't bring that out in me, rather a fascination that has stayed with me to this day. Blood makes me squirm because I know it's linked to pain;

death is a different matter. I'd make a great pathologist if I was scientifically inclined.

'Maybe it's a kid,' someone suggested.

We all stopped. I really hoped it wasn't.

'We'll have to go to the police before we disturb it any more.' I wiped my hands on the damp moss of a nearby rock and turned to the others. 'This is too big. We have to tell them.'

Everyone agreed. I knew they would. I've always been the smallest in any group I'm in, even as an adult I never made it past 'five-foot-nowt', as we say in these parts. In fact, at that point in my life I was wearing hand-me-downs from Jane, my sister three years my junior—total embarrassment. However, I have also always had the biggest mouth and was generally elected unofficial leader of whatever group I happened to be in at the time, mainly because I was so arrogant I didn't think anyone else was up to the job, so I just took charge. And anyway, in this case I was the nearest thing to an adult, so they took their cues from me.

'Someone will have to guard her,' someone suggested.

'Me and Alice will go to the police; we're the oldest. Jane, you and Jenny and Jillian can guard the body.'

'Okay,' my little sister replied, 'me, Jen, and Jill will look after her.'

'Jane do *not* disturb her anymore. Leave it all exactly like this. There might be forensics.' I barked the order, a diminutive sergeant major.

'Yeah,' said Jane, not looking at all convinced she could follow this order if curiosity got the better of her. 'Hey, Lea,' she suddenly looked at me with an odd expression on her face, half fear, half excitement. 'What if the murderer comes back?'

I hadn't thought of this and considered it for a moment. On the one hand, I really didn't want to look like an idiot if I dragged the Sergeant all the way down from the police station, only to find some homicidal maniac had returned to retrieve his victim and knowing the police would never believe it had ever been there, on the other, not wanting my sister to meet the same grisly end as the red-haired corpse.

'Get the hell out of here if anyone dodgy turns up.' I'd made the right decision, best of both worlds. Janey would be safe if she just legged it. She might be an annoying brat, but she was my annoying brat and probably the most important thing in my world at that time.

'Okay. Don't be too long,' she said, and moved herself into position, along with the twins, Jenny and Jilly, three little sentries, sitting in a circle to keep best watch at the graveside.

Alice and I scrambled up the bank. We were full of questions. 'Who do you think it is?' she asked me.

'No idea. Has anyone gone missing? Anyone's wife suddenly "left them"?' I did the quotation marks with my fingers. We racked our brains for a few minutes and walked in silence up through the shade of the beeches in the wood, past the *Pennie Way* sign—it really said *Pennine Way* but I'd misread it as a small child and always thought of it as the Pennie Way—up towards the cobbled Main Street and the police station at the top of the town.

'I bet it's Mr Catchpoll's wife.' Alice was adamant in her choice of killer once he had occurred to her.

'I didn't know he was married, are you sure he has a wife?'

'I don't know, but if he does, he'd definitely kill her. Probably with a carving knife.'

I wasn't convinced. Mr Catchpoll was an old man who lived in a house on Park Terrace. We'd have to pass his house on the way to primary school every day before we'd moved up to secondary, and we baited the poor guy terribly with knocky-nine-doors and other childish tortures. We only did it because he'd give chase, not because he'd ever done anything terrible to us. Honestly, I'd always felt bad about our treatment of him, but you don't tell other kids that at that age or you're next.

'Could be. He is an old bastard,' I agreed, though guilty and half-hearted in my statement.

'It's definitely him, I bet you a quid.' There was no shaking her conviction on this.

I said nothing more as we reached the town hall and cut through the grounds onto the long lonnen, the quickest way up the steep hill. We were out of breath but didn't slow down, I was sure the younger girls keeping watch would get distracted playing in the river if we were gone too long, leaving our poor dead woman to the ravages of wild beasts, other older kids, or worse, her killer if he returned to the scene of the crime.

We finally reached the top of the hill and rounded the corner, passing Betty's shop, where we'd normally nip in for sweets or pop, but not today. Our mission was too important. The cop-shop was quiet but there was a police car outside, so we knew it was occupied, and we banged the huge brass knocker on the door. It was one of those old Victorian buildings, opened in 1850 as a local lock-up, and stood on a hill at the top of the town—I'd learned that the week before in Miss Mundy's history class. It was certainly imposing for the errant child who was unlucky enough to be dragged up there after being caught trespassing or shoplifting sweets from the penny mix-up boxes in the paper shop, Betty's, or Cathy's Cafe. You could get twenty half-penny sweets for ten pence in those emporiums in 1984, but to us kids even ten pence was hard to come by, so these crimes happened. It was certainly imposing enough for two thirteen-year-olds on our way to do our civic duty and report a serious crime.

The huge door creaked as it opened, and I suddenly felt a little foolish as I told the Sergeant, who could put the fear into the toughest of inebriated miners in our little community, 'we've found a body, we've come to report a murder.'

'A murder, eh?' asked the Sergeant. He had a smirk on his face, and even at that age I could tell he thought we were making it up.

'We're not lying!' I was vehement, I've always hated being accused of lying.

'Okay, okay. It's just not the kind of town you expect to get a murder. It's a bit out of our usual duties,' he said mustering as much gravitas as he could, but he was still amused, and I felt patronised.

'Come and see for yourself. It's a body, I felt the bone and hair myself. It was disgusting.'

'Okay lasses, I'll come down with you, you lead the way.'

I was relieved he had agreed to come but didn't much believe that he was taking any of this seriously. I was sure if this was *The Sweeney* they would have put us in the back of a fast car and screeched down the road in a hail of bullets, rather than the gentle amble we were on.

Janey and the twins were still on guard, I saw with some relief when we got back, albeit whilst practising the moves to Agadoo beside the hole in the sand. I'd half expected them to be catching fish or trying to get across to the other side of the river on the slippery rocks without falling in, leaving the poor corpse all alone to whatever fate might befall her, so the dancing was a relief.

'Here she is,' I told the Sergeant, as I brushed the sand aside to expose her.

I actually saw his face drain for a minute, realisation that maybe these stupid girls were right as he clocked the auburn hair in the muck.

'Right kids, get back,' he said, suddenly sounding serious at last. Before he went any further, he got out his little black notepad and asked us why we were there and why we were digging—pretty stupid questions for a bunch of kids on a sunny day with buckets and spades by a river I thought at the time, but I supposed it was his job.

We explained everything that had led up to the grisly find and he wrote it down dutifully. He had brought a crowbar with him which he now used to scrape further and expose more of the remains. We were silent as he worked away at it like an amateur archaeologist. First the cardigan came fully into view, the Sergeant looking more and more concerned as it did so. Then he hit the bone that I'd been so confused about. It was barely bigger than a tennis ball and it had felt, to me, as though this was where the red hair was attached. But surely it would be attached to the skull, and this was far too small.

'It's not a kid, is it?' asked one of the twins.

'Can't be, nobody's gone missing,' said the other.

'Could be one of the gypsy kids, Appleby Fair has just been on, and they've been around,' said Alice. She was just full of theories. I rolled my eyes at her and turned my attention to the policeman.

'Now girls, let's not get ahead of ourselves,' the Sergeant told them.

I could see that he was as confused as me now that he'd uncovered more and felt the body for himself. I was feeling smug that I'd been the first to discover this, even before any grown-ups had got involved, and pleased to see that the conundrum was not lost on this seasoned professional.

Suddenly I saw something dawn on him. His face relaxed and the worried expression disappeared. 'You know, I think it's a dog.'

I was pretty disappointed, I can tell you! All that excitement and potential intrigue for a damn dog. Sure enough, as he tugged at the cardigan and got further into the burial site, we could see that it was a Cocker spaniel, explaining why the skull was so small. Bedraggled wet red hair stuck to the lifeless cadaver, probably buried within the last day or two judging by the lack of decomposition.

Suddenly the horror of a wanton killer gave way to a sadness for whoever had lost their family pet. Sympathy washed over me, and I felt bad for them, and guilty for desecrating the grave. I still felt indignant at the laughing policeman, once again talking to us like we were idiots for expecting the worst. But I'd seen the look of panic on his face, just for a minute when he first saw it. We weren't the only ones that had murder on our minds. Unlike many adults, kids tend to be honest about it.

As the Sergeant walked off back to the station, his warning about over-active imaginations still ringing, Alice, Jane and I left the twins and walked home, a little disappointed with the eventual anti-climactic resolution to our adventure.

'Mr bloody Catchpoll,' I shook my head at Alice. 'You dickhead.'

The Glistening Man
by Robin Montgomery-Smith

Arkansas, USA, 1993

Three police cars, their lights flashing, blocked the road on our way home. Jake pulled the car over to the side, got out, and reached for his badge from the back pocket of his jeans. I rolled the window down so I could listen to the conversation.

'Everything OK?' he asked as he flipped the cover open to show his identification.

'You're out your home patch, son.'

'Yeah, well, we live over there,' he pointed to our house less than a block away.

'Ah. I see. Seems your neighbour's had a bit of a problem.'

'What kind of problem?'

'The kind of problem that'll get him arrested for trying to kill his wife.'

Three officers led a tall man, glistening with what I assumed was sweat, from the front door. His hands were behind his back and there was blood covering his dirty white shirt. I covered my mouth.

'That's not his, ma'am. His wife's, unfortunately,' the officer said as he leaned around my husband. 'She's in that ambulance, there.' He pointed with the mic from his radio.

'Is she going to be OK?' I was curious and worried. I knew her but not her husband. She would often sit outside her house in a lawn chair whilst her children played in the front yard.

'Looks that way. She's beat up pretty bad, though.'

The glistening man lifted his head in an upwards nod at Jake.

'Hey, you! Tell them I ain't done nuthin' here. Get 'em ta let me go, buddy.'

'I ain't your buddy. This isn't my jurisdiction anyway.'

'Aw, c'mon. Tell 'em you know me, brother.'

'I don't know you. I'm not your brother, either.'

One of the officers put his right hand on top of the glistening man's head as he guided him into the back seat of one of the cars. He bent over to put a seat belt across the man's middle, then slammed the door.

'Y'all can go on through to your house, if you want. We'll be done here as soon as DHS shows up for the kids.'

Jake sat back down in the car, and we drove the rest of the way home. I watched as they drove the glistening man away, turned the corner, and headed north towards the county jail.

After dinner, Jake dressed for work. He had been on night shift—from eleven until seven the next morning. As a patrol officer, he was home late more often than he was home on time. I packed a lunch for him, and he kissed our three-year-old daughter, Holly, as she slept. I walked him outside and watched the lights from the back of his car disappear around the corner. He always left about nine-thirty, to give himself time to drive the busy route into the city, get parked up, and find out where his patrol was for the night.

The house was quiet. My abdomen was uncomfortable in my advanced state of pregnancy, so I shifted around on the sofa until I gave up and decided to go to bed. I walked around the house, switching off lights, checking the locks on the doors, and was about to walk down the hallway to my bedroom when the phone rang.

What did he forget this time? I answered the phone, expecting it to be Jake, explaining he forgot something which was vital for his work and to have it ready for him to drop by and pick up in his patrol car.

It wasn't Jake.

'Can I speak to Officer Skipton?'

'I'm sorry. He's sleeping, early shift tomorrow. Can I take a message?' I never announced to strangers over the phone that I was on my own.

'Uh, yeah, this is Officer Thompson, with the North Little Rock Police Department. Officer Skipton has some unpaid parking tickets, and I need to discuss it with him. Can you wake him up?'

I knew Jake never went into North Little Rock. I also knew that the police never made calls like this, especially this late at night. I tried to hide the suspicion in my voice.

'It's ten-thirty at night. It can wait 'til tomorrow. If you give me your number, I'll pass on the message to him in the morning.' I felt my face flush as fear crept into my entire body.

'I'll only be a minute. Go on, wake him up.'

'I'll give him the message in the morning. I'm not waking him for traffic tickets.'

There was a long pause on the other end of the line.

'Olivia, I know you're alone. But you won't be for long.'

The click from the other end felt as if it were an explosion. My head pounded with every beat my heart completed. I stood frozen in the hallway for a few seconds to try and work out what to do next. It was as if a voice in my head dictated my next steps.

The gun.

I rushed into the bedroom and opened the drawer next to my husband's side of the bed. My breath was shaky, but I was in control of every motion. After fumbling around for the piece of masking tape which stuck the key underneath the drawer, I ripped it off, ran across the room, and threw open the doors to the closet. Underneath a pile of folded bedsheets, I felt around until I found two boxes and pulled them out into the floor. My movements were sure and even, as I pushed the key into the hole of one box and heard it click. I pushed the lid open and lifted the foam cover which rested on its cutout counterpart—the cutout in the shape of a Glock forty calibre handgun. I picked it up. The short, black plastic stock fit into my grip as if it were made for my hand. I used the same key to open the second box which held the magazine, full of bullets. Without thinking, I pushed the magazine up into the hole in the stock, pulled back the action and heard a single bullet load itself into the barrel. It was ready to fire. The magazine held fifteen rounds, but with one in the chamber, I released the magazine and loaded another single bullet to give me sixteen rounds in total, then replaced the magazine back into the stock.

The voice on the other end of the phone was a threat. He'd let me know he knew Jake was away and he had one of two things planned. He was either trying to scare me—*and a fucking good job he did*—or he was letting me know he was coming for me. As I held the gun in my hand, now heavy with the ammunition loaded, I thought, *the bastard will have to get past me and this gun first.*

I reached for the phone, which I had tossed onto the end of my bed. I called Jake's pager. That was always the most efficient way to reach him when he was on patrol. In the past, when he received a page from me, he pulled over and used a pay phone to call me back. As I hung up, a loud vibration rattled the bedside table—Jake had left his pager at home! I let out a yelp when the pager went off, because it startled me and because I knew that was my only way to reach him.

With every move I made, calculated and composed, I flipped through the address book in my bedside table and located the non-emergency number for his police department. I pressed the numbers into the phone. A controlled female voice answered the call.

'Little Rock non-emergency. How can I help?'

'I really need to reach my husband. His name is Jake Skipton, and he is on patrol tonight. It's an emergency. I'm his wife, Olivia.'

'Hang on a sec. Lemme see where he's at. I'm going to put you on hold for a few seconds, OK?'

'Please hurry.'

There was silence on the line, and I felt relief there was no happy music playing whilst I was on hold.

'Mrs Skipton?'

'Yes, I'm here.'

'I'm afraid your husband is involved in a chase at the minute. I don't think he'll be able to call you. What's going on?'

'I've had a very threatening phone call, and I think someone might try to come and try to get into the house. I'm here on my own with our daughter. She's sleeping. I'm pregnant and I'm scared he might try to break in.'

'Hang up with me and call nine-one-one. I'll do what I can from here. Give me your address. I'll have it here somewhere, but it'll be faster if you give it to me over the phone.'

I rattled off my address, thanked her, and after hanging up, I made the emergency call. This time a man answered.

'Nine-one-one, what's your emergency?'

I explained to him what I had explained to the first one a few moments before.

'We'll get someone out to you as soon as possible. Are your doors and windows all locked?'

'Yes, they are. I was getting ready for bed when he called.'

'Do you know who it was who called?'

'I don't. But I think—'

'Do you have an idea of who it might be?'

'Well, earlier today, one of our neighbours was arrested for a domestic. But surely he'd still be locked up, right?'

'Do you know his name?'

'I don't. But he was arrested on our street earlier today.'

'Hold on,' there was a pause, 'yes, I see it now. Oh.'

'Oh? Oh what?'

'He was released about seven thirty tonight, O-R.'

'Released? On his *own recognisance*? He almost killed his wife!'

'That's all the information I have here, I'm afraid. Let's get you someone out there.'

'How long is this going to take?'

'I'm not sure, but I have put it out as a priority call.'

'You should know I have a gun.'

'Are you comfortable using it?'

'Very comfortable. And I'll just say that if that bastard comes into my house, you'll have a homicide to work because I *will* kill him. I won't even try to talk to him. If he gets into this house, he'll be dead.'

'OK, Olivia. I need you to keep calm for me, OK?'

'Oh, I'm calm. I've never been more calm. There's only one reason he'd be coming in here and it ain't for coffee. But it'll be the last thing he'll do.'

'I need to inform you that when the deputies arrive, you'll need to put the gun down before you answer the door.'

'I'm aware. Don't worry.'

'That's fine, Olivia. Stay on the line with me, OK? Where in the house are you now?'

'I'm walking around. There are about five or six ways to get in and I'm keeping an eye on them all. Hang on.'

'Olivia?'

'Shhh, I think I hear something. Hang on.'

'OK.'

I held my breath so I could listen. I tiptoed into the living room. The lights were still off, and a streetlight shone through one of the windows which faced the street, casting linear, orange-tinged shadows on the carpet. Footsteps tapped on the sidewalk outside, but then a dog barked, and a woman's voice hushed it. I let out my breath.

'I think it was only someone walking their dog.'

'OK. And you're sure that all the doors and windows are locked, right?'

'They are. I have a routine.'

'Olivia? Deputy Barry is pulling up outside your house. Can you see him?'

'Hold on. Let me walk over to the window.' I pulled back the lowest part of the drape to peer outside. I saw a car pull into the driveway with a visible light bar on top. 'Yes, I see his car.'

'He's going to get out of his car and approach your front door, but I need you to place the gun on a table or something on the other side of the room, OK?'

'Yeah. It's on the coffee table.'

'I'm going to hang up now. Will you be OK?'

'Yeah, I think so. Thank you.'

'You take care now, Olivia. Stay safe.'

I put the phone down next to the gun on the coffee table and heard a knock on the front door. I was trembling as I approached and looked through the peephole. The porch light illuminated a man wearing a brown uniform, standing a few steps away from the door. He was holding up his identification. Switching on the overhead living room light, I unlocked the door and opened it, only wide enough for my face.

'Mrs Skipton?'

'Olivia, please,' I stepped back and opened the door wider. 'Come in.'

'Dispatch said there is a gun in the house. Is it secure?' He stepped into the room, eyeing room for the gun.

I pointed to the coffee table behind me. 'It's over there.'

He stepped further inside and looked around again. 'I understand you had a phone call tonight?' He pulled a small spiral notepad from his front pocket. He reached onto his hip to turn down the volume of his radio.

'Yes. He said he knew I was alone, but I wouldn't be for long.'

'That must have been a bit scary, huh?' He leaned towards me, his mouth in a pout, as if he was talking to a toddler waking after a bad dream.

'A *bit scary*? My three-year-old daughter is sleeping and I'm seven months pregnant. I'd think this goes a little further than *scary* wouldn't you say?'

'Well, these things are usually just to spook ya, right?' His voice was almost jovial.

Is he being serious?

'Do you know who it was that called you?'

'I don't. But I understand the guy down the street who was arrested this afternoon got out tonight.'

'What's that got to do with this?'

'My husband and I were driving by, and he asked Jake to get him out of it.'

'And?'

'Don't you think that's suspicious at all?'

'Well, maybe a coincidence,' he said as he stuffed his notebook back into his pocket. 'I think you're all tight and locked up in here. I'll write a report, and we'll see if we can't get some patrols to drive by tonight to keep an eye out. If that'll make you feel better.'

I had expected him to take the situation much more seriously, but it seemed he was not that concerned about our safety or even convinced there was a valid threat.

'I'll tell you now that if he ends up getting in here somehow, I'll kill him.'

He patted me on the shoulder, a smirk beaming from his face. 'You do that, Olivia. To tell you the truth, it'd save us the trouble—less paperwork.'

He told me the report would be available in two business days if I wanted a copy and handed me a ripped piece of his notebook with an incident number on it, folded over his business card. He left after telling me to lock the door behind him. I was relieved when he left. He had made me feel as if I had overreacted, twisting his condescending tones into an attempt to make me feel guilty he wasted his time taking the report from me. I dared not voice my opposition to his manner or he might not follow through with his offer to have patrol cars come by the house.

After I closed the door and checked the locks several times, I propped a chair from the dining room underneath the handle. I walked over to the coffee table and picked up the phone and lifted the gun, feeling a strange comfort in the weight of it.

Four hours passed as every sound startled me. The rush of blood pumping through my own veins was deafening. If a spider took a step, I could have heard it that night. Every so often, about every half hour, I heard the tyres of a car passing by the house. I expected it was the sheriff deputies driving by as Deputy Barry had told me he was going to request. As the sun started to trickle through the front window replacing shadows with light, I heard the distinct roaring engine of our Camero at the corner of the main road about a mile away. I found myself exhale, as if I had held my breath all night, waiting for Jake to come home. I moved the chair from under the front door handle and as soon as he pulled into the driveway, I ran outside to hug him. That's when I started to cry.

I had to push back my sobs to explain to him what had happened. His sergeant had let him off work as soon as he had completed the paperwork for the car chase. I told him there had been a lot of passes by the sheriff whilst I waited for him to come home.

'That wasn't only the sheriff.'

'What do you mean? There were cars driving by here all night.'

'It was cars from about four agencies around us who were taking turns keeping an eye on the house. Sometimes they were stopped out on the road. Wanted to make sure that guy didn't get near the house. None of them said they saw anything, though. He prob'ly just wanted to scare you.'

Two years later, Jake came home from working a rare day shift. When he walked into the living room, he looked worried about something.

'What's up? Everything OK?'

'Yeah. I arrested Reggie today.'

'Reggie?'

'Yeah, the guy who used to live down the street? The guy who almost killed his wife?'

'Oh! Reggie. That doesn't surprise me. What'd he do?'

'That's not important.'

'Why not?'

''Cause it's what he said that was important.'

'What did he say?'

'When all that happened, I wasn't sure there was a real threat. To be honest, I thought you'd overreacted—put it down to you being pregnant and all.'

I felt his words sting. Of everyone I dealt with that night, I had expected my own husband to believe me—to understand the threat was genuine.

'But he was here that night.'

'I know he was. He told me he was. On the phone.'

'I know that now.'

'How?'

'I had him in handcuffs and was leading him into the jail. He stopped and looked at me. He said, 'You know what? If all those police cars hadn't been in front of your house that time, you'd be single now. I was gonna kill your wife and that little girl of yours."

Reggie was dead less than a year later. He was at home when someone broke into his house in the middle of the night. The intruder filled his glistening body full of bullets as he slept.

Launch Day
by Laura Scott

I primp in my pastel-pink uniform and lip-sync to 'Unstoppable' by Sia playing on the radio. As I swivel, the light from my bedroom mirror glints along the silver threads of the embroidered freestyle script lettering—*Love Beauty*: my new brand and registered trademark. I buff and bronze my face, concealing my tired eyes and pale skin and even as my hands tremble, I expertly apply black liquid liner along my top lash line, creating an upward flick at the outer corners. I halt when my insides begin to twist and coil; I begin to repent gulping down a takeaway and a glass or two of rosé wine last night. My heart jumps when I hear a clatter from downstairs. Then I realise it will be my sister-in-law Darcy arriving. *She never knocks before entering.*

'It's only me!' She shouts as she traipses up the stairs.

Through my husband's persistent persuasion, I had agreed to employ her full-time. I wasn't even sure I could afford her wages. *At least she's arrived early, good start.* Attired in the matching pastel-pink uniform, she struts into my bedroom. She dumps her bag and hairdressing equipment on the bed and tells me about her best friend Gemma, who is currently having an affair with the postman. She prattles on while wrapping my hair around hot curling tongs and I gaze into the rising steam reflecting in the mirror … I begin to think back to the beginning of my career when I would travel around to provide treatments, having just completed three years at college to become a qualified beauty therapist.

My first client Jolene answered the door. 'Do you need a hand?' she asked, eyes wide.

'I'm OK thanks, no problem at all,' I gasped with crimson puffed cheeks.

I hauled my portable bed into her living room, then went back and forth to my car for the remainder of my waxing equipment. Jolene's three-year-old daughter continually got under my feet while she questioned every move I made. The contemplation of cash in my hand kept me motivated. I was grateful when she danced along to the Teletubbies in front of the television, which let me get some work done. When Jolene removed her socks and leggings and clambered onto my bed, my money mindset was interrupted by the malodorous smell. I breathed through my mouth while I continued to work. Every hair was waxed and plucked from Jolene's legs, then soothed with lotion. When I was finished, she handed me a tatty five-pound note barely held together with yellow-stained sticky tape. The remainder was paid with small change that she carefully counted from her ragged brown woven purse.

I shudder back to the present moment and take comfort in knowing from now on I will be offering luxurious treatments from my very own beauty salon. Darcy and I get ready to leave my house, and I lift the flyers displaying: '*Love Beauty Launch Day – Saturday, 17 March from 11 a.m. to 3 p.m. – Receive a FREE goody bag and raffle ticket.*'

It had been a dusty and demanding six months since I had collected the keys from the estate agent. With my family's support, we had converted the lower level of a bedraggled building that had been an old car accessories shop into a minimalist, modern-style salon. Inside, spotlights had been installed to brighten the pristine white walls and polished pinewood flooring. Situated in a prime location, right on the corner of a busy main street, it was inevitable that many passers-by would notice the freshly painted building and new sign.

Now, as Darcy and I walk towards the salon, dark clouds creep over, and the wind begins to pick up. Once we open up the shutters, my heart lifts as I turn on the outside light, illuminating the pink and silver *Love Beauty* sign I spent months dreaming about and endless evenings designing and redesigning. We arrange clusters of metallic pink and silver balloons, entwined with curling ribbons. I smooth and roll the soft pink, fluffy Egyptian cotton towels and place them in rows above the gleaming glass sinks.

Outside, we position a sandwich board advertising the grand opening event and attach some balloons to the windows.

We set out refreshments, and Darcy pours the Prosecco. She takes a glass for herself and hands me one while chattering about her friends' superficial dilemmas. Uninterested, I sip warily from my glass. My stomach is uneasy as bubbles percuss around my mouth and down my throat. Other family members arrive to help out, and a trickle of clients enter…

'Hi, it's lovely to see you,' I beam, as I hand over a goody bag. 'Would you like to try some of our new products?'

I scoop out various creams and scrubs and spread them onto clients' hands as we revel in the scents: lime and ginger, jasmine and neroli, coconut and frangipani. The noise of the wind crescendos outside, and the balloons join in as they pound against the windows like kettle drums in an orchestra. I notice a couple of the balloons float off onto the road, and I cringe as I watch cars slow down and manoeuvre to dodge them. The sandwich-board outside blows over occasionally with a clatter, and Darcy ventures in and out to prop it back up.

At the end of the day, there are final exchanges of farewells as the remaining clients and friends make their way out of the salon with their *Love Beauty* goody bags in tow. I notice my diary is looking busy with appointments over the next few weeks, which is a relief, although I didn't sell any products. I wipe a bit of sweat from my brow as I think about how much I have spent on everything.

The snib clicks as I secure the front door. I close my eyes whilst I press my forehead against the cool glass of the door, releasing a ponderous sigh. The cramps in my stomach, which have been coming and going throughout the day, are beginning to ease, and then I become aware of a low, humming noise vibrating through the floor. I turn around, and Darcy is relaxing on the pedicure throne, soaking her feet. The massage chair shakes and the water from the foot spa froths while she sips from her glass of Prosecco.

'Come on you,' I groan. 'It's time to get out of here …'

Red Suede Heels

by Laura Scott

The black leather of the seat squeaks as Layla shifts closer to Sam. His hand clasps around her fingers, pinching the skin around her wedding ring, and when he looks up into her eyes, it's like glancing at her own reflection.

'M—m—mum …' Sam says, his bottom lip trembling.

'What is it?' asks Layla.

The driver has the windscreen wipers at maximum speed; *swish-swash, swish-swash, swish-swash.*

'Sam …' She lays her other hand on top of his and shakes gently. 'Are you OK?'

The rain bounces off the car like pennies being thrown in a scramble.

'Please … talk to me.'

His blue eyes widen, and he stares straight ahead. Red patches form under each eye in horizontal half-moon shapes, marring his pale skin. *This is your fault*, she thinks as she turns to look out of the window. Maybe she shouldn't have allowed Sam to come along today. The rhythm of the rain changes, tapping on the window like a troupe of ballerinas dancing *en pointe.* Layla is glad she is sitting down when the driver approaches a tall black board displaying the name: GORDON GIBSON in white pegboard letters. A familiar pang in her jaw recurs as they follow the arrow on the board and she realises she is clenching her teeth. Layla ruminates over the last words she said to him … the last words he said to her. On the Saturday evening, Gordon's dilemma had been what to watch on television as the F1 racing and football were coinciding. Layla had been more concerned about the colour his skin had turned over the week: it was similar to the Jack Daniel's Honey whiskey he enjoyed. Twenty-four hours later, he was hooked up to a kidney dialysis machine, and she was told his liver was irreparable.

The rain ceases when the car slows to a halt, and the clouds part like stage curtains, revealing a glare of honeydew light. Layla squeezes her eyes shut; a tear escapes and drops onto her black waffle-weave dress.

Layla and Sam walk along the edge of the memorial garden, brimming with wildflowers, and her throat tightens when she spots a cluster of thistles. A murmur arises from the people congregating outside the glass facade of the crematorium. Some are still sheltering underneath the high apex portico from the recent downpour. The weight of Layla's red-suede shoes feels like her personal trainer is adding an extra kilo to the outer soles with each step she takes as they approach the flock of black attire.

'I've not slept a wink; been up all night being sick,' a voice reverberates from underneath the portico and lingers within the labyrinth of Layla's ears.

'It's such a tough day for you all …' She catches the response of the humanist that she has organised and paid for.

'Layla!' Hannah approaches and embraces her. She finds the familiarity of Hannah's perfume comforting, although the hints of coconut and vanilla remind her of faraway places she wishes she could fly off to right now.

'Oh, Sam, my darlin', how are you?' Hannah bends down to hug him. A smile flickers across his face, but his body is rigid.

'Have you seen my mother?' Layla asks as she looks around, avoiding any possibility of eye contact with Martha, her mother-in-law, or, to use Gordon's nickname for her, 'The Wicked Old Witch'.

'No, sorry, I haven't babe,' Hannah says as she looks around and purses her lips.

Layla begins to recognise a few other faces, boys that Gordon went to school with. Well, they are grown men now, with wider faces, projecting an assortment of stubble and beards, either standing with their hands in their suit trouser pockets or shuffling from foot to foot, chatting as if they are waiting for the football to begin. She offers an upwards head nod and closed-lip smile, and they offer an up-nod back. She remembers how they used to know everything that would go on in each other's lives; she resists the urge to run up to them and blurt out everything she has been through recently. She remembers the way they all used to vent to each other, every weekend in their local pub.

Hannah stares at Layla and points towards Martha with her eyes. 'She … she is just over there …' Hannah says while gritting her teeth like a ventriloquist.

'I noticed,' Layla replies under her breath. 'I'm trying to keep my distance.'

Sam looks up at them both as though he's searching for clues.

'Love your shoes, by the way,' says Hannah as she glances down at Layla's feet.

Gavin appears as if he has teleported from a foreign place. 'Alright, Sam?' He says while reaching for a handshake, his one-sided dimple appears. Sam reciprocates reluctantly.

'Oh, hi Gav,' Layla says. 'Did you drive over with Martha?' Not really knowing what else to say. She notices one side of his white shirt hanging out like the quadrant of a kite.

'Eh … no, just drove over on my own,' Gavin replies.

'Oh right, that's good; we've not long arrived … glad I missed that downpour, at least it's dry now,' Layla says.

'Look, sorry about having to message you about the ashes, but Mum was going on and on and on about them,' Gavin says as he tucks his shirt in, and Layla can't help noticing his once-toned torso now resembles a soft bun shape.

'It's OK, I know what she's like … I hadn't really thought that far ahead to be honest. I need to focus on getting through today,' Layla says as she looks down and takes Sam's hand.

'Alright, Hannah,' Gavin nods as he begins to shuffle closer towards the glass doors.

'Hello, Gavin,' Hannah replies.

He glances at Layla's shoes and then walks away.

'So … you are allowing *her* to have some of the ashes?' Hannah asks as she side nods in Martha's direction.

'No … well … I said we could sort it out after the funeral. He messaged me the other day asking.'

Hannah crosses her arms in front of her while taking a deep breath. 'You know Gordon would've hated her having his ashes.'

'I know, I know … but I knew I would have to face them today and … I didn't want to say no.'

Hannah sighs.

'I feel sick right now, please, just let me get through… this,' Layla says while she waves one arm around as though conducting an orchestra, the wide sleeve of her dress swaying while Sam hangs onto the other.

'OK, OK …' Hannah says as she calms Layla's flailing arm, then puts her own arm through hers.

For the first time at a funeral, there are no rows of pews in front of Layla. She shivers as she shifts on the hard seat and looks around. These high ceilings hold no heat and the festoon of white flowers fade into the fresh white walls. Scattered behind her are fragments of family and friends, and some, since the last time she saw them, have grown lines around their eyes that creep outwards like tree roots. She looks along the row to her right and notices that her mother's red, glossy lips seem plumper. Layla presumes she is dealing with an 'important client' as she looks down at her phone, typing, the rings on her fingers sparkling.

Layla looks down at the order of service on her lap, and her eyes twitch as Gordon's face beams back at her from the wedding day photo she selected. She traces her finger over the thistle design surrounding him, a reminder of the tattoo he sported on his upper arm. All she gets to feel now is the taffeta touch of the paper. *If only you could see this today,* Layla thinks, *the amount of people here for you. Some of them are friends and family that we haven't seen in years, some of them you thought didn't even like you. Your mother sits across the aisle, on the front row pew, like it's her show. She had the cheek to request a certain song to be played: not even a song you liked; certainly not a song I ever heard you listen to.*

'Can everyone please stand?' the humanist announces, and there is a ripple of scuffling shoes, knocks and coughs.

Layla stands and turns around. She watches Gavin help to carry the coffin as he inches down the aisle, his pale blue eyes round and wide, like a sprinter focusing on the catafalque as the finish line. The thistles that lie on top of the coffin seem to contort and float along in a realm of their own, releasing a subtle musky scent. She begins to imagine Gordon's body inside the coffin, and suddenly her legs feel as though she has been running on a treadmill for an hour. She thinks of the suit she picked out for him, his favourite one, and how baggy it will probably be on him now. She couldn't bear to see him at the viewing as Martha and Gavin had done. She had said her goodbyes at the hospital. She closes her eyes, attempting to remember happier times.

She remembers Gordon buying his suit and how handsome he looked when he first tried it on, his broad shoulders filling it. She recalls Gordon and Sam running around their garden, playing with a football—she breathes in the memory—the sound of Sam shrieking and giggling, the noise echoing around their safe enclosure as Gordon would lift him up and swing him around. She realises she will never see them like this again. An image of Gordon writhing in pain returns, him lying, dying on the hospital bed, fighting for every breath. She wonders if he knew what was happening to him. She wonders if he was aware of her presence; she hopes he knew she was there till the end. With each thought it's as though someone is tapping Layla on the head with a mallet, lowering her into the ground like a tent pin.

The microphone crackles and the humanist, Diane, introduces herself and speaks about Gordon—as though he is not here. 'Gordon was unique and so too is this ceremony …'

Layla glances across the aisle to her left, noticing the young man sitting beside Martha. She presumes he must be her new husband as he reaches his arm around Martha's shoulders, pulling her close, and she buries her head into him. Guilt washes through Layla's veins for a few heartbeats. They hadn't been on speaking terms before Gordon's death, and she didn't let them know he was in the hospital. Maybe she should have contacted Gavin sooner. But would Gordon have wanted that? She wasn't sure; he couldn't communicate after he'd arrived at the hospital. If he'd been able to talk, would he have asked for them to be there? She didn't think so. But Gordon is no longer here to reassure her. She wonders what Martha is thinking; she knows Martha likes to have things her way. Although Martha hadn't offered much towards the eulogy when Layla had asked her to fill in parts of Gordon's past that she was unsure of.

'I'm now going to read out a poem that Layla requested,' Diane says. 'She was hoping to read it out herself, but she has asked me to read it for her today.'

Diane begins to read Auden's *Funeral Blues* and Layla agrees that every clock in the world, should be stopped.

While Diane continues to speak of Gordon, Sam rests his head on Layla's arm, as though its weight is just too much. Layla lifts her other hand, stroking and smoothing his hair a few times. Then there is a rustle of laughter around the crematorium as Diane relays antics about Gordon on a lad's night out. Martha raises her head at the mention of her name:

'Martha would say, "if you can't find Gordon, check his local pub, he's sure to be there."'

Layla clasps her hands, and a tight-lipped smile forms on her face as she remembers the earlier days of their relationship—calling around friends, trying to get hold of Gordon, searching and worrying about him—when Martha said this to her. And lo and behold, Layla located Gordon in their local pub. The humanist begins to talk about their wedding, and Layla shifts in her seat again—Martha wasn't invited. She notices Martha overplay, dabbing her face with a dishevelled tissue; it's as though she exaggerates her shaking hands while she receives a fresh packet from Gavin. Thoughts of regret stab at Layla as she attempts to raise her emotional armour, batting away recollections of past family arguments. Martha side glances at Layla, then looks down at her shoes. And Layla quickly turns to face the front again, focusing her attention back on Diane.

Layla picks at a hangnail, which begins to smart, and then the theme tune *A Gift of a Thistle* plays through the speakers. Gordon watched the film *Braveheart* so many times that Layla got fed up with it. But now she wishes to go back to those times when they would sit and watch movies together. The tone of the tin whistle floats around her, and it's as though every person in the building has been paralysed by the sound. She imagines the *London Symphony Orchestra* performing in front of her, the Uilleann pipes play, tears flow, and not just from Layla's eyes. She struggles to swallow, and it feels as though the violinist is drawing their bow across her windpipe. Another shiver passes through Layla's body as the navy velvet curtains in front of her begin to move. Their deep folds straighten, and she realises Gordon's coffin will soon disappear behind them. She watches the bottom of the curtains drag along the stone-cold ground, creeping closer together. The view of Gordon's coffin is diminishing. She wants to run up to it; she wants to lift the lid and hold on to him one more time, lie beside him, go with him. It feels as though the curtains are wrapping around her chest, squeezing and tightening. Then the curtains close, swaying a few times.

Layla gasps while she sits on the bench in the memorial garden. Her relentless sobs slowly subside as Sam sits snug at her side, like a magnet, while Hannah sits at the other. She tilts her face towards the sun and notices the sky grow into a cornflower blue. She begins to appreciate hints of orange blossom, sweet-musk and fresh-cut grass from the array of wildflowers that surround her. The scent of the buttercups, comfreys and forget-me-nots, mingle together and flutter along in the breeze while the kaleidoscope of colours calms her.

'M … mum,' says Sam as he tugs on her dress. 'I need a pee.'

Layla sighs, 'I don't think I can go back in there.'

'I'll take him,' Hannah says. 'I need to go anyway, come on my darlin' …' she stretches her arm out towards Sam.

Layla watches them walk away. Sam's gait like Gordon's, his blonde curls bounce in time with his step. She rubs her temples in a circular motion with her fingers, then combs them into her hair, holding her head as she rests her elbows on her knees. She looks down at her shoes; this is the first time she has worn them in a while. She tilts her left foot inwards to admire the red suede trim and tassel, with its cone heel. Her feet never seemed to return to their pre-pregnancy state, but they still look good on her, she thinks.

Layla had admired them in the shop window on the day of her 30th birthday. Gordon always said she suited red, and that she deserved them for putting up with him for so long. It had been a lovely day out, celebrating together, just the two of them. That had been before they met up with family later that evening for a meal. She had said to herself that she wouldn't drink too much, but while watching Gordon knock back whiskey after whiskey at the dinner table, ending eight months of sobriety, she thought *why not,* and ordered another bottle of wine.

When they arrived home after the meal, Gordon crawled upstairs and crashed face-first on top of their bed, one side of his face squashed into the duvet; it was wrinkled like a bulldog pup. He rarely snored when he had been sober, but his breathing slowed and then rhythmically growled, and his sweet honey breath turned metallic. Layla stumbled down to the kitchen where Gavin had been helping himself to a beer from the fridge. It should have been a cup of tea she made but instead she poured another glass of wine. She kicked off her shoes when she walked into the living room and slumped on to the sofa, the white wine sloshed around in her glass. She rubbed her throbbing feet with her free hand while laughing at Gavin as he mimicked his mother. She liked his sense of humour and his ability to make jokes about family dramas, unlike Gordon. Gavin tripped over her red shoes, and Layla laughed so much she spilt some of the wine onto her red dress and the sofa. Gavin had suddenly emerged with a tea towel and had been wiping her dress when he looked her straight in the eyes. She looked away and began sweeping down the ruffles of her dress with her hands when Gavin leaned closer, and his soft lips pressed against hers. She pushed her hand against his chest, although not hard enough. The lights of the chandelier above her blurred and squiggled, reflecting off the crystal pendants and then mizzled down. She remembers the headache the next morning, the nip when she urinated and how her stomach churned for days.

Now, cigarette smoke swells around her, suffocating the floral scent in the air as Martha walks towards her. Gavin, Martha's husband, and a few friends, follow her like a fan club and stop in front of Layla.

'You alright?' Martha asks, smoke puffing from her nose and mouth.

'Not really,' Layla replies, her eyes hot. She presses her cold hands around them, attempting to cool herself.

'You say I crave attention ...?' Martha nods down at her shoes.

Layla fires a glance at Gavin.

Gavin looks at the ground and pulls on Martha's arm, 'come on, Mum, leave it.'

'It's disrespectful to wear red at a funeral,' Martha says.

'Pfft! You are unreal ...' Layla starts.

Martha raises her thin pencilled in eyebrows that are too dark in comparison to her strawberry-blonde bobbed hair.

'Well, one thing you would know about your son is how he liked to go against the grain. He would probably have liked people to mourn in red—there is certainly no sense in all this,' Layla finishes with her hand waving around in the air.

For a moment, Martha is silent. She folds her arms across her chest and looks at Gavin. He shrugs, puts his hands in his pockets and looks at the ground again as though counting the gravel.

'I just want to make sure I'll get some of the ashes,' says Martha.

'I don't want to discuss this right now,' Layla says as she combs her fingers through her hair. 'Just do your messaging through Gavin, like you always do.'

'Well, Gavin seems to be better at getting his way with you,' Martha says.

'What's that supposed to mean?' Layla asks.

Layla notices Hannah and Sam walking towards them. Layla's feet begin to tap, and she wants to say to Martha that she's not getting a grain of Gordon's ashes; he wouldn't even have wanted her to be at his funeral. She wants to say all the hurtful things she heard Gordon say about her throughout the years. How he would say he couldn't wait for the chance to dance on her grave, singing 'Ding Dong! The Witch Is Dead.'

Martha turns and notices Sam. She drops her cigarette and stubs it out with her shoe.

'Sam …' Martha says while putting her arms out towards him.

Sam stares for a moment, then runs towards Layla and sits beside her on the bench, gripping onto her arm.

'You've had your show, Martha,' Hannah says with one hand on her hip.

'This is a family matter,' Martha glares at Hannah.

'Family! Do you even know what age your grandson is?' Layla asks.

'He's seven …' Martha looks at Sam.

Layla raises her eyebrows.

'I—I mean eight …' Martha stammers.

Layla looks at Martha's fan club. 'There you go; she doesn't even know what age he is. And the last time she bothered to buy him a birthday card was when he was two years old!'

'All I want is a little piece of my son, a spoonful of his ashes … that's all,' Martha pleads.

'No, he wouldn't even have wanted you here, never mind have some of his ashes,' Layla says, her voice rising.

'She's showing her true colours now,' Martha turns towards her followers. 'She won't even give me a little bit of my son's ashes.'

'You should have bothered more when he was here,' Layla says.

Gavin pulls on Martha's arm again.

'You knew he had a drinking problem … and you did nothing about it; you did nothing to help!' Layla blurts.

'I didn't know …' Martha sobs.

'You did. He's always been like that, you said to me. His dad was the same … you said.'

Martha's tears are flowing. She pulls out overused tissues from her pocket, blowing her nose. 'I … I didn't know it was that bad.'

'You never asked. And you don't even have the nerve to contact me about the ashes. You get Gavin to do it. And then you demand a certain song. The one thing you ask for at your son's funeral, and it's about you, not Gordon.'

Layla stands up, clasping Sam's hand. 'I feel sorry for you,' she says towards Gavin. She walks past them, flicking her brunette waves, while Martha weeps and receives some conciliating shoulder taps.

Hannah steps towards Layla and takes her arm. 'Come on, we are getting out of here.'

They walk the weaving steppingstone path of the memorial garden and Layla notices a thistle projecting higher than the others. It waves in the wind. Gordon is gone, and there is nothing she can do to change anything. It doesn't matter that Sam isn't biologically Gordon's; he loved him as his own, and that's all that matters. No one else has to know. Not even Hannah. Gordon always said the best day of his life was when he married Layla: 'My wife, my life,' he'd say to her, and then a short time later, Sam was born.

Sam reaches out and touches a daisy; its long green stem bends. And when he lets go, it springs back, releasing a shower of droplets.

A Perfect Arrangement
by Charity Reed

The doorbell chimed. Catherine knew who it was. Police. She prepared herself to greet them.

'Catherine Cater-Smith?' They'd sent two plain clothed officers. Catherine was a little surprised.

'I am she. How can I help?'

'I'm Sergeant Walker, and this is my colleague, Detective Inspector Morrison. We'd like to speak to you in connection with the attempted murder of Mr Neil Galloway,' said one of them.

He looked like he'd been to the Columbo school of style, and she couldn't help but wrinkle her perfectly sculpted nose in distaste. The woman beside him wasn't much better. Appalling hair. Then it hit her. Her stomach clenched into a knot as she realised that this sounded very much like a detective on a case, rather than the kind-faced officer bearing bad news. Her mind spun.

'Attempted? Pardon?'

Catherine had arrived at her former home just before her soon-to-be ex-husband. She had let herself in through the back door—the front had a doorbell camera—heart beating like a broken clock at the thought of what she was about to do. It was excitement she felt though, not fear. Neil was due home from work in ten minutes. Always late home on a Thursday. She'd arranged it perfectly. Catherine arranged *everything* perfectly.

She slipped silently past the Miele washing machine, caressed the kitchen's marble tops and bespoke cedar doors. She'd selected them herself and it irked her that Neil lived with them, oblivious to the elegance of her impeccable taste. He'd be living surrounded by Ikea's finest if it wasn't for her. Good grief—can you imagine? She slid smoothly along velvet-flock walls and up the exquisite Axminster-clad stairs.

She'd entered the master bedroom so many times over the last five years, but this evening it seemed different. Hollow somehow, although nothing had changed. The same crimson cushions, Persian rug on polished parquet, Neil's single malt bottle on his night-stand. This she headed for, taking the small packet of crushed pills from her pocket; she tipped them into the golden liquid, replaced the top, dropped to the floor and positioned herself under the bed to wait. Neil arrived six minutes later. In her covert cocoon she checked her watch, 9.45, she rolled her eyes in disgust at his predictability.

Lying there, alone and unnoticed under the bed was less tedious than spending an evening with Neil she ruminated, lying motionless listening to his muffled movements. He had a routine. He'd come upstairs, throw his tie and jacket on the chair—he did. He'd kick off his shoes and replace them with comfortable corduroy slippers—he did. Back downstairs for a beer while his ready meal heated. Eat. Another beer. A look at the FTSE—God he was boring. Then, at last she heard him re-enter the bedroom, undress and climb into bed. Her heart sounded too loud. Apparently unaware, Neil poured his usual dram, and she heard the pages turning—Bravo Two Zero! She'd almost laughed when she'd seen it on the night-stand, Neil was no Andy McNabb.

No. Neil was predictable. Worse, he was tasteless. She'd put up with his lack of style and ambition for years. He'd been quite interested in travel—not the good kind, backpacking of all things—until she'd knocked it out of him. Other than that, nothing. Except his shed. His damned 'man cave' as he called it. Catherine had no idea what he did in there, but it smelled of neanderthal and he was always in his scruffy old moleskins when he went in or out. The very idea. Moleskins are all very well for a shooting party—at a pinch—but really, around the house and garden?

'Hey Cat, how about Vietnam?' She remembered him flicking through those God-awful adventure holiday brochures.

'Vietnam? Are you insane?' Catherine hadn't been able to believe the audacity. 'I suppose you want us sleeping in a bivouac in the jungle, do you?'

'Don't be ridiculous. They have hotels in Vietnam, nice ones.'

'What's wrong with Monte Carlo?'

'Nothing *per se*, but we've been there the last three years Cat. Don't you fancy something a little different?'

'I *like* Monte Carlo. I like the people. They like us. They *know* us.'

'Yes.' Neil had sighed. 'That's rather the point of doing something different. Anyway, they like *you*. And if I'm totally honest I find them pretty boring.'

'Don't sigh at me—and don't be absurd.'

Neil had put down his coffee cup. 'Monte Carlo it is then.'

'Don't you have any respect for antique furniture? Use a coaster like a civilised person, *please*.'

They'd split up soon after that and Neil had actually gone to Vietnam. Catherine couldn't believe he'd had the gumption. He'd come back quite tanned as well, hair different.

She thought back to when they'd met. He hadn't impressed her much—until he'd invited her home. My goodness *that* was impressive. Catherine had her rather lovely apartment overlooking Holland Park, bought ten years ago with an inheritance, but it paled in comparison to Neil's Highgate house. As soon as she saw it, she'd fallen in love.

It hadn't taken long to convince Neil he was in love with her. By God it had been hard work though. Catherine had spent months being the perfect companion. She'd wanted to scream at him most of that time, but she'd held her tongue until he finally proposed. She'd worn Wang. A stunningly elegant mermaid cut that gave her the look of a young Grace Kelly. Perfect. They'd honeymooned in the Maldives. Catherine shivered at the memory of the hotel. Exquisite. Neil had wanted Scotland, of all places. She'd almost walked out on him when he suggested it, but she'd just had the kitchen redone in Italian marble and was working on the attic conversion at the time, so she kept quiet and promised him Scotland would be simply divine for their first anniversary. As if.

There was one drawback to Highgate, of course. It was further from her haunts in Knightsbridge, and Neil did go on about the cost of taxis. They'd even taken the Underground at times. Catherine could see why people called it 'the tube.' She'd felt like the only colourful Smartie in a packet full of browns.

Disgusting, filthy place, full of disinterested commuters, jobless layabouts, druggies, and smelly youths. On one occasion she'd confronted a scruffy looking girl who had her feet on the seat opposite her. Catherine was standing.

'It's people like *you*,' Catherine had said, 'that make people like *me* have to sit in filth.'

The girl had looked genuinely surprised, removed her Dr Martens from the ugly velvet seat and apologised in an awful northern accent.

'Well, it's a bit late for that.' Catherine was incensed. 'Sorry isn't going to clean the seat for decent people to sit on.'

The young man sitting beside her had looked at Catherine, steady in the eye, and replied in a dreadful yank drawl, 'So tell me, who pissed in your cornflakes this morning?'

The doors had opened, the couple skipping off the train at Charing Cross Road, giggling like plebian children who'd just found a penny in the dust.

Almost apoplectic, Catherine had looked to Neil for support. He said nothing but she caught the hint of a smirk on his lips. He'd paid later. He'd pay again now.

She heard him beginning to snore and checked her watch. Three drinks and just half an hour had done it. Quicker than she'd expected. Excellent. She waited five minutes more to be safe and slid out. Neil's head lolled back, corpse like on the plush pillow. She eyed him with loathing. Quickly, she swapped the drugged whiskey bottle for an uncontaminated one, lifting Neil's heavy hands and covering the bottle with prints, rinsed the glass, swishing a little clean whiskey round it and, once again adding Neil's fingerprints—not forgetting the lips. After placing a photo of the two of them, taken in happier times, into his hand, she took a Sainsbury's plastic bag from her pocket in her gloved hands and slipped it over his sleeping head, making sure the bottom was tight enough to stop air getting in or out. She'd retrieved this from the kitchen on her way up. Neil kept them in a box under the sink, reusable. She'd had to be sure the bag would have his prints on and not hers, so she couldn't bring one from home. If she had it would have been Waitrose, she despised Sainsbury's. Cheap and tatty.

She'd considered slashing his wrists, but quite apart from the mess there was the cutting angles to consider. She'd heard about hesitation marks and such like on a podcast and it sounded like the type of issue that might crop up at postmortem. This was cleaner. A student in her form at Wycombe Abbey had committed suicide in exactly the same way, so she knew it would work. Strange girl. She'd not had many friends—always in the library, little swot—but she'd just been accepted into Oxford, so Catherine had assumed she could have expected some dreary future in publishing or the like. Some people are so ungrateful. Anyway, she mused, this way there's no chance of blood spatter or luminol tests on her clothes, God forbid.

Then, the *pièce de résistance*, a note he'd left her some weeks earlier containing a single word "Sorry." He'd stayed out until after midnight with Gary and slipped it through the letter box in the morning. Seething, she'd bolted the doors so that he learned his lesson, sleeping in his beloved man cave. Ugh. She hated that shed, and the time he spent in it. She wasn't sure why she'd kept the note, nor why she'd never touched it with bare hands. Had she always subconsciously planned this? Catherine looked around, was there anything she'd forgotten? Oh yes. She dropped a couple of the sleeping tablets she'd crushed into the drink on the floor, almost under the bed but just visible enough for the police to find. Perfect.

She was elated as she left the building, carefully checking that no one was around. She knew there was no CCTV nearby and the neighbouring houses were empty during the early summer, the occupants away on business for another month at least. Dark now. She jogged home, blending into the night in the elegant ebony Gauge 81 Activewear she'd chosen for her expedition, just another health-conscious Londoner, quite sure she'd left no loose ends. The last two hours might be difficult to explain should an alibi be needed, but she'd left her phone at home so it couldn't be traced to Neil's house. She'd left social media logged in; peers would presume her idling over Instagram or working on her latest reel. She was gathering followers on her Insta business, *CatLifestyleGuru*; there were so many tragic people that needed her lifestyle advice.

Nearly over. Catherine entered her immaculate if uninviting flat, chic, but nothing compared to her former house, to which she could now soon return. They were separated but not yet divorced and everything would go to her. Once inside she grabbed her phone to check for messages. Only one, and that was sent seven minutes ago. Perfect.

Liv asking about their lunch date. She replied.

Sorry darling, I was running a bath and didn't hear the tinkle. Yes, Saturday is great for me. The Ivy at 1? Mwah xx

Liv replied. *Perfect. Tootles xx*

She poured herself a large glass of Morey St Denis '94, stripped and slung everything into the machine, finally, sinking into a steaming Chanel scented bath. Reliving the evening she smiled. Everything had gone like a dream. She'd slept better that night than she had since she'd left Highgate.

'If you wouldn't mind coming with us Ms Cater-Smith,' said Detective Inspector Morrison.

'Why? What's happened?' Catherine composed herself, feigning ignorance.

'As we said, an attempt was made on your husband's life. We have reason to believe you were at the scene,' said Walker.

'I—I'm not quite sure I understand.' Catherine was genuinely confused.

Morrison scratched her scruffy ponytail and said, 'Your husband, Mr Neil Galloway, was seriously assaulted on Thursday night. We know it was you that assaulted him Ms Cater-Smith. We'd like you to answer a few questions.'

'I—I don't understand.' Catherine could hear her own voice, high-pitched and whiny. What had gone wrong?

'Mr Galloway had recently installed CCTV at the back of his house. I believe he was concerned that his shed might get broken into, what with the neighbours away an' all. We know you entered the house, we know you drugged him, and we know you attempted to murder him. We just need to get your side of the story. So, if you wouldn't mind coming with us.'

'Neil's al—? I mean—Er—' Catherine was as disgusted with her own lack of composure as she was shocked by the revelations that Neil was both alive and had installed a camera she'd failed to notice. 'Look here, I'm not sure what is going on.' She regained some self-control. 'Do you know who I am?'

'Well, Ms Cater-Smith, right now you're a suspect in a serious crime.'

Her phone buzzed.

'I have to be at The Ivy at 1. Can't this wait?' She checked her phone. Not Liv.

Why? It was from Neil.

'Ms Cater-Smith, I don't think you understand the serious trouble you're in,' said Morrison.

Catherine barely heard. She was staring into her iPhone. She couldn't believe it. She'd thought it was all so perfect.

'If you could come with us.'

Catherine looked up from her phone in disbelief. 'Thank you, *Detective Inspector*,' she spat. 'If you don't mind awfully, I'll call my lawyer and get my coat. But I warn you, I'll be expecting a full apology.'

'Yeah, yeah, it's all been a huge mistake. They all say that.' Morrison was smirking.

Catherine spluttered and her eyes widened. 'But—but—don't you know who I am?' She knew she was repeating herself, dumfounded by the shambling imbecile.

'Yes love, you're just another failed murderer. Now let's get these cuffs on and search those pretty pockets. Make sure you're not carrying eh.'

Cuckoo
by Heather Grossart

I liked black dogs, but not the one lodged in my mind. Samuel Johnson has permanently given them a bad name. He might have given us dictionaries, but that didn't make up for it. Depression is not a black dog.

'Do you know about the black dog?' I asked.

'In what context?' Dr Smart Arse answered.

'In the Samuel Johnson sense of the words.'

'What about it?'

'Do you think it's fair on the dog? Why does it have to be black? Why can't it be golden?' I genuinely didn't know.

'What do you think of the dog?'

'Like I said, it's picking on black dogs. I'm sure that some kind of … what's the word when you have a go at someone 'cos of their colour or height? Bigotry! You are a bigot!'

'Do you worry about things like that? Bigo—'

'Do you ever answer a question?' I was annoyed and kind of worried about the dog. I didn't know why, but it was all that was on my mind.

'Explain what you are asking,' she said.

'Another question, that's just rude,' I tutted. 'You obviously aren't worried about the dog.'

'Are you worried about the dog?'

'I'm worried about *you*,' I answered, 'your brain is stuck on questions.'

'The dog isn't real. It's just an expression. Do you want to call your depression your black dog? We can if you want.'

'It's silly, dogs are cute.'

'We need to move on. How are you feeling?' my psychiatrist asked.

'Dr Smart Arse. I'm feeling fine, apart from the dog thing.'

'Why do you call me that?'

'Because you always think you know what's best for me.' I started picking at my nails, which looked red, raw and hurt, but I couldn't stop.

The psychiatrist started typing on her laptop.

'What are you writing about me? How your crazy, demented, deranged, loony, lunatic and nutty patient has an imaginary dog in her head?'

'Why do you insist on calling yourself these things?'

'You're the one that gave me a label. I'm just adding to that.' I shrugged.

'Bipolar Affective Disorder is not a label. It's a diagnosis.'

'It's a label I shouldn't have; I'm not depressed or manic. And why did they change the name from manic depressive?'

'Because that term belittles the illness, it's so much more than mania and depress—'

'Of which I have neither.' I'm determined.

'Do you remember how you felt when you came here?'

'I felt fine.'

'But how were you acting?'

'There is nothing wrong with the way I was behaving.' I was only half sure of that at this point.

'You were selling everything you owned.'

'There is nothing wrong with decluttering.'

'I don't think that selling your cooker comes under that umbrella.'

I couldn't argue.

'Or going out naked to hang out your washing.'

I didn't remember doing that.

'How many things did you volunteer for? Can you remember?'

No, I couldn't. 'Being busy gets things done …'

'Being manic makes you think you are getting things done. How many people did you actually help?' She smiled.

'Why are you smiling?' I was annoyed again. 'You are shitting over all the good work I've done…'

'You bankrupted two groups and spent the money of two others.'

'I was *helping*. Where did you get this ridiculous carpet, neon blue and yellow? Luckily, I don't take seizures; this carpet would give you one. See, there is something I don't do or have.'

'You are changing the subject.'

'Where is the couch? Don't psychiatrists have couches and timers? When is my time up?'

'No couches or timers.'

'And why are there two chairs, one big and one small? Do you find some deep, dark meaning in whichever chair people pick?' I was genuinely interested. I always picked the big chair because I was too fat to get out of the low, little chair.

'Do you see that your behaviour was unreasonable? I won't even mention what you did in the co-op.'

I wasn't going to admit *that* in any way. 'They needed help, I gave it to them.'

'You aren't doing a very good job of convincing me you won't do it again.'

'I didn't do anything wrong.'

'You were manic. You weren't looking after yourself or taking any responsibility for the things you should. You were reckless and out of control. I think we need to increase your medication.'

'You are not giving me more antipsychotics. I'm not that cuckoo.'

'Antipsychotics don't mean you are psychotic; they just stabilise your mood.'

'I'm not taking them…' I wasn't psychotic.

'You know what happens if you don't take them?'

'Don't threaten me,' I felt the old anger at her rise.

'I'm not, but we will hospitalise you if you don't take them.'

'I could do with a holiday…'

'It's not a holiday.'

'I know,' I felt deflated.

'Okay, we will up your antipsychotics, your anticonvulsants …'

'Why do I need anticonvulsant medicines?'

'They are used to help prevent low moods, that's all.'

'Why not call them low mood boosters or something like that … like *antidepressants*? Everything you try to give me mood stabilises.' It didn't make sense to me.

'Because they aren't antidepressants. But we will increase those too.'

'You trying to make sure I rattle when I walk with so many pills? And where are the curtains for in here? Anyone can see in the windows and know I'm apparently certifiable. Whatever happened to privacy?

'I'm trying to help you, and we are on the third floor.'

'Yeah, yeah.'

'Why do you doubt it?'

'Because there is always a catch with you.'

'Why do you think that?'

'Just because.'

'Tell me why you think I'm trying to catch you out?'

'Cos, it's always something else I've done, something else that you can cast up. I'm never going to get to forget anything I have allegedly done. I don't like it.'

'You have to recognise the signs when you are suffering from mania because I think you recognise depression.'

'Oh, just fuck off.'

I couldn't think straight. Nothing made sense. Everything was cloudy and confusing. I couldn't be bothered even thinking about it. Nothing was interesting. Cooking and eating were a step too far. Life was shit. I was in this horrible waiting room again. Dr Smart Arse wanted to see me. It was our monthly appointment. I had tried to cancel, but the same old threats came out to put me away. I actually didn't care.

'Did you sanitise your hands?' The receptionist said, it was all she ever said.

'No, what are you going to do about it?' Actually, getting up and doing that would involve moving and actually caring. So, no, not happening. Getting here had been almost more effort than I was willing to expend.

'Get the fuck away from me,' a colossal man came bursting through the door I was about to go in. 'I have rights, you can't jag me on the arse if I don't want you to.'

See? Smart Arse was at it again, pissing people off. Two orderlies were at his back, telling him to calm down. He stormed out, and they followed. Shit, now Smarty would be in a bad mood. Oh well. It obviously wasn't a secure place here if he could just walk out. Maybe I wasn't safe.

'Dr Ferguson will see you now.' The receptionist broke the habit of a lifetime and said something else. Typically, the doctor came out, but I guess not today.

I had to wait to be buzzed through. I guess this *was* a kind of secure unit. Maybe they would lock me up and throw away the key. I didn't care. Though I'd love to know how he had escaped. Nah, I didn't, I couldn't be bothered thinking about it.

'I don't want to sit down today; I won't be waiting.' I told her straight off.

'Why not?'

'Yes, start as you mean to go on, questions.' I sighed. This was tedious.

'Why don't you want to?'

'Can't be bothered.'

'Why can't you be bothered?'

I sat down.

'How are you feeling?'

I felt tears rise; she was being nice to me. Well, she was being *something*. And I couldn't cope. 'I … I don't know what's wrong with me. Nothing makes sense.'

'Makes sense, how?'

'I don't know,' tears ran down my face.

'I guess you are feeling quite low.'

'No shit, Sherlock.'

'What started you feeling this way?'

'I don't know,' I really didn't.

'How is day-to-day life?'

'Confusing.'

'Confusing how?'

'Well, if I knew, I would tell you.' My head started to hurt.

'Are you managing to look after yourself, shower, etc.?'

'Do I look like I've showered? It's too much effort.'

'Why do you feel like that?' She persisted.

'You are the psychiatrist, you tell *me*.'

'That's not my job.'

'What *is* your job then?'

'To help you be the best you can be.'

'Very funny.' It wasn't funny, but I was exhausted with this whole episode.

'Do you feel you are a danger to yourself?'

Was I? It had occurred to me vaguely that it would be easier to not be here, but not seriously. 'I can't think in straight lines, but I don't want to play tag with a train.'

'How bad is the confusion?' she asked gently.

'Bad. I often don't understand what I'm doing.' I would ride her for being sappy, but I couldn't be bothered.

'That's not so good. Do you have support at home, or is it just your husband?'

'I've not to call him '*just* my husband'. He doesn't like that.

'Why? Do you say that often?'

'No, I made that mistake once, and he took it really personally.'

'How did that make you feel?'

'Is this about me or him?'

'I'm just asking about the support you have at home.'

'I think I want a divorce,' I announced.

'Why?'

'Because I'm no good for him. I'm just a waste of space. He could be happier with someone else. Have children and shit.'

'How long have you felt like that?'

'I don't always feel like that. Just sometimes. He does kind things for me all the time. He cooks for me and gives me cuddles. He's a wonderful man, and I am a shit wife.'

'Do you not think he'd leave if it was that bad for him?'

'I think he's scared to leave me, just in case.'

'Just in case what?'

'Just in case.'

'Do you have any other support?'

'Not really, but it's okay. I'm not worth it.'

'Do you think you'd feel better if you came in for a while, get a rest?'

'What? Lock up the loony?'

'I'm just thinking of you. You aren't well. At the very least, we need to increase your medicines. You are on a therapeutic dose, but it's okay to increase it. I think we should.'

'Whatever you want. I don't care. Can I overdose on Prozac?'

'Are you thinking about it?'

'Just answer me.' I didn't like the look on her face.

'I'm not going to tell you that.'

'Doesn't matter, thirty seconds on Google will.'

'Think you should come stay with us for a while.'

'Nah, nah, I'll be fine, I'm just in a bit of a funk today. I honestly don't need to come in here.' I hoped she believed me. I tried to put on my confident face. 'I'm not going to jump off a cliff face.'

'Well, you have to promise you'll phone the number I gave you if it worsens.'

'I will.' I wouldn't.

'Okay, we are done for today, but we are not quite finished.'

I waited for the other shoe to drop. 'What…'

'I'm sorry, but I must revoke your driving license.'

'You have got to be shitting me.' Fuck's sake.

One pill, two pills, three. Four, five, six, seven. I wasn't going to choke today getting them down. Antidepressants, anticonvulsants and antipsychotics. An awful lot of antis. I was anti-*them.* I felt my face flush and felt guilty for a second before I pushed them down the plug hole in the kitchen sink. I was kind of sorry and worried that I hadn't heard them plop in the water. What if they were just sitting there? I felt both relief and trepidation at my actions. But I also felt great. The extra Prozac had kicked me out of my gloom. But I didn't need any of it now. I just needed my driving license back; I had things to do.

Three weeks later, I was still okay. What was the big deal with not taking my meds? I had to be sneaky, though. I'm sure my husband counted them, and "he wasn't going through that again." Wimp.

I woke up the next day and felt an all too familiar but long-forgotten fluttering in my chest. Anxiety. I sat up slowly and wondered why I felt like that. Had I forgotten something? Had to have something to do with the pills. Had I forgotten to get rid of them yesterday? I dashed to the kitchen, got a torch from the drawer, and peered down the plug hole. I couldn't see anything. My heart was beating hard, and the fluttering in my chest wasn't quitting.

I had the GP for a blood test today, because, you know, Smart Arse and her pills may affect some other part of me. Another damn good reason to stop taking them. Maybe I'd missed the appointment? *What was it I was forgetting?* This feeling of anxiety was getting me down.

I slowly got ready as an ache crept over my head. The fluttering in my chest was still there. I didn't know what to do about either of them. I decided to make a cup of tea; the husband wanted one, too. He fucking annoyed me, but I loved him. I couldn't make up my mind. He *was irritating.* Tea ready, I walked through to the lounge to sit on the settee. I missed. I missed the settee, landed on my ass and spilled tea everywhere.

This was typical of my life as a whole. I was flat on the floor, covered in scalding tea. How had I missed the settee? Who had *moved* the settee? The fluttering in my chest got stronger. I felt like I had a lump in my throat.

I didn't know what to do with myself beyond getting changed, which I didn't do.

The doctor's office was busy, people sniffing and coughing, everyone looking at the floor, for shame, they should be seen. Maybe that's what was bothering me, being in the doctors. That would explain the fluttering. I picked up a leaflet. It was about COVID-19. That means the stuff lying around in here was five years old. Maybe the receptionist at the hospital had been here and read the leaflet?

The nurse called me through. Though you didn't call them nurses anymore … she was more than a phlebotomist. They were nurse practitioners. All seemed the same to me.

'What can I do for you today?' she asked, all chipper and annoying. Everything was irritating me today.

'You asked me here, you should know.'

'Just being polite. Are you okay?' She indicated my shirt and jeans, which were still damp.

'I'm fine. Can we get on with this?' I just wanted out of here. 'I heard that the tips of needles split when they go into either injecting you or withdrawing blood. Is that true? Do you like sticking people with needles? How much of my blood do you need? What do you do with the spare blood? Any local vampires? Hah hah. What *exactly* are you testing? You are not checking for HIV, are you? I don't think I've got that. But maybe my husband cheated and gave it to me. Maybe I have AIDS. How could I have got AIDS? It must be the husband. Maybe I gave it to *him*. People don't die of AIDS now, do they? I need AIDS drugs, not Smart Arse's drugs.'

'You are taking your medication?' the bloodsucker asked.

'What's it got to do with you?'

'You just seem a little excitable …'

'What's wrong with being happy?'

'Nothing, you are maybe just a little on the high side.'

'Gawd, who said that was a crime?'

'You are taking your Prozac, Lamotrigine and Aripiprazole, aren't you?'

This was the moment of truth. 'Of course, why wouldn't I?'

'Hmm, you know there are side effects if you stop taking them. Anxiety, mood swings, depression … paranoia?'

'I don't need to be off the meds to have depression, and I'm not bloody paranoid or psychotic.'

'Dizziness, trouble with balance … headaches, fatigue … the list goes on.'

'Just take my blood,' I almost begged, 'I won't look and use the small needle. I have a bend in my vein. I tried to give blood once, and they couldn't get it in … ooh er … said the vicar to the prostitute.' I thought I was hysterical. 'Do nurses and doctors get it on? Have you bonked my doctor? What about the receptionist? They look really game for it.'

'I'm worried about you.'

'I'm absolutely fantastic. There's nothing to worry about here.'

So, she stuck the needle in me without further ado. I did look. It was interesting the way your skin puckered as they stabbed you.

'Do you have the numbers you need to get a hold of your Community Psychiatric Nurse?'

'Why would I need them? I don't think I have one. They are all just wannabe Smart Arses. I don't need more than one of those in my life. Hey, you can prescribe! How about getting me that skinny jab? I could get rid of my fat ass. It's a magic drug. Why not give me that? I'd be ecstatically happy on that, but not too happy. We both know we can't have *that*!'

'Think you need to speak to Dr Ferguson. Think she'd love to hear from you.'

'Nope to the no chance, nada, never. When do you put the bins out here? Where do you put your sharps? I'm going to need a sharps bin to put my used needles in when I start taking the jiggy jags. Well, what are you waiting for? Just write the prescription …'

'It's for diabetics. Weight loss is just a side effect.'

'So, between you and I, we can say I'm diabetic.'

'No, I can't.'

'So, when *do* you put the bins out. I believe our blue bins are collected on Tuesdays. Do you even have a blue bin here? Wonder if they put the bins out in *Eastenders*? Are the houses real? I read they were real. I wonder if they will stop filming for the bin lorry? I'm going to write to Aunty Beeb to find out.'

'Why don't you go and wait in reception, and I'll see if I can find you someone?'

'Who? What makes you think I need anyone? What are you planning?' I knew she was planning something terrible for me. I reached inside my bag and pulled out my pinking shears. I liked the pattern they made when you cut something. I pointed them at her, and she—who was planning something against me—took a step back.

'Put the scissors down. I'm not going to do anything you won't like.'

'Do you think the BBC will answer me? I am sure my husband paid for the TV licence. Do you think I could get gobby Bianca's autograph … Oh, but she'd sign it, "Patsy Palmer".'

'Put the scissors down. We can have a nice cup of tea.'

'Why are you backing away from me? Do I smell? Do you know who smells? At least, I'm sure she does. Dr Smart Arse's receptionist, with her "sanitise your hands," bet she stinks of hand sanitiser.

'I'm just going to call through for some tea, I'm parched.'

'I'm not thirsty, but you can have one.' Anything to make her write me a prescription.

She pressed a button on the phone, and a red light started flashing. 'That's the tea button,' she smiled.

I suddenly felt exhausted, like I could sleep for a week.

'Put the scissors down.' She said, facing the phone.

'Why are you talking to the phone? That's not the tea button. Who have you called?'

'I'm just getting us some help.'

'Help, what for?'

'You are off your meds, and you need help. Put down the scissors.'

'They are not scissors; they are as blunt as anything. What did you think I was going to do? Pink you to death? Death by pinking shears, hah, you really thought that of me? All I wanted was a prescription, which I know you can give me.' I threw the scissors down on her desk. 'I'm going now. I know when I'm not wanted. My nurse has treated me like a pariah, so I've never been so disappointed. Well, maybe I was when I discovered that there was no Santa, that was pretty disappointing.' I didn't want to cry in front of her.

'No, just wait here a little while, let's chat. Do you like *Eastenders*?' the traitor said.

'Who cares what I think or like?'

'You know why you are here?' Dr Smart Arse asked.

I didn't answer.

'You stopped taking your medication, and you need to. It helps you.'

'Why have you put me in the hospital?'

'Because you can't look after yourself.'

'I can, too.'

'I'm going to change your antidepressants. You should feel better.'

'When can I go home?'

'Soon.'

'I'm sorry I've been a pain, but I feel better now. My head is calm, and I want to shower.' I laughed. 'I'll take the pills; I want to be normal.' I really did.

'You can have your license back and live normally, that's what you are after?"

'Thank you, I missed it, but I see why you took it from me. At that time, I could barely put one foot in front of the other, never mind driving. I have so much apologising to do. Starting with my husband.'

'He's stuck by you before you were diagnosed. He will be fine, I'm sure.'

'I tried to divorce him with an internet piece of paper. I was ridiculous. I truly don't know why he put up with me.'

'So, you have accepted your diagnosis?'

'Yeah, there are several famous people who are bipolar. It's quite the in thing!'

'There is accepting it, and then there is embracing it,' Dr Ferguson laughed.

'At least I'm not Bipolar I, I'll always be grateful for that. Though I believe it's some trip when you are psychotic.'

'It's a completely different kettle of fish,' she explained.

'I'm ready to go home,' I pleaded.

'Just give the meds time to work, and you can go.'

'I actually miss my real dog, my big black Labrador … I don't miss the other one.'

I Waited for You

by Robin Montgomery-Smith

I had no idea why I crept up on Jasper, but I assumed that he could hear me if I was anything but absolutely silent. I took one quiet step at a time, in slow motion, and if he turned around, I froze. It was difficult to stifle a giggle, which pushed at the back of my throat. After a few careful steps, and one near disaster with a Lego brick, I peered over his shoulder as he was texting on his phone. I eyed the screen to see what he was saying. I put my hand over my mouth so he would not hear the beginning of a snigger or the sound of my breathing. Come to think of it, I did not detect my breath either. Oh well. I watched as he texted his mother. At least it was his mother, right?

I don't know what to do, Mum.

Don't worry, sweetheart. You get used to it.

I don't want *to get used to it. I feel like something is missing.*

Missing? What's missing? I wanted to ask him so badly, but I didn't want to give away my position—and he would be cross if he thought I was spying on him. Somewhere in the back of my mind, I was trying to work out what kind of jump-scare would make the most impact. We loved leaping out to scare each other—something we had done since we dated.

What about the kids? How are they?

Kids? My kids? I was so confused, but I kept peeking, still trying to push that giggle back into my throat.

They're OK, I guess. They keep asking what happened.

What happened—wait, something did happen. What happened? I glanced over his shoulder again. The urge to giggle seemed to vanish.

Do you need me to come over? I can sit with them if you want to go to the hospital to see her.

No, Mum. The doctor said it could be days—weeks even.

Hospital?

A loud siren pierced the sound of Jasper tapping on his phone and I covered my ears. The light in the room faded. Flashing red and blue lights reflected off the trees.

How did I get here?

I noticed how cold it was there in the darkness with the flashing lights washing everything in vivid blue strobes. I rubbed my arms and watched as two people pushed a gurney into the back of an ambulance. A tow truck was winching a twisted heap of metal onto a flatbed. A car? Or what was left of one. A fire truck was parked in front of the ambulance, but its red lights weren't flashing. Whatever happened here was over.

Two other people in uniform stood together talking.

'Excuse me,' I said, as I cleared my throat to get their attention.

'Will she be OK?' One of the officers, a woman, rubbed her hand on the back of her neck as she spoke to the other.

'I dunno. That was some head injury.'

'Hello? Excuse me.' *Why are they ignoring me?*

I stepped in front of the woman as she turned away to walk back to a police car parked behind where they stood. She reached towards her shoulder and spoke something into her radio mic, but it was too noisy for me to hear what she said.

I thought I might have better luck with the ambulance driver. He jumped out of the back to close the doors. I walked closer to him so he could hear me.

'Excuse me. Nobody seems to want to speak to me.'

He walked right past me towards the front of the ambulance.

'Jesus Christ. Am I invisible or what?'

That was when I saw it. Or her. Or me. I was lying on that gurney they had pushed into the ambulance. I rubbed my eyes because of course, I was not seeing what I thought I was seeing. When I pulled my fists away, I was standing inside the ambulance.

How the hell did I get in here?

I was right. She *was* me. My long black hair was matted with something. Dirt? Oh. Blood. There was a huge gash on the side of her—my head. One of the paramedics was squirting something on it and dabbing it with a folded bit of gauze.

I stood there, watching him work on me. He put a needle in my arm and stuck some circle things on my chest and my ankles, then he clipped wires on them. The beep was not steady like in the TV programmes. He listened to my heart through a stethoscope and pushed a syringe into a tube that was connected to the needle in my arm.

The movement of the ambulance stopped, and the back doors flew open. The paramedic said words I did not understand and the people wearing green and blue scrubs ran next to the gurney to a small room full of equipment.

I guess I am invisible.

'No. You're not.'

I jumped when I heard the voice. When I turned around, a lady in a hospital gown stood behind me. She was shorter than me, her hair white but her face looked somehow young. Her crystal-blue eyes looked just like my mother's from photos Grandad showed me growing up.

'You scared me. But wait—you can see me? I was beginning to think no one could.'

'Of course, I can see you. You're dead.'

Everything in the room went bright. I felt dizzy. The floor became spongy, hard to walk over. I tried to get away from her, but the more I tried, the slower I moved.

'Oh dear. You didn't know? I really need to stop saying that to people.'

'Yeah, you really should! I'm clearly not dead, I'm right here. And, uh, there, I guess.'

'Let's start over. I'm Edith. What's your name?'

'I'm uh—my name is—'

'Right. That's OK. This happens sometimes. Why don't we go sit over there?'

A shout from one of the nurses pulled me out of the conversation with Edith.

'Diane! Can you hear me, Diane? Open your eyes, c'mon, open your eyes.'

'Is my name Diane?'

'It must be. So, Diane,' she said my name as if she was speaking to a child. 'Sit down. I have a few questions for you. Do you think you can answer them?'

'I'll try.' I could not take my eyes off the room across from the bank of chairs where we sat. I heard the *beep-beep* from the heart monitor but nothing else. Well, nothing else besides Edith's voice.

'Tell me, Diane, is time jumping around a bit?'

'I guess so. Yeah, I think so.'

'OK. And are people you're talking to—besides me, of course—ignoring you?'

'They are. Bit rude, actually.'

'Yes, yes. And before you came here, where were you?'

'Well, I think I was at home, but then I heard sirens and there were all these lights. Then I saw her,' I pointed to the me in the bed in the room, 'I mean me, I mean her—in the ambulance. Now I'm here.'

'Right. You're definitely dead. I'm sorry, but that's the truth. You better get used to it.'

'What if they,' I gestured to the nurses and doctors, 'save me?'

'Luv, if they could save you, then all you'd be doing is hovering over your body in there. I *hate* the hoverers. God, they think they're so special. They always know they can go back in and play that 'I'm in—I'm out' game until they're *saved*. They always know. Bastards.'

'So, if I go in there and hover—'

'I'm afraid it doesn't work like that. If you're here—with me—then it's,' she made a noise as she moved her finger from one side of her throat to the other.

'But I don't want to—be—'

'Oh of course, no one wants to be dead. Do you think I enjoy wandering around this place in nothing but this piece of shit?' She tugged at her gown. 'I mean, this thing is hideous.'

'Why are you here, then?'

'It's my assignment,' she sighed and rolled her eyes.

'Assignment?'

'Yeah, don't worry, you'll get one, too. Clarence should be here soon.'

'Oh my God, like in that film?'

'For God's sake don't ask him that! He hates that joke.'

'I'm not—'

'He's the manager. He's no bloody angel, let me tell you.'

'Oh. Is this—'

'What?'

'Am I in hell?'

Edith threw her head back and cackled. Not laughed. Cackled.

'Oh heaven's no. This is the waiting room. I mean, literally. Look around.'

There were people sitting in chairs all around us. The room where my body was, began to move away and the lights it emitted grew dimmer.

'Wait, are we all, you know?'

'You can say it. It's not a dirty word, you know. Death is just another way of living.'

'Except we're dead. Not alive. So not exactly living.'

'Diane, my child, you've a lot to learn,' she smiled as she patted my leg. 'You're new at this. You'll get the hang of it, just like your—. Um, don't worry. And of course, I'll be here. I just wish they'd let me change clothes.' Her voice rose into a shout. 'Out. Of. These. Clothes. Please.' She turned her attention back to me. 'They never listen. Customer service isn't any better here, believe me.'

A man pushed open a swinging door. He was tall, dark hair, and he wore an expensive-looking suit. Edith nudged me with her elbow and pointed as the man poked his head from behind the door.

'Here we go. That's Clarence.'

'Diane Gibson?' He looked around at all the occupied chairs.

'That's you, dear. Let's go.'

Edith took my hand and walked with me through the open door—into the brightest light I had ever seen. I held my hand up to block it from my eyes.

'Clarence, sir,' Edith jerked her head towards me as we entered the corridor. 'She's—er new? Remember? The lights?'

'Right. Sorry 'bout that, Diane.' He waved his hand, and the lights dimmed just enough for me to see. White. Everything was white. 'Have a seat,' he pointed his pen to a set of two white chairs in front of his white desk.

We both sat down, and Edith crossed her legs whilst pulling down on her hospital gown. I could tell she was trying to be lady-like, which looked rather difficult.

'Diane, do you remember anything that happened today?'

'Not really.' I tried to remember, but the longer I was in this white room, the fuzzier the events became.

'Clarence, sir. She hasn't had the—you know.'

'The what?'

Edith pointed to something on the desk.

'Oh yes. I keep forgetting. What would I do without you, Edith? Here, eat this.'

He handed me something that looked like an apple, but it was blue and soft.

'What is *this?'*

'Just eat it, luv. You'll understand.'

'I don't eat things from people I don't kno—'

Edith cackled again. 'What? You—think he's gonna—*poison* you? You're already dead, remember?' Her laugh echoed in the white room.

'You have a point.' I sniffed the blue squishy apple and licked it. Caramel and candy floss.

'What is it? Something you liked?' Edith's blue eyes were as wide as her smile.

I took a small bite; the flavour exploded in my mouth. The next bite was bigger, and the next one nearly finished the whole whatever-this-was. I guess I had closed my eyes because when I opened them again, the room was different. The desk was a rich mahogany, the walls painted in the softest lilac, and the chairs Edith and I sat on were like burgundy marshmallows.

'What in the he—'

'Not hell, remember? The waiting room.'

'Now, Diane,' continued Clarence, 'do you remember now?'

A light flickered behind me, reflecting on Clarence's face. I turned around in the chair and could see an old-timey projector. As it clicked the film through, the events of that night played out on a screen set up on the opposite wall. I didn't remember seeing that when I came into the room, but then again, everything was white when I arrived.

'Yes,' I drew the word out, 'I think I do.'

'Good. Who will be waiting for you on the top floor?'

'Waiting for me?'

Edith rolled her eyes again. 'Who died before you?'

'Oh. Nearly everyone.'

'Everyone?' Clarence asked as he flipped through a stack of papers on a clipboard. Another thing I hadn't noticed.

'My Mum died when I was seven, Dad when I was twelve. I lived with Grandad until I got married to Jasper.' I felt a tear hit my arm. 'Oh, Jasper. And Sadie. And Jack.'

'Your family. Poor Luv.' Edith stood and put her hand on my shoulder.

'What are they going to do without me? The kids are so little.'

'We have someone looking after them, don't you worry.'

'Who?'

'That's someone else's assignment. They'll be OK.'

Clarence cleared his throat.

'That's your mother, your father, assuming your grandmother?'

'I never met her. She died before I was born.'

'And your grandfather?'

'He passed last year. Right after Sadie was born.' I fell back into the marshmallow-chair. 'Wait. Are they—here?'

'No, they've moved on.'

'Clarence! Sir!'

'Sorry. They're upstairs.'

'You mean—heaven?'

'Is that what they're calling it now, Edith?'

'Yessir, for about the last five or six hundred years.'

'So, it's a new thing, then?'

'Yessir.' She turned to speak to me, 'See, what you call *Heaven* has had many names over time. Clarence is a busy guy, so he needs people like me to help keep him right. Isn't that so, Sir?'

'Indeed, Edith.' He turned back to me. 'Now, Diane. About your assignment—'

'My assignment?'

'Yes. You must work your way upstairs, see.' He pointed to the ceiling with his pen.

'There are about eighteen or so floors above this one. What you call 'Heaven'—we just call it 'Upstairs'—is on the top floor. Your assignments will earn credit, or dots. Once you have enough dots, you move to the next floor, where you'll get a new assignment.'

'So, *you're* just new here, too?'

'Oh, Luv. No. I've been here for such a long time. This is my last stop. Once I've collected a few more dots, I'll get to go, up *there*.' She looked upwards and a smile lit her face.

'The system is that you start on the bottom floor and work your way up. Once your final assignment has earned enough dots, you go upstairs,' he pointed to a door near the back corner of the room—another thing I missed. 'That'll take you directly there, where they'll be waiting for you.'

'Do they—know I'm—here?'

'Edith? Have they been notified?'

'Did I just fall off a turnip truck?' I laughed because Grandad used to say that a lot when I was growing up. 'Of course, they've been notified. I told them before I met Diane in hospital.'

'OK, so that's settled then. Here's your assignment.'

He handed me a silvery envelope. Edith moved to the front of her chair, hands worrying her knees.

'Open it, open it!'

I peeled back the seal, and a string of lights floated out of the opening.

'God, I love that part!' Edith's hands were clasped just below her chin. She looked somewhat younger, her cerulean eyes sparkled like a child at Christmas.

I pulled out a card made from the same silvery material as the envelope and unfolded it. It was blank.

'What's this all about?'

Edith was almost jumping. 'Wait for it.'

The room grew bright again, but this time instead of blinding me, it filled me with warmth. I felt safe, happy, I would say even love. A soft voice whispered in my ear.

'Child. Welcome. You are safe now. Your first assignment is waiting for you through this door.'

Without any visual prompt, I knew the door the voice referred to was behind Clarence, who sat back in his chair, writing something on the clipboard. He wasn't paying any attention. I looked at Edith, who was now standing in front of me, offering me her hand.

'C'mon now, Luv. I'll show you in. Let's go.'

I stood up, put my hand in hers, and we walked together around Clarence's desk. As we approached, the door opened and on the other side was a bridge. At the end of the bridge was the brightest rainbow I had ever seen. It filled the sky.

'What is this place?'

'So, I guess now *you're* the one who just fell off the turnip truck. Look around you. What do you see? C'mon, I know you can't be this daft.'

'A rainbow. Light. Grass.'

Edith sighed and rolled her eyes. 'What are we bloody standing on?'

'A bridg—wait! The *Rainbow* Bridge??'

'You thought it was a load of shit, didn't you? Everybody does. Yup, the one and only.' She waved her arms around, presenting me with our surroundings.

'Where are they, then? If this is the *real* bridge?'

'Hold on. Any second now.'

We stood together on the bridge for a few minutes. We didn't speak or make a sound. Then I heard it—barking dogs. And running. Edith squeezed my hand.

'Do you hear them?'

'I hear something.'

Then I saw them. All of them. There must have been thousands. And they were all running right for me. For a second, I was afraid they were going to run me over. But they stopped. Their barking had stopped, but they were panting, mouths open, tongues hanging, almost smiling. I noticed movement from the back of the group, all standing there in the sunshine under the cloudless sky, the colours of the rainbow reflecting on their fur. I noticed another bit of movement in a different part of the crowd and another one still from closer to where we stood. All at once, three dogs emerged to stand in front of the rest of them. Their eyes brightened and they set off at a full run, straight at me. This time I wasn't afraid. This time, I knew what was happening.

'Will! Joe! Rover!'

'*Rover*? Really?'

'I was a kid.'

They jumped up on top of me as I bent down to welcome them into my arms. I couldn't believe they were there. They jumped, tails wagging, licking my face.

'They missed you.'

'I missed them, too. Every day.'

'I can see that.'

The other dogs started running off in different directions and where they had stood was a box. Edith nodded her head.

'Go on. That's for you.'

I walked over to the box, dogs on my heels, and picked it up. I opened it with a bit of apprehension, not sure what might be inside.

'Don't worry. It won't kill you. *Again.*' Edith giggled.

When I opened it, there were three small red balls.

'What are these for?'

'Those are your first three dots, Luv.'

'What do I do with them?'

'Bring them with you,' she said as she walked back towards the door we had arrived from just moments earlier. My three precious dogs stopped just short of the door.

'Aren't they coming?'

'Not yet. You still have work to do.'

I bent down to kiss them all in the soft flesh between their ears—always my favourite place to kiss them. I breathed in their sweet scents.

'I'll see you soon, boys. Take care of each other.'

I swear they were smiling at me. We walked back into the room where Clarence sat, still working away at his desk.

'Ah, that didn't take long. May I?' He held out his hand, and I placed the box in his palms.

'First assignments usually take a bit longer.'

'She's a good 'un, isn't she? I knew she would be.'

'Three? That's impressive.'

'That was my first assignment?'

'Not so much an assignment as a test of sorts. To see if animals loved you.'

'Do animals not love some people?'

'You'd be surprised.'

'Yeah,' said Edith with a spark in her eye, 'there was this one guy—'

'Edith.' Clarence looked at her over the top of his glasses.

'Sorry.' She did not tell the rest of the story.

'Now that's all done—'

'That was it?'

'Yes, and now that's done, here's your fourth assignment.'

'Wait. That was my first one. Why the fourth?'

'You have three dots. You get to skip ahead a bit.'

The next few levels passed by in a blink. I returned once more to Clarence's office to see him sitting at his desk alone. I handed him another box of red balls as I sat in the marshmallow-chair.

'Clarence, where's Edith?'

'You didn't think she was just working with *you*, did you?'

'I—I don't know what I was thinking, but this *is* my first time on this side of things.'

'Of course, of course. I always forget. Edith keeps me right. Here's your next assignment,' he said as he handed me another envelope. I was used to the look and feel of them now, but as I pulled this one out, Clarence put his hand up. 'This one is going to be completely different from the others. Just prepare yourself.'

If I still had a heartbeat, I think it would be banging in my ears. The note said,

'*Assignment:*
Jacob Shiller
Age: 2
Location: Sheridan, Wyoming, USA
Mission: Escort'

'What does *escort* mean?'

'You need to bring him here.'

'Wait. He's only two!'

'I'm aware,' he flipped through stacks of files and pulled out a thin one from the bottom of the pile. 'Here. Ah, yes. He's getting hit by a car later today. You'll need to be there to comfort him and get him here.'

I stared at this figure, sitting behind a huge wooden desk, acting as if this was just part of a normal day.

'He's not yet been hit?'

'He's not.'

'Then—can't I—stop it?'

'You ever heard the term; *it's his time to go*?'

'Well, yes—but—'

'Then—and repeat after me—it's his time—'

'Why can't we stop it?'

'You're not repeating, Diane. Listen, it isn't pleasant what I do here. I'm not *killing* anyone, by the way. I'm just here to help them on their way. Jacob has lived his life—'

'At two?? Are you being serious? What kind of life—'

'*His* life. Some souls don't even get that much time. He's known love. He's had happiness. He's taught lessons. He's needed *here*. He has assignments, too, you know.'

'Eh? How can a two-year-old have assign—'

'You've been here now, what is it, thirteen years—'

'No, I've only been here a few days.'

'Thirteen years. You died in 2012. It's 2025 now.'

'How—'

'It's how time works here. Edith—or was that supposed to be me?' He scratched his head. 'Someone should have explained that to you when you first arrived. Anyway, off you to go to Wyoming. Dress warm, it's February there.'

A door across the room clicked open and I felt the chill of a sharp breeze hit my face. I looked over my shoulder at Clarence, who was waving his hand, shooing me as if I were a cat in his garden.

'Jacob's just through that door. You'll know what to do when you get there.'

I continued through the door and as it closed behind me, I could no longer see where I had stepped through the door. It was cold, but I felt no discomfort. I was standing on a pavement, near the corner of a crossroads. The remnants of ice were built up on the roadside, and the light was dull—the sun shrouded behind the flat-grey clouds. I looked up one street, down another, and from side-to-side before I saw him. I could not explain how I knew this was Jacob, but as soon as my eyes found him, a moment of recognition hit me. I ran towards him, and for a few seconds, I thought I might be able to stop it, but just as I hurried to him, he took the step which sealed his fate. A solid thud echoed, and his tiny body flew out before the car that hit him. Tyres screeched, a woman screamed, a car door was thrown open. Before I had time to process the scene before me, I felt a tug on my sleeve. I looked down and standing next to me, no taller than my knee, was Jacob.

'Where's my Mummy?'

'Are you Jacob?'

He nodded.

'I'm Diane,' I squatted to meet his eyes, but he was still smaller than I could make myself. 'I'm here to take you home.'

'With Mummy?'

'No, sweetheart. Mummy is going to stay here.'

I could hear sirens in the distance. Jacob's face was pale, and his bright-green eyes were filling with tears.

'It's OK. You'll see Mummy before you know it.'

'Can I take Nerkle?'

'Nerkle?'

'My bear,' he pointed to the street, where his slight, broken body lay twisted in a heap. A white bear lay clutched in his lifeless hand. Next to it was a familiar box—my dots.

'You stay right here. I'll see if I can get him, OK?'

His finger dangled from his mouth. I could see he was terrified, and I had to find a way to comfort him. I walked towards his body and bent over to see if I could pick up his teddy bear. I put one hand on its leg and smoothed the hair away from the toddler's face with the other. I lifted the box before I stood up. As I approached his spiritual body, waiting as he was told, I held out his bear. He grabbed it, pulled it to his chest, and hugged it with all his might. He offered his tiny hand for me to hold. As soon as I grasped it, all the surrounding noise was silenced and a door opened in front of us. I led Jacob into a large room—the same large room I had been in just days—years before with Edith. I lifted him up and we sat together on two chairs in the back.

'Diane?'

'Edith!'

She bent down, holding the back of her hospital gown together behind her.

'And who do we have here?'

'I Jakey.'

'This is Jacob and Nerkle,' I said as I pointed to his bear.

'Oh, is Nerkle your best friend?'

'Yeah.' He cut his eyes up at Edith over the head of his bear, which was squished beyond recognition from his clutch.

A door across the room opened up and Clarence walked through, looking at a clipboard. 'Jacob Shiller?'

'That's us. Better go. Good to see you, Edith.'

'You get 'em, hen. I'm so proud of you!'

I smiled behind me as I walked Jacob to the corridor and into the office. Jacob shielded his eyes from the bright light, which Clarence noticed and dimmed with a wave of his hand. When we arrived, there were three older people there—two men and a woman.

'Jacob!' The woman bent over, arms open. Jacob ran to her, and she lifted him in a tight hug.

'I trust you'll be able to help him with his assignments?'

The three of them nodded to Clarence and they walked away, through another random door which opened on the other side of the room.

'He has—minders?'

'Grandparents. You don't think we'd set a toddler on assignments on his own, do you?'

'As I keep saying, Clarence, I'm new at this.'

'Well, new—ish. The box?'

I handed over the wooden box. Clarence opened it, counted dots with his fingers, and nodded before putting it on his desk.

'So, how does it feel?'

'You mean, Jacob?'

'No, I mean how does it feel to be finished?'

'Finished? How can I be finished?'

'You've completed all your assignments. Collected all your dots—more than normal, actually. Remember, you were able to skip a few after all your dogs found you.'

'But—what about Edith? I just saw her—' I pointed to the door behind me.

'Oh yes. She'll be waiting for you.'

'What do you mean? She's in *there*!'

'She's not.'

'We just had a conversation.'

'Trust me. I've been at this a very long time. She's waiting for you.'

'But I thought my family were the ones who would be waiting for me.'

'Yes, that's right.'

'I don't understand.'

Clarence stood and walked towards me, leading me by the elbow towards the big doorway. That one was different from any other doorway I had seen so far. It was taller than the rest. It was trimmed in gold and glimmered in the light from Clarence's office. As it opened, I could hear a crowd of people, who were all standing in clumps on the other side. They were talking in low voices and as soon as we stepped into the room, they stopped and looked at me. I recognised several family members who had died throughout my lifetime. My scruffy dog, Rover from my childhood, and my two greyhounds—Will and Joe—were flanking my family, tails wagging, smiling up at me.

'Mum! Dad! Gran! Boys!'

They all ran to hug me. I felt complete.

And then I saw Edith.

'But how—'

She stepped forward, no longer wearing her hospital clothes, but a flowing white gown that floated around her body like a cloud. She reached her arm out to me.

'Diane,' she pulled me towards her and wrapped her arms around me.

'Edith? What are you doing—um how did you—'

'Diane, I'm your sixth great-grandmother.'

'What? I don't underst—'

'I waited for you. I knew you were going to need some extra help when it was your time. I just waited around for you so I could be the one who brought you here—brought you home.'

'You waited—for me?'

'Of course, my darling. Now come with us. We have so much to tell you.'

Beetroot
by Aimee McGowan

'Hello!' Grace announced, letting herself in. 'It's just me, are you home, dearies?' her voice lifting at the word 'dearies'.

'Katie?' she sang, listening for a reply. The house was silent. Sighing, she closed the back door, her shoulders lowered.

'Hmm.' She wandered down the hall to the kitchen. She filled the kettle and set it to boil. She knew that they said: 'only boil what you need.' But where was the practicality in that? What if the water went off and you desperately needed a cup of tea? No. It just made no sense. She always filled the kettle, just past the MAX line on the inside, so that when it boiled, it nearly jumped right out. That's how it should be done. She nodded to herself as she began to wade through Katie's cupboard looking for her china teacup.

'It's like the Cave of Wonders in here!' The cupboards were brimming, packed until not even a mouse could fit in the gaps. In confirmation, a box of sweetener came tumbling out, crashing on the worktop below her.

'Aha!' Her eyes twinkled, and she grinned, her white dentures on full display. 'This needs clearing. Who needs twelve oddly shaped and unmatching mugs?' It was beyond Grace's comprehension. That's the trouble these days. Everyone wants more, more, more. No one appreciates what they have. It takes the excitement out of everything. You get something, then you want the next thing. Then the next thing after that. The world had gone insane. People walking about, talking to themselves on the street. What had happened to everyone?

'Oh!' she squealed.

Laila might be up in her room listening to her EarPods or whatever they're called. They were oddly small, compared to the

Walkmans of Katie's youth, and unrecognisable from the record players of her own.

'Laila?' She slowly made her way up the stairs, her knees creaking, the bannister bearing her weight. Her breath deepened as she made it to the top, her cheeks flushed from the effort.

'Laila?' She repeated, not wanting to scare the poor dear.

She lifted her hand slowly and knocked lightly on the door. No reply. She tried again, louder this time. Still no answer.

'Hmm. I'm sorry if I'm disturbing you, honey,' she began, opening the door, the hinges pleading for some oil.

The room was empty, the curtains still drawn. She clicked her tongue and opened the curtains to let in the meagre sunlight, attempting to peer through the thick grey clouds. A shrill beeping rang through the room. Her eyebrows furrowed as she tried to find the contraption that was making the noise. She searched the desk, then made her way to the bed. The beeping became louder and louder, until she finally noticed the ball on the bedside table, a little light circling round the bottom.

'Oh! What is this? Ah—Alexandra? Alexis? Alexis!' The light changed colour and the beeping stopped. Then it changed back, and the beeping resumed.

'Alexis. Stop beeping.' She felt incredibly foolish for talking to it like a person. That's another problem these days; people are nicer to their infernal machines than to each other. 'Alexis' complied, and Grace gave a slight nod, the blush turning into a smile.

'See? I'm good with the machines.' She stood and fixed her top, making sure it sat straight, and made her way back to the kettle. She checked it was full; fuller than full, the way a kettle should be, and set it to boil. Her cup was already on the counter waiting for her. She had raised her daughter right, provisions for guests always handy. She made tea and set it on the table next to the recliner, hands wobbling as she tried to keep it from spilling. She sat and pressed the button for the footrest to come up. She closed her eyes and listened for signs of her daughter and granddaughter returning.

Grace opened her eyes, and the sun was gone, there were no lights on, and her arms were covered in goosebumps. She leaned over and pulled the toggle on the lamp as she tried to remember where she was. She'd visited Katie and Laila. They weren't home. She'd made tea. She lifted the cup and took a sip, the cold liquid making her grimace as she set it back down. Did she boil the kettle? Where were the girls? Katie phoned her every morning and night. She hadn't phoned today. Laila hadn't even opened her curtains, but they were nowhere to be found.

'Alexis. What time is it?'

'The time is 10.33 p.m.,' came the reply from the little ball in the corner of the living room.

'Alexis, where are they?' She didn't like the way her voice shook.

'I'm not quite sure how to help you with that,' said Alexis.

'Me either,' she said softly.

She went into the kitchen, refilled the kettle, and set it to boil. Where were they? Had something happened? No, that was ridiculous. This wasn't some James Patterson novel. They'd be home soon. But it was after ten o'clock. Laila's got university. Katie's got work. She had raised them right, not like those hooligans with the tattoos, piercings and baggy trousers. How do they not fall to their ankles when they walk? No. Not her girls. They'd be home any minute. She gave a quick nod to herself and made some tea. On her way back to the living room, she remembered to press the little boost button on the heating 'doodah' on the wall. The girls would come home to a nice warm house. She was there to take care of them. They'd love to come into a warm home. She smiled. The recliner groaned as she lowered herself into it.

'Everyone gains a few pounds in their old age,' she said, her face flushing, before she remembered she was the only one in to hear its protests.

'Alexis, what time is it?' she asked again, the fluttering in her chest growing stronger every minute.

'The time is 10.47 p.m.'

'Alexis, what time is it in the UK?' she tried again, sure that the little ball was wrong.

'In the United Kingdom, it's 10.47 p.m.,' came the reply, quick and sure.

'Alexis, turn on the TV.'

The TV on the wall glowed and made a nice chime as it came on. Grace patted down the couch and found the TV remote quickly, opened the menu to check the time.

'Alexis was right,' she mumbled, the sound too quiet for the ball to hear.

She made her way back into the hall and flipped the light, her heart hammering in her chest, her eyes filling with tears she refused to allow to escape. She needed to help them. She needed to help her girls. If she could just find her handbag, that computer-phone thing Katie had bought for her was in there. She had to phone them; her heart couldn't take much more of this before it would finally erupt from her chest. Or burst through her throat. She found her bag hanging on the bannister and thrust her arm in, causing her purse, manicure set, tissues, and mints to spill out over the floor. She didn't look down, just kept up her hunt, her fingers frantically searching the bottom of the bag. After what felt like a lifetime, she freed the 'computer-phone' from its faux leather confines and tried to find the little button on the side that Katie showed her to power it up. She found it and pressed, and the screen lit up. Then went dark. She pressed it again, and it lit up. Then went dark again.

'Oh, for goodness' sake! This is an emergency!' she screamed at it, her cheeks getting hotter and hotter until she was sure that her face might combust. She had a strong urge to throw the thing back down the hallway, but she remembered she needed the blasted contraption since home telephones weren't a 'thing' anymore, as Laila liked to remind her. Poor Laila, poor Katie, they were God knows where, in God knows what trouble, and here she was about to break the only thing she could use to help them. Tears sprang back into her eyes, and this time she couldn't stop a few from tearing their way down her cheeks.

'Oh, girls.' She sighed, feeling like her chest was caving in on itself. Her heart might have actually broken free, since she couldn't feel it anymore. She was empty. Lost. Alone.

No. She wasn't alone. She had the girls, and they needed her.

Trying once again, she pressed the button on the side and the screen lit up. This time it stayed on.

'Yes!' Her fingers fumbled, and she almost dropped it. She carefully pressed her index finger on the little icon on the screen, and it unlocked. There were her girls staring back at her.

'Don't worry girls, I'm coming.'

She found the little phone picture and pressed it, then dialled the three little numbers she had never dialled in her life.

'Emergency. Which service do you require?' came the woman's voice on the end of the phone.

'My girls haven't come home. They're not here. They're always home by now. Something's happened.' Her words ran into each other, each one tumbling over the last until she was sure the woman couldn't possibly have understood her.

'Your girls? Your children?' she asked, her voice much too calm for the current situation.

'Yes. My daughter and my granddaughter. They aren't home, and the door was unlocked, and I don't know where they are, and they're always home by now.' She couldn't suppress the sob that formed on the word '*home*'. They were always home. Her throat began to swell up, until she was sure she couldn't get words out, growing tighter and tighter as seconds ticked by on the phone.

'OK honey, what's your name?'

'Grace. My name is Grace.' She was sure that her voice sounded curt, she was just in such a rush to find them.

'Hi Grace, my name is Susan. Where are you just now?'

'My daughter's house. They're not home.'

'Thank you. Do you know your daughter's address?'

'Of course, I know her address. She lives on the next street from me. She wanted to stay close to me. We're close, you know. We see each other every day.'

'OK, thank you. I'm going to send some police round to your daughter's house just now. Can you give me the full address please?'

'Yes, it's Number Seven Hillside Drive.'

'OK, that's perfect. I'm going to send a couple of officers round just now. They should be there in about five minutes, is it OK if I stay on the phone until they arrive?'

'Yes. No problem. Thank you.'

'Not a problem. I'm glad to help. I'll just stay on the line with you.'

'They're good girls, you know—my Katie and her Laila. They look after me, and I look after them.'

'They're very lucky to have you. Being so close, I'm sure they love that you live nearby.'

'Oh, we're lucky to have each other. My Katie loves her job at the lawyer's office down the road, and my Laila is at university. She wants to be a nurse.'

'I'm sure she'll be an amazing nurse if she takes after you, with how well you take care of them.'

'You're very kind to say so.'

A deep, rumbling voice followed a loud knock at the door: 'Hello?'

'I think they're here now,' Grace said, taking a deep breath.

'OK, I'll let you go and speak to them,' Susan said. 'Take care, Grace.' The phone went blank.

'Come in officers. I don't know what to do.'

'OK, let's see,' the officer said.

'Mum?' came a familiar voice from the hallway.

'Katie? Katie! That's my Katie!' Grace whirled around, searching the hallway for Katie's face. Sure enough, she walked in, her eyes frantically darting about and her eyebrows drawn together.

'Where have you been? I was worried sick. I thought you were in trouble—I thought—' Grace stammered, her words tumbling out in a mixed jumble.

'We were out tonight, Mum. I told you yesterday, and I texted you this morning to remind you,' said Katie, looking between the officers as her face turned beetroot-red.

'I—I don't have a text! You didn't tell—' Grace paused for a minute, a small niggle at the back of her mind trying to find its way forward. There was something. A conversation, a phone call maybe? With Katie. She had arranged a trip. No. A spa day for Laila … for her … something. Grace flushed; the heat worked its way up from the tips of her toes, through her legs (which began to tremble), into her stomach (which became hot and rumbly), up her arms (which felt like jelly), and into her face. She had never seen a human's cheeks burn right off, but right then, she was sure that's exactly what was about to happen.

'I—I—I—. Sorry, officers.' was all she could manage to say before the room erupted into laughter, and embarrassment threatened to swallow her whole.

A Rare Night In

by Laura Scott

I spray pomegranate and passion fruit air freshener around the living room and inhale the sweet solitude. I put new glittery coasters on my glass coffee table and smile while I think about how much my ex-husband would hate them. The doorbell chimes, and I peek through the Venetian blinds. It's Amanda, she spots me through the slats and waves. Then I feel a bit stupid when I remember I can check who is at the door through the doorbell camera on my phone. I adjust my black faux-leather leggings and walk through the hallway to answer the door.

'Hi, you look fab!' I say while hugging Amanda. I've always envied her figure and bouncy hair. At school, her blonde locks floated in perfect, tight curls down her back, like white-gold streamers.

'Hey Christine, it's been a while—you smell great,' says Amanda as she inhales my *Gucci Gorgeous Gardenia* perfume.

Before I get the chance to close the door, Karen is walking up the garden path with a bottle of Prosecco in her hand.

'Hi … where's Shannon?' I ask.

'On her way …' Karen replies as she walks in the door.

I roll my eyes. She's always late.

Karen and Amanda sit down on the sofa, complimenting my new sequined curtains and cushions. I pour the Prosecco into tall flute glasses and pass them around; the bubbles dance in the glasses, mimicking the excitable atmosphere and the music beating from the soundbar. I think that's why I like having my own space now; I get to live my life my way, the way it should be.

A short while later, Shannon swaggers in with a blue carrier bag, her carry-out clinking. She's wrapped up in a large black puffer jacket that goes down to her trainers and a mustard-yellow scarf.

'Ooft, it's warm in here,' she says as she removes the jacket and scarf. 'You lot are looking very glam, are we going out?'

'No, she's antisocial at the minute,' Amanda replies.

'We weren't planning to,' Karen answers as she crosses one leg over the other, flexing her kitten heel sandals.

'Are your feet not freezing in them? It's nearly winter!' Shannon says.

'I've not had a chance to wear them yet, I hardly get out these days,' Karen says.

Shannon takes out two bottles of wine and lays them on the glass table. The carrier bag rustles as she tips it upside down, and her cigarettes, Doritos and a packet of Skittles spill onto the coffee table—I wince.

'I just heard off the girl in the wee shop that the lollipop lady got knocked down the other day,' says Shannon.

Karen, Amanda and I look at each other in shock.

'Just a matter of time before something happened … some people drive about crazy around that shop,' Shannon says.

'Is she OK?' I ask.

'She's going to be OK, broken leg and a bit shaken, so she'll not be working for a while,' Shannon replies. 'Convenient for me though, there'll be a job going.'

I take a deep breath, 'Well, at least she's going to be OK. Could have been worse …'

'Could have been worse,' Amanda agrees as she nods her head, her face solemn.

'Yeah, could've been worse,' Karen echoes.

'What happened to the job you had?' I ask Shannon while placing an empty wine glass on top of a coaster.

'Och, it's a long story …' Shannon says. Her mobile phone flashes, and she lifts it up, the screen partially smashed, 'Two minutes ...'

'I see you've had one of those Smart Meter things installed,' Amanda says to me, changing the subject as she lifts the small portable 'In-Home Display' that's sitting on the side table.

'Yeah, the guy was around the other day …'

'I'm not sure if I can get a Smart Meter as I use the pre-payment card thing,' Shannon says while pouring her wine and splashing drops on my table. 'They're a pain in the arse. Was in the middle of watching *Coronation Street* the other night and the electric cut out.'

'I think you can still get one,' says Amanda. 'Would be easier for you to top up too.'

'Mmm …' Shannon replies as she taps away on her phone with one hand while managing to drink her wine in the other.

'Anyway,' I continue, 'I didn't think the guy was that attractive at first, but the more he chatted, I thought, *you're not too bad*. He said I didn't look my age …'

'How did you end up telling him your age?' Amanda asks.

'You've always looked younger than all of us,' Shannon interrupts, 'Mind the days when we would try and get into pubs and clubs, Christine was always getting a knock back.'

'I certainly don't feel young at the minute,' I say as I get up off my chair, exaggerating stiff movements. I brush off the compliment as it's not something I'm used to receiving. 'I'm going to the loo.'

I'm already feeling woozy from the Prosecco and realise I was only at the toilet about half an hour ago. I regret my choice of clothing as I struggle to roll down my tight leather leggings. And I wish I'd put on my large, comfortable cotton pants instead of these lacy ones from Victoria's Secret. I mean—who is going to be seeing them anyway?! I think about going upstairs to change, but Amanda and Karen look so good, especially since they have been making the effort to attend so many fitness classes recently. I can't keep up. I look down and notice how much my leggings enhance my belly bloat that appears around this time most evenings. Maybe I should take a break from the drink. Or at least cut down a bit. Then a hot sweat creeps up through my core, my satin top begins to itch as though it has turned to wool, and perspiration gathers in my cleavage. My heart beats hard and I try to focus on my breathing—inhaling for four seconds, then exhaling for five, six, seven … while I place my ice-cold hands on my cheeks. The new meditation app I downloaded recently is proving useful and may be worth the premium subscription fee after all.

When I return, Karen and Amanda are boogying around my living room to dance music, taking me back to the 1990s. I join in waving my arms in the air, but it's as though there are tight elastic bands attached to my hips, pulling them back down. The song ends, and we sit down to catch our breath.

'Put on some music that's a bit more chilled,' Shannon says.

I lift my phone and play 'I Wanna Be Yours', and it smooths my nerves like an iron over silk on a delicate setting. I open the window a crack, allowing in a nip of the frosty air, and it settles my sweats. I lay back on the sofa and think of the engineer who installed my Smart Meter. In fact, I haven't stopped thinking about him. Our conversation has been going around and around in my head for days. I gaze out the window and notice how dark and clear the sky is tonight, the stars twinkling intensely.

'Anyhow, what happened with … Smart Meter Man?' Karen asks as though she has read my mind.

'His name's Martin,' I say.

'Did you manage to get a phone number?' Amanda asks.

'I did actually,' I say, giggling, my face feeling hotter again.

'Thought you were done with men?' Shannon says.

'I'm not sure about dating, it sounds like hard work. I'm quite happy with my self-determined life for now.'

'It's nice to look though, right?' Amanda asks.

'Think Christine, instead of going on one of those dating apps, you could just arrange for workmen to come to your house to "fix things" for you,' Shannon says as she raises her hands and air quotes with her fingers.

'Yeah, it's nice to look … if I did that, Shannon, I'd be able to check them out in real life, rather than a photo,' I say. 'Martin was very thorough. After he fit the meter, I got a full demonstration on how it worked.'

'Ah bet you did!' Shannon says.

'Enough, you,' I say in a shrill tone as I wave my hand towards Shannon, nearly spilling my drink. 'Anyway, I am definitely done with dating ... for now.'

'Really?!' my three friends say in unison.

'Yes. Martin was very polite though, and he listened when I spoke about how I wanted to focus on my career,' I say, as I recall, the presence of his strong, well-built body—

'Why did you take his number then?' Shannon asks.

'I was being polite,' I reply.

The feminine energy circulates around the room like a rabble of butterflies. We dance; we talk about wellbeing and the importance of self-care. We laugh so much, I exclaim that I'll need to remember and wear some TENA Lady next time we meet up. Then Amanda says she's going home; she needs her beauty sleep. Shannon is absorbed in her phone. Karen stays a bit longer; she's asking me more about Martin the engineer, and she speaks of her own relationship troubles.

At the end of the evening, I find myself alone again. I attempt to tidy away the glasses and rearrange my cushions while swaying in time with the music. I wipe over the coffee table, removing a few sticky circles, and give it a polish. Then I flop down on my sofa, exhausted and a bit drunk. Then, my doorbell chimes. I don't even check who it is. I bet Shannon's forgotten something. When I open the door, Martin is standing there smiling.

'Hi, eh, hello, I messaged you to say I was on my way …' Martin says.

'Umm … Hi,' I say. 'I messaged—you?'

'Eh … yeah,' Martin says. He holds up his phone showing a text conversation we seem to have had, but I'm struggling to focus on it.

'I didn—' I begin to say, then think … *Shannon,* she must have messaged him, from *my* phone. 'Oh, sorry, I've had a few drinks. Umm … come on in.' I stand back from the door, gesturing my hand in towards the hall.

Martin smiles as he walks in, 'So, what needs fixing?'

'Well, my dishwasher has been broken for a few weeks now and I'm fed up washing the dishes …' I say.

'So do you want me to start with washing the dishes … or fixing the dishwasher …?'

Phoenix Rising

by Rose Campbell-Smith

Margaret Shaw's apartment was a shrine to her life's interruptions. The air hung heavy with nostalgia, echoing the remnants of life that once filled the space within its walls. Dust danced in the slanted shafts of light filtering through half-drawn curtains, settling on memories and a sleepy cat curled up tightly in the warm sunbeam. A potted geranium sat lifelessly in the corner of the windowsill, leaning into the shadows, its once vibrant green leaves now drooping in defeat. It had been a gift from a neighbour last Christmas; a gesture of kindness Margaret hadn't known how to repay. She had watered it at first, until she didn't. It was long past saving, but Margaret kept it there anyway. 'Water isn't my element,' she often muttered to herself. The plant's withered leaves felt more like a metaphor she wasn't ready to face; nothing felt worth the effort of tending anymore.

The clock on the mantel's pendulum swung softly, its rhythmic 'tick-tock.' Beside the clock rested the key and wallet of a deceased husband, evoking memories of a life once shared, their surfaces coated with a fine layer of dust.

Margaret's life had once been full of laughter and purpose. The home she shared with Frank, her husband of twenty-seven years, was a home where books filled every shelf with careful order, where the scent of Frank's pipe mingled with the pinecones crackling in the fire. Love had been almost tangible here, woven into the very fabric of the space. But cancer had a way of hollowing out not just the body but everything around it.

She hadn't known how quickly time could shift. One day, they were planning a holiday by the sea; the next, she was learning the name of his oncologist.

Margaret became Frank's night nurse when the illness stole his strength. She would brew coffee at midnight to keep herself awake. Midnight had a way of stretching time, making each minute feel longer than the last. She wasn't much of a coffee drinker before, but during those nights, it became her lifeline. Frank never liked it. He hated the smell. Yet there she had been, cup in hand, watching him sleep, hoping he couldn't smell it over the medications and the soft hum of the machines.

He didn't have a lot to say towards the end. They had spent years chatting, sharing their dreams with each other, finishing each other's sentences, knowing each other's thoughts without words, but in those final days, their conversations were different. Softer, slower. The silence between them felt heavier. She'd talk to fill the space, hoping he could hear her even if he couldn't respond. The words were mostly for her, an attempt to keep the night from swallowing them whole.

During the day, the house felt different somehow, probably due to their daughters. They were the day nurses: stronger, more efficient, brighter, more alive, still smiling, despite everything. But the nights belonged to her and Frank. Just the two of them. That was when the house settled into a kind of hush, and she slipped into the quiet rhythm of keeping watch. She was the night nurse, and he was her patient. It changed them, it changed her. She loved him, but she was so tired. Bone-tired. Coffee wasn't just coffee back then. It was survival in a mug.

When she'd make coffee at midnight, not because she wanted it, but because she needed something to do, something to keep her hands moving when the waiting pressed too hard on her heart. Even now, when she makes a cup late at night, it's not just for the caffeine. It's for him, for those nights they shared, for the silence they held together, and the things they never got to say. It's strange how the smell of coffee can still pull her back there, to those nights. Not a memory she holds dear, but one that lingers all the same.

When he was gone, the silence became absolute.

Margaret stopped talking altogether. Days blurred into weeks, and the house, once alive with their shared energy, grew dim and cluttered. She left his wallet and keys on the mantel, exactly where he'd always kept them, and avoided the space altogether. The smell of coffee lingered in the kitchen long after she'd stopped making it, a ghost of the nights she had spent pacing and hoping for a miracle.

Her days were full of rituals, small acts meant to keep her afloat. Margaret swung open the door of the washing machine, the faint creak blending with the steady hum of dryers lining the laundrette. The hum of machines filled the room, a steady background noise that somehow made Margaret feel less alone on a rare outing to the laundrette. The basket perched on her hip tipped forward, spilling its contents in an orderly heap on the machine's rim. White sheets, a few pale t-shirts, and a lone towel waited, a soft, muted palette.

She began feeding the machine, piece by piece, her fingers brushing against the cold metal drum. A shirt snagged briefly on the edge, and she gave it a firm tug before throwing it in. Then her hand paused. There, nestled among the whites, was a sock, bright pink, an anomaly that didn't belong.

Margaret held it up, squinting at it in the fluorescent light. She glanced at the pile, at the machine already half-full. A quiet sigh escaped her lips. Setting the sock aside, she muttered, 'That was close,' ... and resumed her methodical loading, this time with care. The small act left her unsettled. Things like this reminded her that the past had a way of sneaking in, uninvited.

Margaret closed the washing machine door with a firm push, the glass smudged where her fingers had pressed. She reached for the detergent bottle when the doorbell chimed, the sharp sound cutting through the low drone of machines.

'Margaret?'

Her hand froze mid-reach. That voice, soft but edged with surprise, tightened something in her chest. She turned slowly.

There he was, standing just inside the laundrette his basket resting on his hip. David. His hair was streaked with grey now, his jawline softer, but the crooked tilt of his smile hadn't changed.

'David,' she managed, her voice barely audible.

'I can't believe it,' he said, stepping closer, his gaze steady on her. 'After all these years.'

She gripped the detergent bottle tighter, unsure what to say. The past hung in the air between them, delicate but persistent, like the faint scent of fabric softener.

'How are you?' he said, stepping closer still.

Margaret hesitated, unsure how to answer such a simple question—*Lonely. Tired. Trying.*—Instead, she said, 'I'm here.' Her voice steady but quiet.

David nodded as if that was answer enough.

Their conversation started cautiously, like strangers testing the waters. Yet as they talked, Margaret felt something stir inside her, a tiny flicker of warmth, like the first spark of a fire. It wasn't much, a small but significant shift. It wasn't hope, not quite, but it was close, close enough to remind her that maybe she didn't have to go through life alone.

Later that week, Margaret stood in the dim light of her small, book-cluttered sitting room. Books overran the space, each corner crammed: stacked on the floor, piled high on tables, peeking out from windowsills, and spilling from the cluttered bookshelves, creating a labyrinth of stories waiting to be explored. The carpet beneath her feet was once a deep crimson but had lost its vibrancy and was now worn in places. The wooden floorboards, painted black, contributed to the gloom of the room.

Her fingers lingered over the little line caught silver fish around her neck; its inscription a whisper of love long gone. '*Love you always, little fish,*' it read. The words felt hollow now, their echo fading with time. A Christmas gift, exchanged before the word 'cancer' had turned their lives into a series of goodbyes.

She had to sit down.

Her gaze fell on the business card buried in clutter, its edges curling slightly. '*Psychic Readings by Madame Amelia,*' it read in fading script. The sight of it tugged at something deep inside her, a bittersweet reminder of ambitions she had once held so tightly.

Fortune-telling had once flowed through her veins like an enchanting river, vibrant and unyielding, but the past year had worn down her confidence, turning certainty into doubt. Business was slow now, the phone eerily silent most days.

Her gaze drifted to the stack of fortune-telling cards nearby. She reached for them out of habit, only to pause. They had felt heavier in her hands than they used to, as though the cards themselves resisted being dealt, as if they too doubted her touch. Her fingers brushed over the cards, once owned by her Granny Bryce. A formidable woman who always insisted the cards knew everything. She could still recall the way her grandmother's hands, gnarled and weathered like ancient roots, danced over the cards with a practised elegance, the soft click of cardboard edges meeting the air in a melody of mystery. There was a calm intensity in her tone, a quiet power that made you believe she could pluck secrets straight from the ether.

But now? Now, those very cards sat before her, and she stared at them with a silent plea for even a flicker of inspiration. Instead, doubt settled in beside her, familiar and steadfast, like an old friend she didn't quite know how to part with. She paused for a moment before she steered her focus back toward her future.

She was sitting at the rickety desk that bore the weight of her hopes, desperation and frustrations. But the most glaring reminder of her desperation was this brand-new laptop, gleaming with promise and possibility. It had pushed her over her limits financially, but it was necessary if she wanted to try and rise from the ashes of her current spiral. A jar of sharpened pencils sat on the desk, a testament to the small rituals that filled the long minutes on hold with the credit card debt management team. 'Over thirty-five freaking minutes,' she muttered under her breath, annoyance bubbling up.

Social media was the way forward, or so she had heard. She had read the blogs, watched the videos, absorbed every nugget of advice she could find. At 63, the idea of connecting with the world through a screen felt like a leap into the unknown, but she clung to it like a lifeline in turbulent waters.

With a deep breath, she opened her laptop. The familiar startup chime and the soft glow of the screen wrapped around her like a quiet promise of possibility. Maybe, just maybe, with some hard work and a touch of her magic, she could transform the remnants of her past into a brighter future

This new chapter wasn't just about tarot and fortune-telling. It was about rediscovering herself, reclaiming the identity she thought she'd lost. Day by day, she would nurture her dreams, even as the neglected geranium in the window withered away. She would replant those faded ambitions, tending to them with the determination and resilience she had almost forgotten she had.

The world was vast and unpredictable much like the cards laid out before her. Yet, as her fingers tapped away on the keyboard, a familiar spark began to reignite.

Name: Madame Margaret Amelia (psychic-witch)

Email: m.m.a.psychic-witch1864@gmail.com

Password: finlayfloofstar2015

D.O.B: 24/11/1961

Gender: Female

Now came the next step: selecting a profile picture. It felt like a daunting challenge. The image she wanted to project seemed worlds away from the person she saw in the mirror. She felt closer to 80 and perhaps looked older still. Her long auburn hair, streaked with rebellious white strands that defied her hair dye, framed a face that seemed drained of vitality. Her pale skin, ghostlike and dull, was a far cry from the vibrant woman she hoped to become.

She sighed, catching sight of her reflection on the laptop screen. In ten months, she had lost three stone; her entire wardrobe had turned against her. Clothes hung loose and shapeless, draped over her like curtains on an empty scaffold. Once, she had thought herself beautiful.

The cursor blinked, waiting for her next move.

And then it hit her. '*That settles it.*' She wouldn't use a picture of herself. Instead, she'd upload one of Mr Finlay Floofstar her sleek black cat. Mischievous and mysterious. Black cats were iconic for witches, after all; and Finlay's sleek form and mischievous eyes perfectly captured the spirit, she wanted to project, without forcing her to share her own fading reflection.

She smiled, clicking through her cat photos. Finlay, as always, would save the day.

That evening, Margaret sat back down at her desk. Her hands trembled as she shuffled her Granny Bryce's old fortune cards. Turning over the first, she froze. The Phoenix. Granny had called it the card of renewal, of rising from ashes.

Margaret exhaled. The Phoenix card gleamed in her hand: renewal. For the first time in years, belief stirred, not in the cards, but in herself. She could rise again.

In Search of Strawberries
by Charity Reed

'Never regret the past, everything happens for a reason,' is Granny's second rule for living. She should know, she's lived through some of the most regrettable times in history. So now I'm sitting here trying to decide if I wanna become some folk's dinner. To feed or not to feed, that's the question eh. And will I have regrets? Obviously, Granny thinks I shouldn't, so I feel I should be sure. I think I may have already made up my mind though eh.

It all started earlier on the tram, so I better go back to that. When that knacker what calls themselves 'The Gate' started bothering me. No, it's about Granny really, so I'll tell you about her first.

When Granny was my age, The Administration—well it wasn't The Administration then, it was lots of laal local administrations governing the different countries and mostly fighting about the best way to do it—finally woke up to the idea that the world was warming at an alarming rate.

'It wasn't like they weren't warned,' Granny told me. 'They were just greedy, didn't listen because it wasn't profitable.'

Sometimes I think about this, and I actually care. Most of the time though, I just accept that it's the world I was born into. Can't regret the past apparently, even if it was a monumental cosmishambles. After all, Granny's first rule is 'always listen to Granny.'

So, this morning, I was heading down the cred centre for my monthly rations. I ran out of SlowDown last week so I'm feeling vulny, even more than usual, and I hate going to town even when I'm chill. There was some crazymad charver trying to conversate with me on the tram, so I jumped off at Thunberg Park to avoid them and took an amble through the trees to calm me like. We don't get trees in the units, so I love Tunny Park. Granny and me come here together sometimes when the units get real stuffy, and she's always bothering me about being too slow. She's eighty-seven my granny, she's the funniest person I know, and the only one I ever call "she" because she still thinks that personal pronouns are important—see I told you she's funny. Anyways, she's old but she's real fast at walking. Probably because she prefers Quicker to SlowDown. Giggle is our favourite of all the Administration tablets, but that costs big creds so we only have it twice a month, once when I get my cred rations, and once when she gets hers.

The sky had a blue tinge again today, fighting to break through the usual orange. Administration chatter on the net says the blue is a good thing, a sign that the pollution is finally clearing. Granny reckons it was always blue in the old days, and the trees were full of birds, but I sometimes wonder if she doesn't see the past through a heat shimmer. Granny calls that 'strawberry-tinted glasses.' I asked her what glasses were, and she said they're like shades, but with glass in instead of slats, and they were to help people see better before the docs started fixing folks' eyes. Sounds grim. I also asked her what strawberries were, and she went all dreamy and said they were just heaven. I looked it up onscreen later and they were a kind of fruit. She mentions them quite a bit so I'm glad I know what she's talking about eh.

'Aye Aki, birds in all the trees. Tits, sparrows, finches. I went to London before it burned, and there were parakeets in the park. Green they were, same colour as the leaves. Of course, that was before everything went to hell in a hand-blender.' I looked that up too. A hand-blender was a real old-fashioned kitchen tool.

Anyways, Tunny Park is chill as Arctica—I love it. A living, breathing heaven on scorched earth. The air there feels light, almost cool. Fresh, grazing over your skin like eh, lifting the hairs on your arms. I was just passing under the big holly oak tree—Granny taught me trees—when I caught that crazymad geeza from the tram and I was wondering dafuq they doing here. My heart started whizzing like a fuqed aircon and I quickened right up, trying to lose them like eh. I heard that a folk from Block 18—that's the one next to mine—got mugged off for their prints and eyeballs. They use them for access to accounts and such. Granny says always someone wanting a piece of you.

I ducked down the cut leading from Tunny to Main Street, thinking I'd slip them right off, but I clicked it just too late that this was really stupid. If someone gonna grab you it's gonna be down a damn alley. They were about ten metres away when I spotted them, so I sped up and thought I'd have time to get out at the end, lose myself in a crowd I's reckoning, but I looked behind me and the shmucko was catching up. My anziety was kicking right in again. Nothing to take the edge off see. My heart banging, coming out of my chest like. Sweat was dripping down my spine and my hands were clammy. I could see the end of the alley and I was thinking I could get away, when I felt them grab my arm. My heart stopped whizzing. Stopped banging. Just stopped altogether like. I froze.

'Slow down marra, I ain't gonna hurt ya.' They eyed me up. Creepy like eh. Sticky hair plastered on a face like a maggot. Docksider, sounds like from their accent. Dodgy bunch.

'I ain't your marra. Dafuq you want jerkass?' My heart was beginning to beat again, but I still jumped back away, can't be too careful.

'Just wanna give ya proposition geeza, see if ya wanna make big creds like.'

'Dafuq you onabout?'

'You got *commodities* I could sell for ya.'

'I got fuqall,' I telt them.

'Ya got dem legs dude.' They looked me up and down. Lascivious like eh.

'Dafuq you on about legs geeza?'

'Dem richies want 'em—not dat average upsider mind—dem government types, da ones what run De Administration, dey pay good money for leg like yours.'

'Dafuq would anyone want some charver's leg for eh?' I asked before I could stop myself. Too curious like, that's what Granny says.

'Eatin' marra. Wotcha think for, sitting on a shelf lookin' pretty?' They laughed. It wasn't funny.

'Eating?' I could totally feel my eyes popping out my head, I really wish I'd never got involved in this converse. 'Dafuq anyone want to eat a leg for?'

'Dey missin' da meat marra. Dey love it dem richies. No animals left, wey not many. Dey can't get enough of it. Longpig dey calls it. You never see dem eating dat textured proteins like us.'

'What about lab-grown? Couldn't they just eat that, like they make organs for sick folks?'

'Dey like da real ting marra,' they shrug. 'Divven ask me why. Weird proclivities.'

'Well, I like my legs so I'll keep 'em thank you very much.'

'Just saying marra. Tink about it is all. Ten million credits an' a toppa da range new cyber-limb if ya sell me ya leg,' they said. Suddenly, the folk jumped forward and grabbed me again. Real quick all of a sudden. My anziety hit the sky and I was ready to scream when I realised they were just scanning their wrist over mine.

'Dere you go pally pal. Ya got ma deets now. Da Gate, remember dat. Screen me up if ya wanna make da good cred.'

Sell them my leg? No chance—nutter. 'You're nuts. I'm not selling my damn leg for no-one.'

'Ya could buy yassel outta dem downside units. It's only a leg matey mate.'

'Yeah, *my* leg. Now fuqoff, sell em *your* damn leg,' and I pegged it, half running to the cred centre as fast as I could manage.

The credit centre was as dismal and depressing as ever, it's cooler than outside but the incessant whine of the antique air-con goes through me every time, scrapes down my teeth like eh. I waited my turn, hiding behind my mask and scrolling through my indiscreen, turning up the volly on my earbuds to try and drown it out. It didn't. There was an oldie standing too close, and they looked like they might have a virus. Poor old freaky looked like they had a dozen viruses, so I stood well back. I hate getting sick. Their hair, what was left of it, was stuck to their head with sweat, but at least it covered up some of the scabs. There was a sour stale smell coming off them too. Mank. I shifted. The queue was slow to move but I eventually reached the screen and pressed the comm key, rubbing my hands in Sansize—can't be too careful. The familiar sound of the buzz signalled that it was my turn. Same old. I faced the screen pressing my print into the pad as the scanner read my retina. Then I waved my wrist under the chip scanner and the screen voice chirped:

'AR28092090-086. Top up 100 credits. Have a nice day.'

'Not sure what one of them is,' I replied, knowing nobody would hear or care.

I headed down the walk, shuffling my way into the food queue, smearing my hand in more Sansize, those print pads are covered in germs. I get the palpitates just thinking about it.

'CREDITS AVAILABLE—57' the screen flashed me as I retrieved my week's edibles from the cubicle and headed towards the drug dispenser. 'CREDITS AVAILABLE—35' said the screen as I picked up my tablet rations. Fuqsake I's thinking, there'll be nothing left by the time I scan for power.

I was trying not to stare at the upsider charver waiting for the tram. I knew they's an upsider on account of their clothes. In the units we cover up with Administration issue baggies, which are pretty well designed for keeping us as cool as possible. Granny says humans weren't meant to withstand fifty-degree temperatures, and it was way colder when she was young, but it's just how it is so I'm used to it. Of course it's not nice, and I might even go outside more if there was air-con in the sky, or more trees like Tunny Park, but there's nowt you can do eh. Anyways, this folk I'm trying to avoid eye contact with, they have massive chests that are barely covered by the filmy tunic they're wearing. It's ladgeful the way they stick out like that. It's a weird phenomenon with the upsiders, all this sticky outy stuff. Granny says it's all to do with finding a mate. That's for making babies. We don't really think about it in the units, the TP keeps us dosed so we don't reproduce. Legit sounds disgusting to me anyways eh.

The tram stops are roasty and full of big slow flies that remind me of the folks that wait here. No interest in life, no future. Well, not us downsiders anyways. I managed to get a seat in a pair mercifully unoccupied by anyone else. As we rolled on towards Block 17, I's finally calming down. I's thinking about Granny. It's sad to think of her remembering the old days and the animals, and the birds. Life today must be worse for her. I've never known any different. Maybe that's worse, who knows. Who cares. As the tram passed the big houses I seen a folk in a garden, they got a cyber-leg. They were trimming a green bush, I don't know what it's called—Granny would know, what with her once having her own garden. I noticed their arm was false too. A few houses down I seen another. Some geeza with all cyber-limbs. They look all perfect on the edges, with a squishy belly in the middle. It's weird, but the folks in the upside often have limbs missing. The big chesty charver from the tram stop got off here. I knew they was an upsider. I got to thinking, as they waddled past, that chest is unnatural too. I was wondering if it's a genetic thing. Born with money but missing bits. Balance is what Granny would call it. Then I suddenly realised, maybe they've sold their limbs to The Gate. I shuddered, but I couldn't shake it once it occurred to me.

When I got back to Block 17 Granny was sitting outside her unit with Shaina from next door. They're even older than Granny and their face is like the bark on the trees in Tunny Park. Granny looks terrible.

'What craic Granny?'

'Haven't you heard Aki love? They're kicking us out of Block 17.'

'Nah man. How like?'

She's about in tears. 'Reutilisation they call it. My arse.' Everything with Granny is 'my arse'. 'Moving us all down to Block 12 they reckon.'

'Nah Granny. No way. Block 12 is all laal teenytiny units.'

'I know Aki, they don't care about us. Couldn't give a flying piece of shite if we live or die.'

Poor Granny. I'd never seen her look this sad. 'You sure about this?'

'Yep. Got an Administration message onscreen after you left. *Priority*. Bastards.'

'Bastards.' Shaina echoed in a voice of split granite as they spat on the concrete.

'How long we got?' I asked.

'Six weeks.' Her eyes crinkled and started leaking, looked like she's not gonna stop until she's cried a month's water ration.

'What am I going to do with my books, Aki? And it's far from the park.'

I felt proper helpless. I wished I could do something like. 'I got us some Giggle Granny.' That seemed canny futile at this point, but it's all I had. 'We could go inside, get a bit of dinner and have a bit laugh together. You can tell me a story 'bout the old days eh.'

For a minute Granny looked like a lost laal kid. Then she sniffed, tugged her pants out her backside and said, 'I don't think I fancy the Giggle tonight, but you're a good kid Aki. Come on.'

I served up the TP and Granny said, 'chicken my arse.' She seemed to have a bit of her spark back as we tucked into our dinner. 'This textured protein all tastes of cardboard whatever flavour they choose to call it.'

'Hey Granny.' I gave her a smile. 'You gonna tell me a story? About the old days?' I know she loves telling stories. Reminds her what it was like being young. Really, I just love to hear them. It's nice to think of a time when it would rain every day, well that's what Granny says anyway. Probably the strawberry glasses again.

'Yes lovey, what do you want to hear about? The big flood? The tsunami that covered the States?'

'Nah—tell me about the last strawberry you ate Granny.'

She looked real sad eh. I was surprised because she usually loves gabbing on about her life. She said, 'I don't want to.'

This is even more of a shock. Granny has never had a story she doesn't want to tell me. 'How comes?' I asked. Maybe I shouldn't but I wanted to know now.

'It's just that I was selfish. I don't like to think of it.'

'You're never selfish Granny. Go on, tell me. Might even make you feel better.'

Granny sighed. She did look geet sad. My heart hurt as I studied her face. It was so soft and kiddylike, her skin reminded me of the soft wrinkled paper in the books she loves so much. I held her hand.

'I was selfish Aki. It was when your mam was in the hospital having her new kidney.'

'What?' I'd never heard about this. 'My mam had a new kidney? When was this?'

'Before you were born. She needed one to stay alive and she wanted to have a baby so she had to get better before she could have you.'

'Why couldn't they get a lab-grown?'

'They weren't invented then.'

I think of The Gate. I wondered, have people been selling bits of bodies forever? 'Where did they get a kidney from then Granny?'

'Oh, from me lovey. I gave her one of mine.'

'You gave my mam one of your kidneys?' I's real proper astounded. I'd definitely never heard about this before.

'Well she might have been your mam, but she was also my daughter remember. You do anything for your kids, Aki. Maybe one day you'll find out.' Granny looked sad and all faraway starey like.

I doubt that I will, but I just said, 'it doesn't sound like you were selfish at all. How dafuq you selfish in this story?'

'Hmm?' She was like in a reverie now and it took a few minutes before she continued. I let her be. She's often like this when she's on remembering stuff. 'What did you want to know again?'

'Your last strawberry, Granny.'

'Oh aye, that.' More sighing. 'Well, we were in the hospital— hang on. No. I need to tell you what was going on first.' She's gone all thinky for a minute. 'So, it was after the flooding started, Brighton, Portsmouth, Southampton, they were all gone. People were moving up into the hills—that's how we're stuck in downside quads, the ones with money all wanted to be up in the hills, and that's never changed since. Folks scared of the seas rising any further. They pushed us all out the houses. Escape goats we were, said we were all using more power and making the problem worse. My arse.'

I went and got us both a hottie to drink while Granny went into another of her silences. She does it a lot, so I'm used to it. 'Here you go Granny,' I said as I slipped it into her hand.

'Eh, oh thanks Aki love. Where was I?'

'Granny, you had any Quicker today? Usually sharpens you up a bit.'

'Nah.' Her eyes were twinkling at me. 'I figured I would rather not be too sharp after I got the news about Block 12. It'll just make me madder. I might opt for some SlowDown instead, take the edge off. You seem to cope better being numb.'

That worried me a lot like. Granny never likes losing her edge. 'Come on man,' I said, 'it's not that bad eh?'

'Aki, I've been through a whole heap of shite in this life, but getting moved into a unit I can't fit my books in might be the last straw for me.' It *was* that bad. She sipped on her hottie and gave it that look like she's just sniffed some shit, apparently it's not like they got in the old days—what is though eh? Then she carried on. 'Oh yes, so anyway, things were changing a lot at that time. We must have just been relocated to the downside. The economy probably started it really, when it went tits up over in Yankeeland, the world seemed to get smaller somehow. But then with the waters rising it really got smaller. Then with all the fires, nobody knew their arse from their dildo. Sad times.'

She does this does Granny, she starts in one place and then goes off on a tangent. Getting her historical bearings like.

'Anyway, we were in the units, and it was a big change for us at the time. You have to remember we were used to a bigger place, and fresh air—well, as fresh as you could expect with all the fires and whatnot—your mam had been getting worse so I asked the doc if a transplant would work. That's what the operation was called before all the cyber-surgery came in later—that was all after the new energy of course. So, the doc said sure it would work, but there weren't many kidneys going at that time, on account of people all dying of diseases from the floods and the bad water. So, I said what if she had one of mine, and they did some tests and job's your uncle, bob's a goodun. They said we could do it.'

'So, where's the strawberry come in?'

'I'm getting to that.' Granny put her cup down, still half full, but tepid. 'We were in the hospital, we'd just got the business over with. Your poor mam was sleeping, but I was awake on account of me being young then and healthier than she was. They brought in the dinner tray. It wasn't as bad as TP, but hospital food was never the best, and there was strawberries for our afters. They liked patients to get some fruit and veg in them, for health and whatnot. Anyway, these strawberries were so delicious, especially after the sloppy dinner, so I gobbled them up. Then I got to eyeing up your mam's. They were just sitting there all red and juicy. I feel shame to this day Aki, but I couldn't help myself, I nicked the lot. Not one left for your poor mam, and her all ill.' Granny's eyes were shining so much that I knew it was with tears, not mischief like usual.

'Granny, you'd just given them your kidney fuqsake, I think they'd be okay swapping their strawberries for that.'

'Aki, that is neither here nor anywhere, they were her strawberries. I stole them.'

'But you gave them your kidney.'

'Ach, I had two. What's a body part between friends? A strawberry, on the other hand… They were the last ones I ever saw. After the volcano went off in the States we were rationed. Never saw another one in the shops since. Not downside anyway, not for the likes of us.'

So that's it. Granny gave my mam a kidney so they could have me. That's canny generous of her if you ask me, even if she did have two.

Granny fell asleep after a bit and I headed into my unit. The lights flicked on as I entered, a sure sign that my credits had topped up not only my wrist chip but the unit chip as well. Thankfuq. I was getting sick of living in the dark. I was making a mental note to turn off the lights more and not fall asleep with the screen on this cycle when I started thinking on about what it would be like to not have to fret so much about it. Daydreaming like. Imagine getting a big place with a garden for Granny and not worrying about the power rations. I watched a bit of screen and turned off the lights.

So, now I'm lying in bed thinking over all that's happened today, especially Granny's story and how I wouldn't be alive if it wasn't for her. Mam died when I was a babby, but they lived long enough to have me, and Granny's been like my mam ever since.

Now I'm thinking, ten million credits for a leg. Ten million credits eh. I'd have to give up my leg for some richie to eat. It makes me feel a laal bit howky. But ten million credits eh. That would buy a big house and somewhere to grow more strawberries, I hate the thought that her last one is tainted with guilt. I'd get a brand spanking cyber-limb—fuqknows the dudes in those gardens seemed alright. But *my leg*. But *ten million credits.*

I stare at the screen. Fuqit. Life here in the units is shit. Gonna get a whole lot shitter when we get moved to Block 12. I screen them up. It's only a leg.

'Yeah?' I hear the same whiny voice from the tram as The Gate's pale beardy face fills the screen like a hairy moon, greasy eyes shifting all over the place.

'Er, we met on the tram this morning.' Dafuq am I doing?

'Ah, yes—dat kid wid da legs eh? Changed your mind? Dey all do eventually.'

'Yeah. I was just wondering—'

'Wondering what?'

I'm stammering a bit, it's kind of overwhelming thinking of someone eating me, but I persist. Fuqknows living in this hole is no life for me and Gran. 'Sign me up geeza.'

'You sure?' They sound suspicious. 'You know dere's no going back once I contact a buyer?'

I think of life in Block 12. I think of them big gardens up on the hill, and I think of Granny, and mam, and strawberries. Suddenly I feel this weird joy bubble up inside my belly. I hear myself laughing. Actually laughing. Not like when me and Granny are on the Giggle. This is a proper laugh, and I realise I'm actually *happy* at the thought of a life outside Block 17. I'm happy that Granny could sit in a garden, under a tree and eat some vegetables. Hell, I might even like them too. My sides start to hurt like I've been running and I'm still laughing my head off.

The Gate looks at me through the screen, kind of half smiling and half frowning. 'You in then marra?'

'Yeah. Hang on.' I take a minute to compose myself. I'm not used to feeling like this. 'Aye marra, what's a body part between friends eh? I got two.'

My Bridge to Nowhere
by Rose Campbell-Smith

Each time I head to Belhaven Bay, a familiar thrill rises in me. The sun glints off the water, and the salty breeze carries a promise of freedom. But before I reach the waves, I cross what many dismiss as a strange little structure: the Bridge to Nowhere.

To most, it looks like a footbridge with no purpose, dropped into the landscape by accident. But to me, it's a threshold. As I step onto it, the noise of life fades; responsibilities loosen. I breathe deeper. The bridge, draped in greenery and arched above the Biel Water, becomes a place of pause and reflection. Each step is a ritual, a quiet crossing back into myself.

On the other side, the bay opens wide. Surfing here is more than a sport; it's a dance with the sea. Paddling out, I feel both small and strong. Each wave brings a lesson: courage in the face of fear, joy in fleeting moments, and resilience after every fall.

But it's the stillness between the waves that stays with me. Floating on my board, sun warming my face, I remember who I am beneath the surface of daily life. A seeker, a soul in motion.

Later, crossing the bridge back to the car park, wetsuit dripping, hair tangled by wind, I feel changed. The view behind me— open sea, shifting light, the arc of the bridge— reminds me of what I leave behind and what I carry forward.

The Bridge to Nowhere may look like it leads nowhere, but it always brings me back to myself. We all need spaces like that, whether found in nature, in our passions, or in the quiet pauses of life, these bridges, real or imagined, are forever sacred.

Mother's Day
by Michele Hinchliffe

One hand holds the baby, the other tips a jigsaw onto a round, white table. Outside the spidery branches of a bare cherry tree reach into a solid grey sky, but the large bay window allows her the best of the daylight at least. Looking down from her first floor flat, she sees the world continuing as though everything is normal. Couples share coffee and conversation at the café opposite, parents herd children along the street, people in suits make haste to important places. She is behind glass, simultaneously visible and invisible.

Across the street, there is a red sandstone block of tenements mirroring her own. She sees a woman opening her living room curtains then flopping down onto a sofa to watch television. The woman is heavy-set with tied-back blonde hair and wears an oversized sweatshirt with 'GAP' on the front in large varsity font. This woman appears from time to time when normal people are at work. She wonders if the woman is trapped too. Perhaps she is depressed. She feels a sense of solidarity with this woman, someone else living on the outside of expectation. But her heart sinks as it occurs to her there may be another more plausible explanation for the odd hours she keeps. The woman may be a doctor or a nurse perhaps or some other job that requires working nights and back-shifts. Her shoulders drop and she sighs as she presses her hand against the cool glass of the window.

The toddler child breaks her reverie by instructing her to sit at the table. There is work to be done with this jigsaw. So she sits down, baby on her shoulder but moving his head back and forth, woodpecker-style. Demand Feeding they call it, and it could not be a better description, for it is nothing if not demanding. She lifts her pyjama top and, in a frenzy of instinct, he locates and latches onto her breast before settling into a rhythmic gulping. With her free hand she attempts to make herself present to her toddler child, by talking and trying to help place the pieces. While her mouth moves her mind is in ten different places at once. Wondering how in this moment she can do this. Make the jigsaw, talk to her toddler, feed the baby, think about what to make for lunch, and then dinner. How she will manage to wash clothes, or herself? Her stomach growls and she shifts in her seat, feeling pressure from her bladder, reminding her of her inability to fulfil even the most basic tasks of eating and visiting the toilet. These facts add to her sense of failure as she wonders, *how do other people do this?*

She thinks about her own mother, who has chosen to weaponise her experience of early motherhood against her. Her mother tells blithe tales of babies blissfully asleep in prams outside for hours, happy trips to high street shops with baby, cake baking in the oven. 'We just got on with it!' her wounding refrain. She always felt different and unacceptable to her mother. She suspects her mother might have preferred that she left school at sixteen, got a job as a typist, wore a nice white blouse, navy pencil skirt with heels, and a full face of makeup. She thought perhaps motherhood would be the plain on which they would finally meet. *Yet here I am,* she thinks, *university education, a husband more hands on than my own father ever was and on my fucking knees while my mother stands over me gloating. Why is she in a competition with me over this? I just want her to throw me a rope.*

There is a park two streets away with swings and climbing frames and benches. She would like to take the children out. Yard time. But the logistics involved in getting everyone dressed and wrapped up for the cold, managing down the close stairs balancing baby in pram and holding toddler child's hand, crossing the main road – it feels impossible. There is the terror of meeting someone, and the still greater terror of not. And yet the alternative is being stuck in this flat all day, trying to occupy a baby and toddler for ten hours alone. Memories of an attempt at a local play group burn fresh in her mind. Her toddler child clinging to her leg, the baby mewling to be fed, her sweating and surrounded by the cacophonous din of chattering children, rubber shoes squeaking on polished wooden church hall floors and the side-eyes of middle-class mothers in cosy cliques. The devil and the deep, dark blue.

Her toddler child is talking non-stop and it is hard for her to keep up. The baby has settled at her breast for now. Her mouth is so dry, she would love a cup of tea. She can't remember if she managed to eat breakfast before her husband left for work this morning. What she can remember is standing in the living room doorway, holding the baby while her toddler child ran in circles behind her singing loudly, begging him to work from home today. Her eyes searching his face for any sign of acquiescence before the words left his lips like hammer blows confirming the worst: 'I can't'. It isn't his fault; it is after all still a man-shaped world out there.

There is a song from her early teens which sometimes gets stuck in her head, about something being wrong with mum and the dad and kids not understanding and everyone saying it's just a bad day. It used to feel like a neat distillation of her family dynamic growing up, yet somehow it has fermented through time and is now about her. Except that her mother was angry, angry at her father and all his alleged failings and she is … what is she? Not angry, but like the song said, something's wrong. She feels like an untrained circus performer, juggling and walking a tightrope, looking down to see no safety net, living in a kind of terror that her next step will be her undoing. In trying to right the wrongs of her own childhood she has swallowed the myth of motherhood whole, and it is now choking her.

The toddler has had enough of the jigsaw and slides off the chair in pursuit of a fresh diversion. The baby is still at her breast, dozing. She would like to lie down with him, and just sleep. But domesticity is her jailer, and he has other plans. She gently slides a pinky between her baby's mouth and breast to break his latch and, like a bomb disposal expert, she places him on a changing mat on the floor. Pressing her index finger to her lips, she eyeballs her toddler child and creeps gingerly across a living room floor, strewn with books and toys, to finally get to the toilet. As she nears the door, she stands on the ear of a large stuffed elephant, a concealed landmine. It starts blasting a fearsomely cheery rendition of 'Nelly the Elephant' in that loud and tuneless way peculiar to children's toys. The toddler child jumps up and begins to dance and sing along and the baby startles awake and starts to cry. There is a rushing sound in her ears, and everything feels like it is crowding in on her, like the world is tilting. There is no escape now, so she picks up the baby and her discreet tears mix with his as she holds her toddler's hand to dance around a little to the nightmarish ditty. At times it is like being eaten alive.

Somehow, as it always does, morning gives way to afternoon and faces are miraculously washed, lunches are conjured and a pilgrimage to the park is successfully made. She is cooking dinner now. The baby is asleep in the sling and the toddler child is watching TV. She has even managed to wash some clothes. Everest was scaled again but nobody was there to see it.

The sound of a key turning in the front door.

'Daddy!'

The toddler child jumps up and runs to greet her husband.

'Hello-ello,' her husband says cheerily.

He scoops up the toddler child and she squeals with delight as he holds her high and blows a raspberry on her tummy.

He plants her on his hip and asks, 'So, what have you all been up to today then?'

From the kitchen she replies, 'Oh, nothing.'

Reflections
by Charity Reed

'Mandi. Mandi?'

Is that me?

She lay on her bed. The voice seemed so far away—if it was even real. The evening summer sun shone through the gap in curtains dulled by grime. The once crimson velvet curtains, now cobweb-covered, open halfway to allow the smoke from her cigarette in the overflowing ashtray access to the outside world, flapped like gentle waves. As it made its fragile airborne escape, the shafts of light came in by the same passage to dance on the rust-red walls and over the cluttered furniture. Shabby, not chic. The smoke swirled around the mobile in the middle of the window-frame, its cascade of miniature mirrored discs spinning in the light. 13 mirrors in all, dangling and winking amongst pretty pink beads with a single crystal, cut to refract the light into a thousand, tiny rainbows, shimmering iridescence at its centre. The only thing shining in the neglected space.

As Mandi sank into the cocoon of her unwashed duvet, the mirrors caught the greasy sunlight and flashed it into her eyes. An involuntary blink as her dull eyesight caught the source of her momentary blinding. She began to watch, mesmerised, as the mirrors began a slow seductive spin in the ochre evening glow.

As she gazed on, one of the discs spun alone in a tiny tornado frenzy of its own. As it caught her focus, she saw a little piece of her bedroom reflected upon its silver surface. The dusty Monet print above the decaying drum kit. *Water Lilies*. Water lilies that now rolled and tumbled, spinning in front of her eyes, making her dizzy in their tempestuous violence until, suddenly all was quiet.

She found herself surrounded by water and beautiful flowers, floating, serene. The unhindered peace she could feel to her very core. The utter bliss of being. She bathed in the beauty of her surroundings and soaked up the equanimity of being alone. Gone was the dust, the grime, the pain. All she knew in this moment was the still of the pond, the sickly-sweet smell of the floating blooms. Then, too soon she could feel herself pulled, sucked back into the reality that was her room. Everything as it had been, the disc at the window twisting delicately. Left, then right, with little enthusiasm. Her cigarette had burnt itself out.

She blinked slowly and looked harder at the mobile. Another of the discs was beginning to twirl. Another flash of silver, turning gold as it twisted into the sun, then once more silver as the rays spun on. The mirror caught a reflection. A broken bedside lamp, superglue holding it together in a mutant patchwork.

'Bitch!'

She heard the voice before she saw what was coming. The lamp in the centre of the disk whirled and grew in size until Mandi realised that it was speeding through the air right toward her face. She couldn't move.

'Ricky, no.'

The lamp hit her on the left temple and smashed into three pieces that she saw slowly tumble and crash to the floor. A familiar face snarled at her from across the room and his sick laughter echoed in her ears. Her stomach churned with the fear of him stalking across the room toward her as she waited for the next hit.

'Stop snivelling. I wouldn't have to hit you if you weren't such a stupid cow.' Ricky yanked at her hair, pulling her off the bed as he spat the words into her face.

'I'm sorry. I'm sorry.' She didn't know what she'd done wrong this time. She knew he would tell her.

'Why the fuck can't you just be normal? Eh? Like any other wife. Dinner on the table at a reasonable hour.'

'I just wanted to catch up on this last chapter before I started. I'm sorry Ricky.' Mandi wept. Apparently escape, even into a book, wasn't allowed now.

'I'll show you what you can do with your chapter.' Ricky took the paperback from her hand and began ripping out the pages and throwing them out of the window. Printed confetti caught on the breeze and danced its way to the ground. 'You're lucky I don't shove it up your fucking arse. Get my dinner. Now.'

Mandi crawled to the door dabbing at her bloodstained face with her sleeve. She didn't dare go to the bathroom for a plaster.

Abruptly this time the vision ended, and the disc hung limp. She was lying in the same position on the bed, face turned toward the window, a drop of blood trickling down her face, mingling with her tears.

Another disc spun; another vision reflected. This time an old rag doll that had comforted her in childhood. She couldn't see anything but a sliver of pale moonlight as she hugged the Hollie Hobby close to her in the dark.

'Mandi, candy, cuddly child, kissed her daddy and made him smile.' Her step-father's voice came towards her in the darkness.

No.

'Who's a flirty little girly then?

Sorry. I didn't mean to be.

She screamed silently, knowing what was coming.

To her relief the memory faded, and the sun shone once more. She couldn't take her gaze from the glinting, gloating illustrations pictured in the mobile. They lured her. Within a moment she noticed in the largest of the discs, perfectly reflected poppies. Opium poppies she'd collected on her earlier foray from the flat. One of the few things of beauty to be seen in the city's filthy streets, roughly plucked and transplanted into a dirty pint glass, already dropping their petals, forlorn, onto her bedroom floor. In the mirror there seemed to be an entire field of them, petals lost, and seeds not yet ripened. Creamy liquid oozing out of each bulbous seed head and browning in the dry sun. She was encompassed by the acrid smell of fresh opium, the waving heads as far as she could see, spinning inside her head and out. Waves of multicoloured delirium washed over Mandi, and visions of nothing and everything filled her mind. Dreams took her. Floating. Flying, through clouds of honeyed happiness. She knew nothing, and nothing mattered anyway. Nothing mattered at all. Then it was gone.

Another disc drew her into the vision held in its circle of silver. She could make out misty figures. Herself and a long dead lover. She floated above them as the two naked bodies became almost solid, brushing and bumping against her. They gripped and licked and grasped and bit at each other as the image enveloped her. Their sweat dripped upward onto her tingling skin. The heat from their bodies hit her like a drug. As if she were within the scene and yet set apart from it. As if she were part of the excitement and the passion whilst simultaneously holding it within her. Watching. So overwhelming was the lovers' emotion that the three climaxed together and, as she lay panting in the affair's aftermath, she felt herself pulled away from the dream and found herself once again on the quiet bed, with its dancing rainbows, shaking gently.

Mandi wasn't sure she could take any more, but she was transfixed. Staring at the window and its many mirrored horrors and delights, as the sun sank slowly, and another single disk contorted its winding way. Silently reflecting an old khaki hat that sat, gathering dust, on top of her wardrobe. She had bought it years ago from an Army Surplus shop and not worn it for ages. She wondered vaguely why she kept it.

It felt like falling this time as she slid into the image. She found herself sitting on a bed, but not her own. The room was grey and stark and felt lonely. There was no shade on the light, and the atmosphere was apologetic yet without empathy. The hat sat on a table beside her.

'It's for the best Mandi.' Dave was never particularly affectionate, but this felt colder than usual. She wondered if they would stay together once it was over.

'Whatever.'

'Don't be like that Mand, we both agreed.'

'Well, it's not you going through it is it?' Mandi was less angry than she thought she should be. She was just empty.

'It's not even a baby yet for God's sake. It's just a bunch of cells.' Dave was so matter of fact about it. About everything.

'We're *all* just a bunch of cells Dave.'

She couldn't tell him that she'd felt like a mother since the first day she'd missed her period. That she'd felt such joy at having someone she could love. That she'd genuinely thought Dave was 'the one' and she couldn't wait to tell him, to share this with him. 'Whatever,' she repeated.

The doctor interrupted their conversation with a chirpy 'and how are *we* today, Miss Sharpe?'

'We're good thanks doc,' Dave replied. Mandi said nothing. Doctor Blennerhasset didn't press her.

'Well then, if you just pop yourself into this chair an orderly will be along to take you to surgery in half a tick. Hubby will be waiting when you come round.'

'We're not married,' she said, voice flat.

'Well, quite. Err …'

'*Thank you*, Doctor.' Dave shot her a glance and gave the doctor his smarmy used-car salesman grin. Mandi watched as he rubbed his hands together. He looked as though he was actually enjoying this.

Mandi said nothing. She lowered herself into the chair and waited to be wheeled to the room where she would soon kill her unborn child.

Sorry.

She felt the pain seep into her chest, gaining strength and speed, rushing as if it wanted to burst right through her rib cage. Giddy with hurt and rage and loss and emptiness. A part of her gone, and no matter how hard she tried to replace it with men, drink, drugs, she knew it was gone forever.

The thin air around her thickened in her lungs as she was tugged back into the weeping, shuddering body on her own bed.

As her body adjusted back into the controls of her own mind, she felt only numb. She shivered slightly as her eyes refocused on the mobile. She wanted so badly to tear her gaze away, but she was trapped now. She knew it had to play out.

One of the small outer mirrors on the mobile winked at her. It turned. She averted her face from the spinning disc but could not move her eyes. As she held the image in sight she saw, reflected in it, herself. Her own pale face looked back at her. As it weaved its way into and around her with its spell, she noticed it was cracked and her still revolving image distorted and awry. The perverted visage overthrew her. Defeated her with her own inner horrors. Conquered her with her own weakness. Her own guilt. Fear ravaged her. Fear of what was within her own flimsy essence. All that was negative pulsed through her veins. Pulsed relentlessly, uncovering, exposing, baring a crooked psyche. Yet again she could not look away.

She'd watched her life play out in the visions, each one furious in its gripping and tearing of her emotions. Each intense and lasting, leaving its own impression of cold or warmth, joy or sorrow, passion or pain.

Her gaze rested on the disc that now spun in the glowing embers of the day. This disc reflected reflections. In its face was mirrored the mirror that hung upon the wall by the door. Reflected in the hanging mirror was the small mirror on the bedside table and reflected in its surface was the little spinning disc. Mandi could see each reproduction with alarming clarity and the spinning mirror consumed her entirely. It was as though her brain, heart and lungs, her liver, spleen and womb were all being stretched out wide enough to encompass the earth and then squashed down to the size of a marble, thrown into the air, simultaneously and at different times over and over again. She thought of nothing and could see only mirrors reflecting mirrors endlessly. She felt the feeling would go on forever. All her senses were confused, and she could only smell, rather than see, the distorted illusions that resonated around her.

Then peace. Slowly, very slowly, Mandi found light and vision coming back to her. She looked about her at nothingness and out, through the disc that trapped her. She could see herself on the bed, pinned pupils still fixed on the mirror mobile, the needle still in her arm, eyes dimming, surrounded by a mess of her own making, a mess that she would never be able to clear away.

Am I free?

She watched a smile creep across her own face on the bed.

'Mandi. Mandi?'

Sorry.

Josie's Secret
by Robin Montgomery-Smith

Josie felt her heart thumping in her ears as she pulled into the car park. A young woman with white blonde hair tucked inside a woolly scarf and hat—Josie's daughter—sat on a bench right across from where she had parked. She sat across from the swings in the park where it happened so many years ago. Josie was about to face her darkest moment, and her daughter knew it all. Otherwise, she would not be there in the park on that very day. Twenty-four years ago, Josie had done something terrible, and this was the day she would have to answer for it.

She sat in the car for a moment to gather her thoughts. The leaves had all turned burnt shades of orange and brown. They were in heaps and dotted all around the paths that ran through the park. A soft breeze swished by as though some unseen entity had walked through, disturbing the unique pattern they created on the path. Josie's chest tingled with nerves, as it always did when she was scared.

When she opened the car door, she broke the seal which separated the worlds she had created for the better part of two decades. She stood behind the door, shielding herself from her daughter. The spell lifted when Ella turned to look at her mother.

Josie shivered. She felt a tickle as sweat popped out along her hairline, just under the fuzzy, green knitted hat she wore. She pulled her heavy coat tight around her slim figure, guarding herself against the cold and the words about to be spoken. As she walked towards Ella, she was surrounded by the crackling, rustling of the leaves underfoot and around her. The air was full of decay and of endings.

'You found the key?' Josie asked, her voice no more than a whisper.

'I found the key.'

Without making eye contact, Ella waved her hand at her mother, indicating she wanted her to sit on the bench. Josie sat down, with as much distance between them as possible.

'What are you thinking?' Josie asked this question often because she could never tell how Ella's mind worked.

'Tell me how this happened.'

'I … I don't remember exactly,' Josie began. 'I saw you and you looked so much like her.'

'Your daughter, you mean—your *real* daughter.' Ella's voice was sharp.

'Yes. Ella.'

'The *other* Ella.'

'You need to understand what I was going through back then. My daughter had just died. I was heartbroken and I …'

'But you … you *stole* me.'

'Yes, well, *we* took you. I wasn't alone in this.'

'We? Tell me what happened and don't you dare leave out a single detail. I'll know if you do.'

That was it. Josie had to say the words aloud she had stifled all these years. She stared into the distance, as if her gaze took her back.

'It was cold, like today. We were walking, your father and—'

'*Father*? Really, Josie?' Ella rolled her eyes, tilting her head back in frustration. 'Go on. *Paul* and you …'

Josie stared at her gloved fingers wringing in her lap. 'We were walking here, in the park. He saw you first and stopped. I asked him what was wrong, and he nodded in that direction,' she said as she angled her head towards the swings. 'I couldn't believe my eyes. For a moment, just a tiny second, I thought you *were* Ella. I nearly called out your name—her name.'

'And then?'

'We sat on that bench over there,' Josie pointed to a bench near the slide, older now. The wood had faded, the metal legs rusted. 'We watched you for such a long time. We couldn't take our eyes off you. A family came by and the woman who was with you—'

'My *real* mother.'

Josie cleared her throat. 'Um, yes, well, she walked over to the other family and started talking to them. You jumped off the swing and headed for the slide, which was closer to that bench. We couldn't stop staring at you.'

'So you just … took me?'

'No,' Josie took in a deep breath, 'that wasn't the plan. We didn't even *have* a plan.' Josie grabbed her knees with her gloved hands. 'It simply happened. You had something in your hand that you dropped. Your mother didn't notice so I stood up to give it back to you. When you slid down the slide, your fath—,' Josie stopped short, correcting herself. 'Paul, well, he was at the bottom of the slide and caught you. He lifted you onto his hip and started walking back to the car. I barely kept up with him.'

'Didn't I cry for my Mum?'

'You were busy playing with whatever it was in your hands.' Josie's forehead wrinkled as she tried to remember. 'A bear, I think. You were so small.'

'Then what?'

'Then we put you into the car and drove you home. To our house.'

'And you passed me off as your *dead baby*?'

'No one really knew us, and we didn't have any other family. After Ella—we couldn't stay in that house, you understand. We had moved to a new house—a different house, miles from here, a few villages over. We needed a clean slate. Then you …' She trailed off, the events of those years before, fresh in her mind. 'I still had Ella's birth certificate. We used that to register you at the local surgery and school when the time came. No one ever questioned it.'

'How did you live with yourself?' Ella's voice was low but firm. Her blue eyes were dark as she wiped a tear from her cheek with the back of her coat sleeve. She shivered, but Josie was not sure if it was because she was cold or angry.

'I was grieving, Ella. I could scarcely function after she died. When we had you, afterwards, I picked up where I left off. I was so happy just being a mother again.'

'Why on Earth did you keep all those clippings?'

'I don't know why I did that.' Josie shrugged. 'I thought maybe one day I'd tell you the truth.'

'But you didn't. The only reason you're talking to me about it now is that I found the key.'

Ella was right. The key had opened a lockbox that Josie had kept since that day. Paul never knew about its existence. Inside were newspaper clippings about the kidnapping of a little girl at the park. Over the years, the family renewed their search for their missing little girl. One of the clippings was an obituary of the girl's biological father that mentioned he had a surviving daughter and son. The most recent article snipped from a newspaper and stashed in the box, was one where the son, Ella's little brother, was appealing for information about his sister's disappearance. In the article, he said his mother was ill with cancer and he wanted to help find his sister before she died. Josie knew Ella must have read all the articles she had saved. She watched as Ella slipped through her fingers, right before her eyes.

A bus drove past, whipping up the drying leaves in the road with a loud *whoosh*. A dog barked across the street. Josie recognised the momentary distraction from the conversation—a conversation that she knew was going to shape how she and her daughter would move forward, if that was still possible.

'What are you going to do now?' Josie continued to avoid eye contact with Ella.

'I want to find my real family.'

She looks so composed and cool, Josie considered. Although Ella's body language suggested she was calm—almost relaxed—the tone of her voice gave away her emotions. A woman walked past pushing a new black pram, followed by a small boy attached to a harness to keep him close. Josie felt Ella's eyes on her. She had dreaded this day but hoped that Ella would never find the box until long after Josie had died.

'How did you know I was here?'

'The last article that was on the bed—the one on top—was about that day and a photo of this park was with it. I figured you were either here or at the police station. I saw your car as I drove by.'

Ella sat in silence, staring off into the distance as if she was holding her breath, gathering the energy to shout. Josie's legs were growing numb from the bitter, icy wind. Her fingers were stiff with the chill through her gloves. *This cold is from the inside.*

'I'm so sorry.'

'Are you?' Ella's expression hadn't changed, but Josie now knew she was in this moment. 'Are you, really?'

'Of course, I am.'

'Why? Because you're caught out? Because I discovered your dirty little secret?'

'No. Well, yes, but not like you think.'

'Then how? Enlighten me.'

'I know what I did. It has haunted me since the day we were here. I wanted to turn myself in, but every day that passed was another day I had with you. Your smile, your eyes, your laugh. You are *mine*. I couldn't leave you—give you back. Without you, especially when Paul died, I would be nothing. You have always been my life, Ella.'

'What happens now, *Josie*?' Ella said Josie's name with such contempt, her heart felt the physical blow. Ella sat forward, with her elbows on her knees, her limp wrists allowing her hands to dangle. Josie recognised it as something Ella did when she was uncomfortable in conversation.

She watched as a squirrel scurried up a tall tree on the far side of the park.

'I don't know. What do *you* want to do?'

'I want to go back to yesterday when I didn't know all this. I want to go back to my life.'

'Nothing needs to change.' Josie was hopeful. 'We really can go back to the way things—'

'Are you serious?' Ella interrupted. 'To be honest, Mum—*Josie*, things were never great between us, were they? Now I know this, you expect I'll look the other way and go on like nothing's happened? You're delusional, woman.'

'Then where does that leave us?'

'It leaves *me* damaged for the rest of my life, no matter what happens next. And with any luck, it leaves *you* in jail, where you belong. And if Paul was still alive, that's where he should be, too.'

'Is that what you want? You want me in jail?'

'Isn't that where kidnappers belong? You took me from my *family*. You raised a stranger's daughter as your own because you couldn't be bothered to do what *normal* people do and just grieve the loss of your *actual* daughter and get on with your life. I'm simply a substitute for Ella. I've *never* felt good enough for you. You must realise how empty that makes me feel.'

Josie swallowed to clear her throat. *I must keep it together.*

'I know it has to. I can see that now. There's no changing the past. God knows, if there was, I would.' Josie's voice broke as the lump in her throat refused to clear. The sadness she felt seeing Ella upset was rising, the tears were pushing their way to the surface.

'You may not be able to change the past,' Ella said as a matter of fact, 'but you can pay for it.'

'Ella, I've been paying for it every single day of your life. Every time I look at your beautiful face, I see images of your parents in the newspapers and on the news reports. I listen to how you talk about Paul and feel sad that you will never know your real father. Don't you think I know these things? You must know I feel them.'

'Well, the guilt didn't get you very far, did it? Because here we are,' she said as she threw her hands up in exasperation. Josie felt the anger aimed at her through the eyes of a girl who was not her daughter; the girl who had always called her, Mum.

Josie pulled her mobile from her coat pocket. Looking away from Ella, she pressed nine three times. She paused and said to the person on the other end of the phone, 'Hello. I'd like to report a kidnapping.' (Another pause.) 'No, it was me. I am the kidnapper.'

Ella touched her hand to her mouth as a sudden, fat tear fell onto the fabric of her glove.

'I'll meet them at the station. I'm on my way now.'

Josie stood up and faced Ella who was still holding her hand over her mouth. 'I can't change the past, but I can do something about the future. I'm so sorry, Ella. Please know that I love you. I've always wanted the best for you.' Josie teased out a bit of Ella's blonde hair from under her scarf. One last gaze. 'I hope someday that you can look back at your life and know that you were loved. And I hope you can find it in your heart to forgive me. Forgive *us*.'

She put her hand on Ella's shoulder and nodded her head. Ella remained still. Josie walked back to her car retracing the steps from her arrival. However, this time only the sound of her heartbeat fell on her ears, and she felt it pounding inside her thick winter coat. She knew better than to turn around to look at Ella still sitting on the bench, a few feet away from where she was stolen all those years ago. As she drove from the park, she saw the figure of Ella in the corner of her eye, still sitting on the bench. She dared not stop for fear her mind would change.

Moments later, Josie parked her car in front of the police station in the town centre. She sat for a moment, expecting her chest to tingle from the fear of what she was about to do, but she felt nothing. The brown and orange leaves danced with the wind as she stood up outside the car. The courage she needed to walk into the building before her, swelled inside her heart, filling her soul. She left the car unlocked as she walked into the station, with her head held high. For once in her life, she was doing the right thing.

'Yes, I'm Josie Taylor. I'm here to turn myself in for kidnapping Valerie McIntosh twenty-four years ago today.'

Close to the Edge
by Laura Scott

Charlotte followed the ivory gossamer train of Donna's wedding dress as it rippled up the pebbled steps in front of her. She watched the father-of-the-bride as he supported his daughter, their arms linked, and she noticed the wrinkles around his eyes deepen as he gazed at her. Then, she felt a tug at the tail end of her bridesmaid dress, and she fell forward. Her knee hit the edge of the step, and she dropped her bouquet.

'Oh, I'm so sorry,' Karen said, the other bridesmaid who was walking up the steps behind her.

Donna's father, Michael, turned around and bowed down to help her up.

'You, OK? These steps are a bit wonky,' he said.

'I'm OK … I think,' Charlotte said, rubbing her knee.

He picked up the bouquet, straightening the fawn roses, before handing it back to her. Charlotte wished for an attentive father like him.

Donna smirked towards Karen before she looked down at Charlotte. Her Swarovski Crystal drop earrings were swinging and glistening in the sun.

'Come on, can't have you holding up my day,' she said. Then she about turned and sashayed up the steps, the skirt of her mermaid-style dress swishing.

'Lottie—I am sorry,' Karen whispered.

Charlotte brushed down her dress, drew in a deep breath and gripped her hands tighter around the bouquet. Had Karen stepped on her dress on purpose? Maybe not. But still, she hated being called 'Lottie.' School day chants played in her head: *Potty*

Lottie, Potty Lottie … With heavy legs, she carried on up the steps of the Amalfi coastal path.

About nine months ago, it had been her 21st birthday and Craig, Charlotte's brother, had taken her out to celebrate. They downed Midori shots and released their woes, bopping together on the smoky dance floor of the club. Their bodies flickered in the kaleidoscope of flashing lights. Donna had come into their lives like a battering ram when she barged into Craig.

'Whoops,' Donna said, almost spilling her drink.

Charlotte had been convinced she had knocked into him on purpose. Her party of two became three, and Donna tossed her dark, wavy hair, swaying in her minuscule-black-sequinned dress around her brother. When Craig had gone to the bar and bought drinks, Charlotte sat down at a poseur table, and Donna glided onto the barstool across from her. Charlotte felt the consumed alcohol swell from her stomach, which burned her throat. Her short legs dangled from the barstool, whereas Donna had been able to perch the tip of her black velvet strappy sandal on the footrest as she crossed her legs. There had been an uncomfortable silence between them, even though the music had been booming. Donna propped her elbow on the table, resting her chin on the heel of her hand and tapped her fingers on her face. She leaned closer to Charlotte and spoke:

'I can't believe he's your brother. He. Is. Gorgeous.'

'We have different dads,' Charlotte said.

'Ah, makes sense …' Donna continued to tap her face as she looked over at Craig at the bar.

Charlotte had been used to Craig getting attention from women over the years that he usually evaded. But when he walked over to the table carrying the drinks that evening, there had been an expression on his face that Charlotte had never seen before. She shifted in her stool as she watched them talking, her glass sliding in her sweaty hand as she sipped her drink. Donna's teeth dazzled in the dark as she smiled at Craig, and her pink-and-white French-manicured nail extensions flickered around in the air as she spoke. Charlotte clung to the edge of the barstool while she watched Craig listening to Donna. He seemed to be melting into her chocolate-brown eyes. Craig was the only family she had: a father, a best friend, and a brother, all rolled into one. No way was she letting this woman come between them. Charlotte gulped down her drink and complained of a sore stomach. She had convinced Craig to head home before Donna could work any further incantations on him.

As Charlotte reached the top of the steps in the Amalfi Coast, her heart thumped hard, and a few fawn petals fell from her bouquet. The path leading to the gazebo stretched out in front of her. Craig was waiting with his best man; the tartan of their kilts was blurry. There were family members and friends sitting on white wooden folding chairs, many of whom she had met for the first time the previous evening in the hotel. One by one, they turned their heads and gazed at the bride.

As she approached the white chiffon-draped gazebo, Craig ruffled his hair with his hand before staring at Charlotte. She lifted her head and smiled but struggled to meet his eye. Michael leaned forward, lowering his head briefly as he handed his daughter over to the groom. His lips pressed into a tight line, and then he clasped his hands behind his back before he raised his chin and puffed out his chest.

Not long after being made redundant from her job at the local bank, Charlotte was offered a job at Michael's Skip Hire company. Most of the high street banks were closing in their area. Craig had said it would be a good opportunity for her to get back out there, but she refused. No way could she tolerate working with Donna in an office all day. She imagined Donna ordering her around, asking her to make tea and coffee for all the staff—the thought.

Charlotte looked down at her dress; there were a few spots of blood seeping through. She must have cut her knee when she fell on the steps. Charlotte lowered her bouquet to cover the stain. As Donna turned towards Craig, the Swarovski crystals covering the entire bodice of her dress flickered and flashed in the sunlight. Charlotte thought the light from them would probably be bright enough to send SOS signals to the island of Capri. Her stomach tightened as Craig looked into Donna's eyes and smiled. Charlotte took in a deep breath, then breathed out hard, puffing her cheeks.

Karen looked at her, concerned. 'Are you OK?' she whispered.

She managed a nod and hoped that her eyes didn't look too watery as the celebrant talked about Craig and Donna. Charlotte rolled her eyes as she listened to how it was love at first sight and how strong their love had become. They had not even known each other a year—Craig had rushed into this. Before he met Donna, he had never been interested in getting married, or believed in long, loving, lasting relationships with just the one person, forever—happily ever after. No such thing, they had agreed. Particularly given their parents' history. She was listening to her brother make a lifelong commitment to a woman she didn't like. How he promised to have and to hold her, even if she became sick or poor. Until the day he died. As she stood listening to Donna proclaiming her vows, comments that were made by her at the dress fitting suddenly chimed in Charlotte's head: *I'll need to get you some padding to put in that bra.*

In the bridal shop, after Donna's hurtful comments, Charlotte had to walk away and go to the bathroom for a bit. When she returned, she had overheard Donna talking to Karen as she stood at the edge of the changing room door. She heard Donna going on about the Swarovski Crystal jewellery set she'd convinced her dad to buy, and how she wanted to try for a baby as soon as possible. Donna mentioned how much hassle it would be to get Charlotte's dress altered to fit. It wasn't as though Charlotte had had any say in what she would be wearing. The fawn colour of the bridesmaid dress didn't exactly flatter her skin tone. But Donna had told Charlotte, 'just put on some fake tan.'

At the gazebo, Charlotte was aware of sweat collecting at the middle of her back as she watched her brother kiss the bride. She reached behind her and tugged at the charmeuse material, fanning herself. She wanted to be happy for him. But she was struggling to release this knot in her stomach.

Donna's family and friends rose from their seats and gathered around to congratulate the married couple. Charlotte stepped away to inhale the fresh sea breeze. She needed a moment to herself. Their voices grew garbled in the background as she drew closer to the edge of the cliff, the waves crashing below. After a few deep breaths, she looked around and realised how high up she was; she appreciated the warmth of the late-afternoon sun and the view of the bay surrounding her. She noticed the seagulls as they soared and called, the wisps of white clouds against the dream-blue sky, the colour fading like a gradient into the water. On her left, the mountainside jutted out like the shape of a tortoise's shell. It looked as though it was topped with waves of apple and forest-green moss. To the right, there was a cluster of houses, each one with its own charming character, in a variety of yellow shades, pastel oranges, and dusty pinks. From this height, they looked like doll houses, and the array of windows resembled shapes from a child's sorting cube. It must be nice to live there, Charlotte thought.

Donna approached Charlotte and said, 'Are you not coming over to congratulate us?'

'I'm working up to it,' Charlotte said.

Donna held out her left hand showing the wedding ring that had been made to fit around the fashioned engagement setting. Charlotte wondered how many pharmaceutical sales Craig would've had to make to afford them, along with the new clients he'd probably had to acquire.

'You could at least pretend you're happy,' Donna said, raising her hand closer to Charlotte's face.

'It's not in my nature to be fake,' Charlotte said. 'But the rings are gorgeous.'

'You're just jealous,' Donna retorted, then she turned and walked away.

The low, deep pain in Charlotte's stomach expanded throughout her chest and almost erupted. She imagined throwing the bouquet at Donna and it hitting her, the petals and green foliage flurrying around her like confetti. Charlotte smiled to herself. She envisioned Donna's face flushing through her fake tan and makeup. But no, she would not lose her temper. Not today.

Not at her brother's wedding. She worried about how she would adapt to Donna being a permanent fixture in Craig's life. She'd never been good at making new friends. What would she do? She heard spongy steps on the grass and then a cold hand grasped her arm.

'Are you sure you're OK?' Karen asked. 'I really didn't mean to step on your dress.'

'Donna didn't seem to think so,' Charlotte said.

'Donna thinks everything's about her,' Karen said.

Charlotte smiled again. 'I thought she was your best friend?'

'Oh, she is,' Karen said. 'Doesn't mean I agree with everything she says and does.'

There was a quiet moment between them, making the seagull's playful calls apparent.

'I feel like I'm losing everything,' Charlotte said, looking down and twisting her fingers together.

'No, you're not,' Karen said. 'Come on,' she continued as she put her arm around Charlotte's shoulder. 'Let's go and enjoy this fancy meal we're getting.' Karen winked, then pulled her close as they walked away from the edge.

The air became still, wrapping around Charlotte like a warm cardigan as she approached the dinner table. The sun was setting, creating a peachy-pink glow. The table was set under a large pergola, twisted with climbing roses and fairy lights; the green grape leaves draped across the entrance provided a welcoming bow. Charlotte noticed her name was on the place card at the seat beside Michael. When she pulled out the chair, he looked up and smiled.

You know, maybe she would consider working for the family business after all. Well, she was officially family now, wasn't she? It would beat sitting in her pyjamas all day, eating cheese puffs and watching daytime television. As she sat down, she thought this would be the perfect opportunity to have a chat with him.

'Is it red or white wine you prefer?' Michael said, pointing to the bottles on the table.

'Oh, the champagne looks tempting,' Charlotte said as she pointed to the bottle posing in the ice bucket at the end of the table.

Michael politely ordered the waiter to bring over the bottle of Champagne. It looked expensive, and the condensation trickled down and dripped from the bottle. As the waiter poured, the Champagne was almost bubbling over the top of the glass.

She looked along the table, and Craig grinned at her. He raised his glass and mouthed, 'are you OK?'

He looked happy—maybe it was time she accepted the decision he had made?

Donna had been chatting and laughing with Karen, and she tapped Craig's arm to include him in their private joke. He told Donna to wait as he was already turned towards Michael and Charlotte. The bubbles fizzing and hissing in her glass, she raised it towards Craig, looking him straight in the eye and nodding. She mouthed a 'yes.' She was determined to get a new job and get back out there, even if that meant putting up with Donna at Michael's Skip Hire.

Untangling Time
by Rose Campbell-Smith

(The Time Weaver spins existence itself, weaving past, present, and future—yet even she meets a knot or two.)

The wide-toothed comb glides through tangled strands,
untangling whispers of thought and dreams
weaving through moments—as time gently expands.

In a hidden realm beyond mortal sight, the Time Weaver plied her craft. With a loom that stretched across the ages, she spun the threads of existence, intertwining past, present, and future into a single tapestry. Each strand whispered of a memory, a dream yet to unfold, or a fleeting moment slipping through the hands of time.

Yet even she encountered knots—tangles of fate, twisted paths, and moments too stubborn to be smoothed. With patience and care, she worked to untangle what was, what is, and what might yet be. And then there was Kala, one such knot.

Kala was small and petite, with a fiery crown of red hair threaded with flashes of gold that caught the light like embers in the wind. Her green eyes, ever watchful, held a questioning intensity, as if she were constantly searching for answers hidden just beyond reach.

On the eve of her nineteenth birthday, Kala stood at the threshold of destiny—a thread waiting to be claimed. Every soul, when they came of age, was meant to claim the thread woven for them—a strand, that bound them to the path that had been spun for them since the moment of their birth, which would bind them to the tapestry of existence. But when the moment arrived, Kala hesitated.

The loom pulsed before her, its strands shimmering like woven starlight. Her thread, a delicate golden strand, awaited her touch. Her fingers hovered over the golden thread, and her heart thrummed with uncertainty, each beat a silent plea for control. It wasn't the thread that scared her—it was the certainty it represented.

A certainty she couldn't escape, of a future not of her choosing—it was suffocating. And yet, something inside her rebelled. To accept it was to submit to the path laid out for her; the weight of inevitability pressed against her chest, and for the first time, she felt how small and fragile her life was against the vastness of time itself. Would she ever be more than the choices someone else had made for her?

Memories surged, unbidden. Her mother's soft voice pressing a kiss to her forehead, whispering of the day she would take her place among the woven fates. Just as every child had before her. But did that mean she had to accept it without question? Was she not allowed to dream of something else—something of her own making? Her father's firm hand, steady on her shoulder, guiding her toward the moment they had all awaited. And yet, woven within those tender recollections were the echoes of something else—a longing for freedom, the uneasy pull of the unknown. She remembered stolen moments under the vast night sky, tracing constellations with her fingertips, dreaming of paths untethered to a single fate.

What if she accepted and lost herself? What if her dreams, her choices, became nothing more than echoes in a predetermined story? What if, in taking this thread, she severed every possibility of something more? The thought sent a shiver down her spine. She clenched her fists, the air bursting with the unspoken battle within her. Her mind spun in circles, her body tense with the impossible weight of choosing between safety and freedom. What would become of her if she did not choose the thread?

Her name—Kala—meant *'time'* in the old tongue. It was a name whispered with reverence, a name passed down in stories of fate and flow. But now, standing before the loom, it felt like a weight, like a prophecy she never agreed to. Was she meant to move with time—or bend it?

'I refuse,' her whisper barely audible. And whether from fear, defiance, or something she could not name, she turned away from what was meant to be.

At first, nothing changed. The stars still wheeled in the heavens, and the world spun on as it always had. But the Weaver does not take kindly to missing threads, and Fate does not suffer defiance lightly.

Soon, the fabric of her existence began to fray. And the Weaver was watching.

The changes were small at first—insignificant to others, but to Kala, they were like the first crack in a dam. Time slipped unpredictably; her reflection in the mirror one morning appeared hazy, as though someone had smeared the glass. Her fingers, when she reached out to touch it, left no marks, no trace. Later, when she spoke to an old friend in the marketplace, she noticed that the words didn't seem to flow as they always had. There was a hesitation in her friend's voice, their eyes clouded with uncertainty, as if Kala were a stranger she'd never truly known.

And so—the knot tightened, and the fractures deepened. Time itself faltered around her, slipping like sand through unseen fingers. The next day, she awoke to find the sun hanging low in the sky, unmoving, as though time had forgotten to push forward. The bells of the town struck the hour, but the sound never reached her ears. It was as if reality itself was disentangling, leaving jagged gaps where certainty once was.

Days stretched too long; nights blinked by in an instant. And when the world around her suddenly froze—people suspended in mid-step, their lips parted in words forever lost—Kala's stomach twisted. The stillness was wrong, the air dense with a silence too deep to be natural. Time itself had faltered, as if a forgotten page of a book had been torn out of the universe's story. She knew in that moment—she had broken something far more delicate than she had ever realised.

And then came the dream. It did not come as sleep nor as wakefulness but as something in between—a slow unravelling of the world around her, as though the edges of reality had frayed beyond repair. She reached out to grasp at something solid, but each time her fingers closed around an object, it slipped away, dissolving into the zephyr as if it were never there. The air thickened, pulsing with an unseen rhythm. The walls of her room wavered like mist, and then, with a breath, they were gone. Kala floated in a sea of twilight, weightless, untethered, as if caught between moments.

Every movement felt like it was happening in slow motion, as though the very act of existing was becoming an effort, each second stretching into eternity. At that moment, a dreamscape unfolded around her—an endless horizon where the sky shimmered like a restless ocean, rippling with shifting light. The stars flickered, unstable like the frantic beating of her heart, their glow waxing and waning as if struggling to hold their place in the firmament, pulsing in time with something unseen. Her feet did not touch the ground—there was no ground, no direction. Only the great loom that stretched endlessly, its threads glowing in shifting hues, writhing like living things. Out of the vastness, she saw her. The Time Weaver stood at the heart of it all, an unmoving figure in the storm of unravelling fate, watching her with eyes like the turning of centuries.

The Time Weaver was tall and slender, her presence both ethereal and commanding. Long white hair flowed around her like drifting strands of silk, catching the shifting light in strange, impossible hues. Her robes, woven of time itself, shimmered between the past and future, never quite still. Her hands never ceased their work, fingers moving in elegant precision, adjusting, guiding, correcting—yet the loom shuddered beneath them, fraying at the edges where Kala's refusal had left its mark.

Kala tried to speak, but the aether stole her voice, swallowing her words before they could form. The Weaver turned her gaze upon her, and in her eyes, Kala saw the vastness of eternity—centuries unfolding and folding upon themselves, moments stretching into infinity and snapping back in an instant. There was no anger in that gaze, nor disappointment—only the quiet weight of knowledge.

'You have undone what was meant to be,' the Weaver said, her voice neither cruel nor kind but vast, like the hush before a storm. 'You are a knot in the tapestry, Kala.'

Kala lifted her chin. 'I did not ask for a path I could not choose.'

The Weaver's fingers glided over the loom, and images flared to life in the threads: a village crumbling into dust before its time, a child vanishing mid-laughter, an old man staring at a door that no longer led where it should. The fabric frayed, the threads loosened, twisting wildly as the tapestry fought to mend itself.

'You believe you have freed yourself from fate,' the Weaver said, 'but you have only unmade what was meant to be. The world is unravelling.'

Kala's defiance wavered. She had seen the changes and felt the instability, but she had not understood. Not until now.

Still, she clenched her fists. 'Then let me fix it,' she said. 'I will weave my own thread.'

The Weaver studied her for a long moment, and then, with a slow, deliberate motion, she plucked a single golden thread from the loom. It pulsed with quiet energy.

'This was always your fate, Kala,' the Weaver said. 'Not to follow a path, but to weave it. To mend what others cannot.'

Kala's breath caught. All this time, she had fought against a destiny she did not want, only to find it was not what she had thought at all. The knowledge settled over her, heavy yet fitting, like a cloak she had unknowingly worn all her life.

She stepped forward, hesitating only for a moment before reaching out. Her fingers wrapped around the thread, and a warmth spread through her, as if she had just awakened from a long, restful sleep—and instinctively, she understood the movements and ways of the loom. She could feel the rhythm of the loom, the hum of time itself. As if she had always known, somewhere deep within her bones, how to bring order to the chaos. Warmth surged through her, a quiet knowing, a purpose she had never understood until now. This was not a fate she had to run from. It was not a cage, not a restriction—but a chance to shape the world, not by defying it, but by guiding it.

As the dream faded, the world began to steady. Time, though fragile, held firm once more. And Kala, the weaver of lost threads, had taken her place at the loom no longer adrift, no longer uncertain. For the Weaver had long needed a helper, and in Kala, she had found the apprentice she had been waiting for—someone to tend the knots and steady the fragile strands of time itself.

The Weaver nodded once. 'You will be known as Kala Sevaka.' The name echoed with ancient weight. 'Servant of Time. Mender of threads. Apprentice to the loom.' She fell silent, but there was something in her eyes now—a flicker of recognition, of understanding. Kala felt it too.

She closed her eyes and let the name settle into her bones. 'Kala Sevaka,' she whispered it once, tasting its shape. It felt like home. Like choice. Like beginning again—but on her own terms. Her fingers, now steady, grasped the golden thread, and she felt the weight of it settle into her palm. It was a weight that carried responsibility, yes, but also power—the power to shape the future, to mend the fraying edges of time.

And so, in the hidden realm beyond mortal sight, Kala Sevaka stood beside the Time Weaver. Together, they plied their craft; with a loom that stretched across the ages, they spun the threads of existence, intertwining past, present, and future into a single tapestry. Each strand whispered of a memory, a dream yet to unfold, or a fleeting moment slipping through the hands of time. Weaving and mending together, ensuring that the great tapestry of existence would never again unravel.

It Only Took One
by Aimee McGowan

Lucas arrived at 10:33 a.m. on Thursday, 13th April 2017. I had been in labour since Monday and was finally given an emergency caesarean on Thursday morning. I was exhausted, drained, and complete. But that was only the beginning.

A midwife came and helped me get a bed bath, which consisted of warm water and a cloth rub down. It was harder than you'd think, with all the monitors and IV lines coming from me. Lucas had to be taken away as soon as he was born for antibiotics.

'Take this time to get yourself a little rest. You're going to need it!' Julie advised, turning away to get some sandwiches and biscuits. During my three-day nightmare of labour, I'd only managed to eat half a bowl of cornflakes and three Urban Fruit Strawberries before vomiting them across the floor and wall. My stomach was louder than the machines, the hunger pains felt like an errant elbow swinging around in my belly, making me double-check that they hadn't forgotten to take my baby out during the operation. They hadn't.

I gorged myself on sandwiches and was into the prized Border Biscuits when they brought Lucas in.

Julie stood up, fussing over the swaddled bundle in the Bristol Maid.

'Look at you!' She gasped. 'He's tall!'

She was right. At 9 lb and 11 oz, he was incredibly long. She quickly discarded the newborn baby-gros and held up one for a three-month-old. She laid it out and gave me a once-over.

'Are you ready for some skin-to-skin?' She asked, a crease growing between her eyebrows when she noticed I was still hooked up to the machines.

'Well, we can get these sensors off you now, but you'll need the IV for a few days at least.' I nodded and let her sort me before she picked Lucas up and gently placed him on my chest, manoeuvring around the tangle of wires.

'Will you be bottle feeding or breastfeeding?' It sounded like I was picking something off a menu, or maybe I was just still hungry.

'Breastfeeding,' I said immediately.

She nodded.

'Baby might wriggle down to find the breast,' she said, as she continued looking through his little light blue case, 'but I wouldn't worry too much just now about getting him latched; you might find he'll try and suckle a few times before he gets the hang of it. I'll go and let you get some privacy. If you need me, just press this button.' She handed me the buzzer and pulled the curtain closed behind her.

It wasn't long until she came to say her goodbyes and let me know that the midwife relieving her would be through to take me up to the ward, though we hadn't made it to latching. We were admitted to Ward 48 quickly, though my spirits sank when I saw my new neighbours. The lady in the far-right corner had moved slowly and carefully, but there was no baby to be seen. The lady directly across from me had the curtains drawn all the way across and was in the middle of a heated conversation. I couldn't make out any of the words through her thick throat and sniffling, but I was glad. A midwife came through and asked if I was ready to begin feeding. After several failed attempts to get him latched, she gave up, concluding that we were both tired, and he wasn't hungry yet.

I was up most of the night, after the epidural had worn off, trying to change him quietly, navigating around a catheter, the curtain, and our IVs. By the time I'd gotten back into bed, my face was covered in sweat, and my stomach ached from the movement. By breakfast, I felt like I'd run a marathon. I found myself staring at Lucas in the way all new parents stare at their babies, which, in any other context, would be creepy. I had always, since I found out I was pregnant, intended to breastfeed. It was going to happen, and that was that. I hadn't considered the alternatives or the consequences if I couldn't feed. I lifted Lucas, still moving around, under and between wires and tubes, and settled myself in bed. I pulled down my PJ top, which thankfully still modestly covered me, since the curtains were to be pulled open during the day, and tried to get him to latch. The third, fourth, and fifth attempts were heart-wrenching, and I was beginning to get nervous. By day three, the midwives were concerned enough that they came to discuss the possibility of using formula.

'As much as Lucas isn't losing a concerning amount of weight yet, we don't want it to get to that point. It's time to think about supplementing with formula. That doesn't mean you will never breastfeed, but it's what baby needs.'

I was crushed. My chest felt like it was going to cave in, and my throat felt like it had swelled to three times its usual size. My head suddenly began pounding, and my hands were clammy. There was no way I was going to do that. None. I was going to feed my baby myself. They agreed to let me think about it and left. Sitting on the end of the bed and looking over the crib at my beautiful baby boy, I couldn't stop the tears that finally escaped. I gave in to the sobs that had been threatening since that first attempt to latch him. It wasn't long until the woman in the far-right corner appeared in front of me. Perching silently onto the bed next to me, she gently lifted her arm and put it around my shoulders. She explained to me about the lady across from me, the one who had been crying when I was first brought up here.

'He's lost 15% of his birthweight, and she's refusing to supplement with formula. The thing is, all he does is cry, so he's obviously hungry. They've had midwives, doulas, breastfeeding support specialists, doctors, and nurses in trying to help, but they don't think she's producing enough milk. It's heartbreaking.' She explained, her voice low and soothing. I couldn't find my voice around my tight throat to even reply, but she understood. She was one of those women who tend to collect their daughters rather than birth them and given that she had three sons and only one daughter, she liked having a woman to speak to.

The thought gnawed at me throughout the day. One minute, I was determined to keep trying. My natural birth didn't happen, and as it turned out, I needed an epidural twice and a csection, just to do the one thing that, as a woman, should come naturally to me. It was in my DNA to conceive, carry, birth, and feed my baby, all using only my body. But I'd already failed, and I wouldn't, couldn't, fail at this. Then, in the next breath, my thoughts turned to guilt. How long would it take, of starving my baby, for me to give in and feed him? I mean, really, what did it matter where the milk came from if he was getting everything he needed to thrive? I went backwards and forwards, crying, trying, and crying again, before finally standing at the end of the nurses' station and weakly asking for a bottle of formula. They didn't hesitate and handed over a small bottle with a teat already attached.

'Here you go, honey. If he doesn't like that one, we can try another, not to worry,' she said, her tone confident, but her face was sympathetic.

I fed my baby. With tears streaming down my face onto his, he lapped up a small amount of milk from the bottle. After nights of restless sleep, him trying to latch, being unsuccessful, throwing a tantrum, then passing out from sheer exhaustion, I finally got a good few hours of sleep. The next morning, they came and carried out all his checks, which he passed with flying colours, before the cleaners came through. I wasn't ready to get out of my bed, by now feeling like a complete and utter failure, as a mother, and a woman. The cleaning lady chatted as she worked, though she could tell I wasn't in the mood. Finally, she asked me.

'What's wrong, honey? You seem down today,' she enquired quietly, trying to give me more discretion than I deserved.

'I can't get him to latch. I've tried everything, and now I need to bottle-feed.' I whispered, tears once again flooding my eyes.

'Oh, honey, here.' She gave me the half cuddle that our positions would allow and looked behind her. 'Do you mind?' she asked, nodding to my partly exposed breast and Lucas, attempting to suckle. Unsure entirely what she meant, but figuring I'd lost all dignity during my labour and the events that followed, I nodded,

'Not at all,' I said, a little wary about what was going to happen.

In a flash, she grabbed my boob and pointed it upwards slightly, exposing my nipple for half a second, before gently grabbing Lucas's head, and tilting it back and shoving him against me.

He latched: full sucks, his little neck moving as he swallowed. A smile that I swear could have swallowed the entire ward plastered itself on my face. I stared up at her with tears streaming down my face for a completely different reason.

'Don't mention it, honey,' she said as she turned and continued hoovering,

I have never been so grateful to anyone in my entire life.

Mary Mary
by Michele Hinchliffe

"The being who patiently endures injustice, and silently bears insults, will soon become unjust, or unable to discern right from wrong."

– *Mary Wollstonecraft (1759-1797)*

26 December 1801

I am home. It is late now, and William and Joseph are downstairs. I hear their muffled voices and the sounds of their footsteps pacing back and forth in the drawing-room beneath my chamber. I have bathed and dressed and eaten a little soup. I am in my own bed, a place I thought I would never see again.

It was like a miracle. Yesterday morning I was lying there on that hellish straw mattress facing the stone wall of my room, damp and cold, always cold, my mind in its usual state of torpor. Through the bars of the small window, high up on the wall behind me, came the bells of St Paul's, bringing me to my senses. Christmas Day. Of course, moments later the howls and shrieks of my co-habitees filled that God-forsaken place, bouncing off the walls of the endless, dreadful corridors, followed by the shouts and beatings from the keepers to quieten them back down. Next thing I heard the click of a key turning in the door and I turned over to find Matron standing by the bed.

'Sit up now, Mary,' she said to me, so I hauled myself up and pulled my blanket tighter round me, teeth chattering. I could see my breath.

'Mary, you are going home tomorrow.'

'I am cured then?' I asked her. I had been very, very quiet. I have learned that this is the best way.

'Just get yourself up, you're to be bathed today. Let's try to make you presentable for your husband and son.'

So, I was bathed and dressed and 'made presentable'. Then, early the next morning, I was taken out, put onto the cart, and delivered home to Maiden Lane.

William was waiting at the door for me, his face impassive. Was he pleased to see me? His wife and the mother of his children, well, only Joseph now, for dear Mary Anne was gone with the angels. I thought I saw him glance from side to side as I was helped off the cart by the keeper. I told myself *I must behave, no fuss, don't give them any reason to send me back*. He quickly ushered me inside and into the living-room, out of sight.

Joseph was waiting by the fireplace. He turned and looked at me and said, 'Mother. You are well, I hope?' As if I had just returned from the market. I just nodded and smiled. I need to be very careful with him.

They warned me no excitements. I am not to read, nor write, so I must keep this journal hidden. I asked if they had heard from my dear brother, but they said they had not. I would like to see him. Maybe if I behave, they will allow it. I am exhausted but thank God I am out of that place.

My hands tremble as I write. The badness is behind me now, I am sure. I was a different person before.

Joseph says that that cretinous mad-doctor Monro will be out to see me the day after next. I must behave.

28 December 1801

I slept most of yesterday. For the first time in a year, I was not cold or awoken by the demented screams of lunatics. William did not share my bed last night. He is my husband in name only now, I fear. He looks at me with such distaste, that curious man with the funny accent who appeared in the doorway of my brother's butcher shop more than a quarter-century ago.

I was thirty-three years old then, on the shelf. There had been suitors, but I didn't seem to be like my sisters or other women I knew, all desperate to be married. When Mama died five years earlier and the house sold, my dear brother Joseph took me into his home. My young brother was still unmarried then so, as is the way of things, I became his housekeeper and assisted him in his butcher's shop from time to time. It was a modest home and my brother and I formed an easy alliance. I clearly remember those early mornings alone among the waxy carcasses, hanging dead-eyed and stone still, the air full of their fresh death, metal and sweet. I would scatter fresh sawdust on the shop floor in preparation for the day's trade and with my foot make roads and hills, places beyond Brentford I had read of in my brother's books. It is unfortunate that we only recognise we have been at the peak after we start going downhill.

William was younger than me, tall and though not exactly handsome possessed of a confidence and self-assurance which drew one towards him. He was a barber and wigmaker on his way to London. I found myself thinking about him more and more between his near daily visits to my brother's shop. One morning he appeared at dawn while Joseph was at market and told me he would soon be leaving and wanted me to join him, to marry him, and live together in Covent Garden. He said he had spoken to Joseph, and he was agreeable. I must admit that wounded me slightly – did my brother wish me gone? He was young though, and would go on to marry himself at some point. So, I said yes.

I must stop now, that horrid man Monro is due soon and he must not find me writing.

29 December 1801

That dreadful mad-doctor Monro came to see me yesterday. He didn't stay long thank God. He pretends to care for my health, but I know his game: he wants to keep in with my son, ensure he gets his paintings at a decent price. He told me I had been 'good' this last while.

'Am I cured?' I asked him.

He said I should not worry about such things, that I should not get excited. Yet it is these very sentiments that make the bile rise in me! If I remonstrate, if I question, if I wish for myself the things that men assume so freely, then they think me mad. But if I pose as a supplicant, if I suppress what I feel is my truer nature, which is what Monro, my husband, and son seem to desire of me, I win their favour. But I am not free whichever way I go. It is this which thickens the darkness I feel at times so that I can barely breathe.

They all think it was losing Mary Anne that did me for all those years ago. There is no denying that my heart was shattered that day we lost our dearest, sweetest little girl, but it would be wrong to say that there had not been difficulty before. For several days each month, a blackness would enter me, worsening and growing with each passing year. Things which were usually of no consequence stirred such a fire and rage in me that I could not seem to contain myself. I had headaches that lasted for days on end. I could wake up as one person and be an entirely different one by the end of that same day. I could not sleep and when I did I my dreams were devilish and grotesque and I would wake soaked through in my own sweat, heart galloping like a runaway horse and struggling to breathe. I wondered sometimes if there wasn't some dark external force taking me over, for I felt entirely unlike myself and yet I was powerless to control it. For a long time though, when my bleeding began, that devil which had taken residence in my black heart seemed to up and leave again and I would be restored. Until the next time.

Over time, my bleeding stopped bringing any relief, instead the blackness would build in me and when the bleeding came it was replaced by terror and the blood so abundant I could not leave my chamber. I became convinced that I was somehow responsible for the death of my daughter so many years before, ranting and raving and inconsolable. One morning, having again soaked my bed and clothes in blood and sweat overnight, I stripped off and squatted over my chamber-pot on the floor, holding onto the bedpost to steady myself. The blood seemed to come in gushes with each paroxysm of agony. I felt I would die in those moments. The terror was suffocating. I became aware that there was a banging at the door, and in bounded William. He froze at the sight of me, his face stricken. Even through the wildness of my state I was not immune to mortification, naked as I was by my foul chamber pot and blood everywhere.

I screamed at him, 'Get out! Get out! Do not put your eyes upon me!' He would not listen; he came closer. I begged him, 'Don't come near!' I scrambled backwards, cursing him, and my foot knocked over the chamber-pot and its contents spilled forwards, splashing across William's shoes. I swear I did not mean to.

'Oh Mary, what has happened to you?' William asked in despair or disgust, perhaps both.

I hung my head as I sat there on the floor, wailing and pleading, still, to be left alone. During the course of the next couple of days, the bleeding stopped, and I felt a little more myself again, but the damage had been done. As I sat reading in my chamber one morning there came a loud knock at my door. Two strange men entered. William and Joseph hung back on the landing. I screamed with fright—calling out to William and Joseph for help.

'It's for the best,' William shouted back.

For whose best? I was taken away to St. Luke's Asylum, where I remained for a year before being moved to hell itself, Bethlem Moorfields. I never bled again after that last dreadful time, and though my mood remained black, the wildness and the rages eventually tempered. Once I was afraid of some unknowable horror, but now, I know what I am afraid of. I'm afraid of going back to Bedlam, as it has come to be known, among the repugnance and filth and the worst kinds of suffering. So, I have learned to be quiet. To choose the lesser of evils.

30 December 1801

I am feeling a little stronger each day though remain tired and sleep on and off. I managed to get up and dressed and spent some time in the drawing-room while William worked in his salon. I have been good. Joseph came by briefly. He is very busy now that he is a member of the Royal Academy and his paintings are in great demand. I did not say too much, mindful of behaving myself always. My dear son, he has grown into a strange and brilliant young man. I am guilty every day over sending him away so young. Only ten years old he was, and shy as a violet. I was terrified that he would go the same way as Mary Anne in the grime and muck of this city. I could not lose another child. I myself was in a terrible state then with my moods, and of course, his father was busy in the salon so there was nothing else for it. We have never spoken of it, but I feel the weight of it between us now.

As he came to kiss me goodbye, I placed a hand upon his cheek. I said, 'I am proud of you, Joseph. I hope you can forgive me.'

He hesitated a moment, looked askance, then said, 'of course, mother,' before withdrawing.

I think, at last, he understands. I hope he does.

31 December 1801

I am shaking as I write this and in terror once more. I am in fright at what I have discovered. I was reading in my chamber this afternoon when I heard the door go downstairs, and the voices of men greeting each other. I went to my chamber door to try to listen. The men moved to the drawing-room. I crept out onto the upper landing, curious as to who was visiting. The drawing-room door was ajar, but I could not make out the voices. So, I went down a few stairs closer to the open door to hear better. I could make out William's voice first, then Joseph's and the third I recognised as Dr Monro. Well, at first, I thought it must be regarding my son's art, Monro having supported his work for so many years.

I strained to listen.

'You are sure?' Monro said.

William replied, 'She has been quiet this week …'

Then Joseph, 'But for how long, father? She is a woman of ungovernable temper and will ever be thus! Quite, quite mad!'

'I know, son, I know.'

Monro then said, 'I shall notify the keepers then and arrange for the cart to come for her in the morning.'

Well, I felt some of that old bile rise up and I marched downstairs determined to convince them that I was not mad!

I begged them not to send me back to that place, pleaded with them, promised, 'I am changed, I have been good, and I will behave.'

Monro quickly grabbed a hold of me, then William. Joseph simply turned away.

'I am sorry,' I begged over and over. 'Please don't do this!'

Unmoved, they took me back upstairs to my chamber and placed a chair at the door. I continued to shout on William, banging on the floor. He did not come. Is this Joseph's revenge on me? I pray for a miracle overnight, for I know if I am returned to Bedlam, it will be for the last time.

Note from the author:

Mary Marshall Turner, the mother of the artist J.M.W. Turner, was released from Bethlem Moorfields (popularly known as Bedlam) on 26 December 1801 then re-admitted around one week later. She remained there until her death on 14 April 1804 at around 64 years old.

Little is known about Mary's personal life except that she experienced worsening mental health towards middle-age which led to her being placed in asylums. This was at a time when women could be locked up for an array of reasons, from simply reading and writing, to showing outward signs of hormonal changes or distress.

This story is a fictionalised diary of her final week at home and imagines the events, thoughts and feelings that Mary may have experienced between her release and re-admission. All dialogue and character interactions are fictional and are intended to give voice to a woman who, like so many, has been otherwise erased by history.

A Chat with Pat
by Rose Campbell-Smith

The flickering glow of oil lamps cast golden reflections across the polished marble as I stepped into the lavish hall of Cleopatra's palace. The scent of lotus blossoms mingled with the spiced warmth of Egyptian wine, and the air hummed with distant strains of music. At the centre of it all, reclined on a gilded couch, was Cleopatra herself—the Queen of Egypt, the last Pharaoh, the woman who had charmed the greatest men of Rome and shaped the fate of an empire. She turned her kohl-rimmed eyes toward me and smiled, an expression both knowing and inviting.

'Ah, my guest from afar,' she mused, gesturing for me to sit beside her. A servant approached, offering a delicate goblet of honeyed wine, its surface shimmering in the candlelight.

'To your health, Queen of the Nile,' I said, raising my cup. 'And to your remarkable reign.'

Cleopatra's lips curved as she tilted her head, studying me with curiosity.

'And which of my many achievements do you celebrate tonight?' she asked, swirling the wine in her goblet.

I considered my words carefully.

'Your mastery of diplomacy, for one,' I said. 'You have held your own against Rome's mightiest—Caesar, Antony—and steered Egypt through dangerous waters. Your intellect is legend, and your command of languages, unrivalled. You are not just a queen but a scholar, a strategist, a woman of power in a world ruled by men.'

Her laughter was soft, yet filled with amusement.

'Flattery, my friend, is a Roman art. But I appreciate it nonetheless.' She leaned in, her eyes glinting. 'Tell me, does history remember me kindly?'

I hesitated, then met her gaze.

'History remembers you as it does all great figures—through the eyes of those who write it. But your legacy endures, not just as a ruler, but as a woman who shaped the world around her.'

She exhaled, taking a slow sip of wine.

'Then I have done well.' She lifted her goblet in a silent toast before flashing me a conspiratorial smile. 'Now, tell me—if you had my power, what would you do with it?'

As the music played on and the wine flowed, I found myself caught in the Queen's web of wit and wonder. One thing was certain—Cleopatra was far more than the stories told of her. She was not merely a beautiful queen. She is a force of history itself.

The Dance
by Robin Montgomery-Smith

Arkansas, USA, 1984

Without looking up from her book, she put her half-smoked cigarette to her lips, the ashes glowing as she sucked the smoke in deep. Using her knuckle, she pushed up the rim of her glasses to rest them properly on her nose. Her voice became sharp and terse.

'Not tonight. I don't feel good.'

'Momma, we're only doing the concert tonight. Please.'

'I told you; I don't feel good. You wouldn't even notice me anyway. Just pretend I'm there.'

I knew this was a losing battle before I had even asked. My mother never was one of those parents who showed up. She never attended parents' nights at the school. She never went on field trips. She never came to choral concerts. All my friends' parents did. They filled the auditorium no matter what the performance was about, sat with their children on the school bus for field trips, stood in lines to speak to teachers. But not my mother. Her back hurt, she was busy, she had forgotten—this time she felt unwell. Nothing stopped her from playing cards with her friends when they visited. The odd occasion I was allowed to be included in those games, I noticed how alive my mother was when her friends were there. She smiled. She laughed. She connected. I had not realized it then, but that was what I missed—the engagement, the presence. She was there, but she was never there.

I gathered my costume and my choir dress and told my mother I would return after the concert. I walked out of the front door and closed it behind me with no acknowledgement from the chair in the corner. Whenever I closed that door, I shut out the darkness which lived behind it. Even when it was dark outside, it was brighter than on the other side of that door. I felt an iciness of the doorknob in my palm, as I pulled it closed.

I raised the bag containing my costume and dress higher onto my shoulder and started the mile-long trek to the school. The bag was heavy, but I managed. Although it was only late afternoon, all of us were to meet before the performance to warm up and change into our costumes. Some of my classmates had stayed after school to help decorate and set up the stage. I was asked to stay behind but had decided to try and convince my mother to attend the concert. As I walked into the front doors of the school, I wished I had not gone home. I always felt more at home there than in my house. Marcell, one of my closest friends in choir, saw me as I came into the auditorium and ran up the slope of the floor to meet me. He took the bag from my shoulder and placed it on his with little effort.

'Well? Is she coming?'

'No. She's sick.'

'Oh, I'm sorry.' His voice shifted, 'You're here now, though. Will you help me with this paper back here before you change?'

We climbed up onto the stage, and I held an enormous sheet of construction paper as Marcell taped it to the back wall, completing the set design.

'There, that looks good! Doesn't that look good?'

'It does. This is great. Y'all did a good job. Do you know how many people are coming tonight?'

'Yeah, I think Miss T said it was almost sold out.'

'Well, Mom probably wouldn't have been able to get a ticket anyway, right?'

'Prob'ly not. I'm gonna go change. See you in a minute, okay?'

Marcell handed back my bag, and I took it to the classroom which was reserved as a dressing room for the girls. After I changed, I pulled my long black hair into a high, tight ponytail, then joined the other girls whilst we put on stage makeup for the night. A bit of electricity ran through our young bodies; anxious for the audience to enjoy the concert and worried that we might make fools of ourselves. I was particularly nervous because Marcell and I had been rehearsing several moves and lifts from swing dancing, which most of the audience might remember from their own childhoods. Having practiced our own dance for weeks, we were both comfortable with it when no one was watching, but I think he shared a bit of the nerves I was feeling that night. The first part of the concert was a show choir, performing musical numbers along with choreography. That year, the theme was American Bandstand, and one of our best tenors portrayed the host, Dick Clark. All the girls dressed in white button-up shirts, open cardigans, and poodle skirts, the boys in jeans, white t-shirts, and leather jackets—harking back to the 1950s.

Miss Thomson came into our dressing area and led us in warm-up exercises, so our voices were ready for singing.

'Break a leg, girls! The auditorium is filling up and it's almost curtain time. Are you ready?'

'I'm nervous, Miss T,' one of my classmates said in a small voice. 'What if—if they don't like it?'

'They're going to love it, Jennifer.' She addressed the rest of us, 'I know this is our first year doing something like this, but we've all had so much fun putting this together, right?'

'Yes, ma'am,' we all spoke at once.

'Then they are going to have fun watching it. You've got this!' She winked and left us to finish getting ready whilst she led the boys in warming up in a room down the hall.

We filed out of the classroom and walked into the darkness of the hallway to the stage doors. We heard the low hum of the audience before Miss Thomson took the stage to make a few announcements. The audience fell silent, so we knew it was almost time. The stagehand stood at the door and gave us the cue to make our way inside. From behind the curtain, we heard the music begin. We started dancing with each other as the ancient, dusty red velvet drapes were pulled open, their golden tassels dangling. There was immediate applause, and we all caught sight of each other smiling. It was going to be a good night!

We all knew our parts in the performance—it was as much a play as a concert. The moment Marcell and I had been dreading was coming up fast, and we took our positions. We did a few simple moves, and he leaned his face towards my ear.

'You ready?' he mouthed.

I answered with a nod, he took my hand and pulled me to the centre of the stage, as the other dancers made way for us. He lifted me up and swung me from side to side, my feet flying over his head to the left and then right, as I clutched his hands with a tight grip. In rehearsals, he had dropped me at least twice, but that night, our moves were as smooth as if we had been dancing together for years. After a few quick steps, I was pulled underneath his legs and ended up on my feet, with a well-practiced landing. The audience exploded with applause. We did it! Triumphant, we gave each other high-fives and were both grinning, as much from shock as from relief.

The show choir performance concluded, and a delighted audience rewarded us with a standing ovation. Almost an hour later (and a quick costume change), the rest of the concert was over, and we stood together in our formal choral outfits, on stage for our final curtain call. Every person in the auditorium was on their feet. My skin tingled, my head was woozy, and I don't think my feet touched the stage. The elation I felt in that moment was the greatest feeling I had ever experienced. We waited for the curtains to close then filled the room with the thunder of jumping and running feet, racing towards each other for joyful hugs and high-fives. Everyone ran off the stage and into the awaiting crowd below the stage.

When I made my way from the auditorium into the lobby, it was like a trap door opened underneath me and stole every drop of enthusiasm I had felt just moments before. My classmates had found their parents in the crowd. The realization that I was there alone felt like someone had thrown a glass of ice water in my face. I would walk home on my own—the one student out of many without family there to witness this incredible achievement. Without a word—and trying to move so no one would notice me—I lifted my heavy bag and crept out of the front door, slipping past unnoticed by my fellow students caught up in the energy of their delighted families. The walk home was in the blackness of night—streetlights reserved for the well-travelled roads. Not feeling any danger, I headed home the same way I had walked to the school. Once I reached the road where I lived, my euphoric mood began to leak out of me, like a slow pinhole in a full bucket of joy. The porch light was on, and the chill of the doorknob seized the last few drops of my happiness from the night.

As I opened the door, my mother and her husband were sitting in the living room waiting for me. The overhead light was on and that was when I knew I was in trouble—for something. My mind raced to rewind the last few days, interrogating my memories to work out what I did to upset them. I came back with nothing. I felt my heartbeat in my throat as I sat my bag on the floor. My mother spoke first.

'So?'

'So what?'

'Tone, young lady. So, what have you got to say for yourself?'

'A—about what?'

Her husband was the next one to speak.

'The dance.'

'It was a choir concert, not a dance.' I remember clearly thinking to myself, if you had bothered to show up you would know that, but I dared not speak that aloud.

'You know what I'm talking about.' His voice was firm, and I heard a tremor in his words. He was not only angry—he was raging.

'I—I don't know.' My voice was small, low and hesitant.

He stood up and only then did I notice he was holding a belt in his right hand, dangling by his side. He rushed towards me. I stood motionless. Frozen.

'Clayton was there tonight. He saw what you did, and he called me.'

I was still confused about what I had done wrong. I said nothing. My face was on fire, and I felt tears well up in my eyes, but I never let him see me cry. I willed them not to fall.

'You danced with that—that boy.'

Now I knew what he meant. Marcell was my dear friend—and black. I prepared myself for what I knew was coming, wishing

I had changed back into my normal clothes before coming home. The fabric of my concert dress was thin, and I knew this was going to hurt more than usual.

'I'm s—sorry,' a tiny voice slipped from my mouth.

'You're only sorry 'cause you got caught. You know better than to have anything to do with those people. And you danced in public with a black boy! People there know me! Know your mother!'

He bent towards me, spittle landing on my face, stinging my eyes. My mother sat in her chair, smoked her cigarette, and watched. She did nothing to stop what was coming. She never did anything to stop it.

The next few moments melted into each other. There was more shouting and the sharp pain of the belt on my legs and back. I never cried when he hit me with a belt. I wanted to because it hurt with the relentless sting of rage and anger. I was a small-framed child with very little fat on my bones, and he was a tower of a grown man with a weapon of pain and the strength of a factory worker in his swing. I did nothing but stand there and take the beating. My refusal to cry always made it worse. His fury of not getting the reaction he was after made him strike me harder and more often. If I scream, will he stop? I stood still as the lashes from the belt bit into my skin. I kept my eyes focused on my mother as she smoked her cigarette, refusing to make eye contact with me. With my stare, in silence, I begged her to stop him, but she ignored my plea. He soon tired and wanted me out of his sight. He screamed at me to get away from him and go to my room, to think about what I had done.

My bedroom was my respite. I limped back to the darkness of my room and reached for the wet washcloth I kept in a zip lock bag under my mattress. I took off my dress, which was now streaked with thin, bloody stripes, and dabbed my legs with the cool, moist cloth. I whimpered, but I dared not make too much noise. If he heard me cry, he would get the satisfaction of having caused such pain—such distress. I put on my pyjamas and climbed into bed. No dinner for me. I just wanted to sleep and forget the night, but I never slept after beatings. I was always worried he might come into my room and hit me again. I laid in my bed, staring at the ceiling, the sheets covering me nipped as they brushed against my wounds.

Those were my wishing moments. Wishing I was not me, not in that house, not the me I was then. Wishing I had been born someone else. Wishing one day I would fall asleep and not wake up. I lay awake in my bed the rest of the night, listening to the crickets and frogs outside my bedroom window. I watched as the sky changed from thick ink to murky morning light. Life in the neighbourhood went on as if nothing had happened the night before, as if the neighbours had not heard the raps of the leather against my skin whilst they cozied up on their sofas watching TV. I heard movement in the front of the house, the door opened and closed, the roar of the pickup truck which then pulled away into the distance. He had gone to work.

That was when I felt safe enough to get out of bed on that Saturday morning. I checked my legs, and the blood had dried where he broke the skin. I took my dress into the bathroom and rinsed it with cold water, something I should not have known to do at my tender age. I hung it up in my room next to the window to dry. I walked into the living room and noticed my mother sat with one leg folded underneath her. She was reading a book and smoking a cigarette whilst she sipped her morning coffee.

'Morning,' she said, not looking up from her book.

'I'm going outside.' I knew I was safer outside and anywhere was better than being at home.

'Fine. Be back before dark,' she mumbled through the cigarette which dangled from her mouth.

'Okay, Momma.'

I opened the door—the frostiness of its handle cold in my hand, and noticed the warm, dappled morning sunlight as it danced on the dusty front yard. I filled my lungs with the clean air. The air that was clearer, fresher outside. I pulled the door closed behind me, and once again I shut out the darkness which resided in that house.

Life Is Sweet

by Heather Grossart

She was fat. No ifs, no buts. She was fat. There is a humour in being outsized, at least to others. He laughed and called her the fat bitch who couldn't walk twenty yards without sitting down and who took up two spaces on buses.

She often wondered why people didn't feel sorry for someone in permanent misery: their sore knees and back, the awkwardly fitting clothes. There are hundreds of reasons why it's not funny. But, as he told her, she brought it on herself. She could have stopped eating after all.

The online group was busy this morning, and everyone talked about what they had lost and eaten. She told them she'd lose the weight starting today, but didn't add that it might make him happy. First, though, she'd need a plan of action. This time was going to be different. This time, it would work.

'You plannin' to sit there all day on that damn iPad? Or are you goin' to do somethin' useful… like *walk anywhere*?' he said.

'You know it hurts to walk,' she moaned, hating herself.

'You don't even try.'

'Because it hurts. What part don't you understand?' She wished almost immediately that she hadn't said that. No point in making him irritated.

'The same part that you don't understand, that it's not goin' to get any better unless you actually *do* somethin'.'

She knew he was technically correct, but it wasn't as simple as that; being overweight never was. She didn't need anything practical to help her lose weight; just willpower was enough.

However, she knew that new, shiny things encouraged her. So, she started doing the next best thing to eating; she spent money. New Bluetooth scales and a Bluetooth tape measure went into the virtual basket. Because she had to measure, measure, measure just in case, by some miracle, she lost inches, not pounds. She would have to exercise to build muscle, but that wasn't happening. She bought a portable blender for the protein shakes she had just put in her basket, not forgetting a cup for said shakes. The protein part was only good for protecting muscles, which still meant exercise. But it was a fresh start, a new life.

Doomscrolling through social media because there was nothing else to do, nothing that she *could* do anyway, no housework, cooking, or gardening. She had messed up her internet algorithms, and now her feed was full of adverts for protein shakes since she had bought them on Amazon, and social media knew everything about you. Her only real friend, who could see her and loved her, was her mongrel Cleo. Cleo always sat at her feet.

Social media amused her mostly. Though the 'research' rabbit holes she went down were always interesting, basic things like how to kill someone with minimal effort were always amusing and kind of fun. Even gave her hope. Watching person after person posting shit on every insidious but engaging platform, was another pointless exercise. People posted pictures of their cats and dinner. She spent untold hours wondering about other people's lives. She imagined being like them and walking around the shops. Choosing clothes from non 'fat' shops. Sneakily enjoying the battle of words that some people always get into. She knew she had a sad life.

She sat the following day, tracking her delivery. She had little or no chance of hiding her purchases, but she could open them and pass them off as old.

Four stops away, the dot showed the delivery van in her street. Why weren't these trackers accurate?

'Sittin' there again, doin' nothin'? What's keeping your attention out the window? Is watchin' the neighbours all you do?'

She didn't answer.

'That better not be an Amazon van outside there for you.'

'So, what if it is?' She looked him in the eye. He punched her in hers. She knew any normal woman would have been surprised, but she wasn't. This one felt like a 'good' one, and she felt it instantly swell. He went to the door and took her parcels in. He threw them at her.

She shrank down into her seat, and her head dropped. She knew there was no point in reacting. The best she could hope for was that there would not be a follow up or follow through with another punch. She sat that way until he left.

'Well, Cleo, let's see if we can do this technical stuff.'

Setting up the scales was more complicated than she expected. Who knew how to make Bluetooth talk to each other? Thank goodness for internet videos. She set them down in the kitchen, knowing that he would complain. BMI of 52.4. How disgusting.

She made up a protein shake with salted caramel. It was lumpy. She choked it down. She wondered what to do next. She could go for a walk to the end of her path. That was about her limit.

Doomscrolling again, an advert flashed up for antifreeze. How did the advert god know he'd told her they needed it? Then there was one about being the best you can be. The model wasn't stick thin; it was a revelation. She clicked on the link. It was a miracle weight loss injection. She had heard of them, so she signed up, filled out all the forms, and sent her full-length body pictures and identification. She paid for it and waited to see if she had been accepted into the programme. Knowing her luck, they would refuse her and return her money.

She was surprised when they phoned her straight away. They asked loads of questions she was loath to answer. But she put her big girl pants on and told the truth.

'I need to lose weight for my life, sanity, and marriage,' she admitted.

'We will send it out now. You should get it tomorrow.'

She felt tears well up. This could be the answer. The answer to all her problems. He would be happy if she got healthy. If she got thin. He'd love her again.

With something to look for, instead of mindless scrolling, she googled weight loss injections. Diarrhoea, constipation, nausea, sickness, headaches, feeling cold, sulphur burps, and vomit that was worse than the worst baby's nappy were all side effects. Twenty-two per cent of your body weight is gone in a year. Minimum. Desperation had driven her to it. She knew stupidity had stopped her from researching before she bought, but she was frantic. Suppression, they called it when you felt full all the time, was a side effect she would welcome. 'Food noise' disappeared with this elixir. You didn't think about food and where your next hit would be. It was another kind of hit she was worried about. She thought it sounded like magic.

She had another shake, conscious that too many shakes were as bad as too much food.

She got ready for work. Standing in front of the mirror, though, her black eye was scarlet and purple, which meant she would have to call in sick. One more bruise, and they really would be talking.

'I've got an upset stomach; I won't be in.'

'Are you sure you're ok?' Her boss asked. 'It's not like the last time, is it?'

'No, no, I'm really sick.'

This was the sort of speculation she was trying to avoid, trying to hide from. She'd have to change jobs if the wrong questions came up many more times.

Her job was thankfully sedentary, meaning she could rest her knees and back. Also, it meant there were a lot of cakes around. Not because the job was sedentary but because all the girls were skinny and could eat cake without fear. She was jealous but still ate the cake.

She jumped back on the scales again. Up three pounds. *For fuck's sake.* Tears again.

He got home from work in a good mood. She wasn't so glad; good moods usually meant he would feel frisky. That was the last thing she wanted or needed. It wasn't technically rape, that's what she told herself, but it was a beating if she didn't concede. So, she usually did, grudgingly. Luckily, tonight, the food was enough to distract him. The downside was the alcohol, which raised a whole distinct set of problems. Well, no, it's the same problem as the good mood. She'd just lie back and think of her injections if it came to it. She hated this too about her life; she knew what an advice columnist would tell her to do, but she wasn't brave enough to leave. And it was rape, she knew that. Coercive control, they called it.

The postman was late, and she had taken another day off work. She was going to lose her job soon, she was sure. She couldn't, though. She needed it to afford the injections. She almost ran towards the door when the postie approached.

Sitting on the toilet with the injection in hand, she was scared to inject herself. *Just do it.* She opened the pen, screwed on the needle, primed it, and held it over her stomach. The needle was only half a centimetre. She closed her eyes and plunged. Didn't hurt a bit. Glad *something* didn't hurt.

She felt no different, but it had only been five minutes. She went back to her usual perch. She didn't do anything, no scrolling through social media or looking for potential problems with the injection. Waiting for something, anything to happen. Suddenly, her stomach made a weird gurgle. She just made it to the bathroom, sitting on the toilet, throwing up into the sink. This would be the side effects, she decided.

Eventually, she felt empty.

She spent the rest of the day running between her chair and the bathroom. She wondered if her knees would hold up to all this dashing around. Surely, she must lose weight today. On the scales again … back to where she started. She stupidly wondered if he'd notice she'd lost weight.

He came strolling in just before teatime. Her heart sank.

'We are going out,' he announced. 'The boys and their wives are meetin' up for dinner.'

She sighed for about a hundred reasons. No clothes, no ability to chatter to people, black eye, the volcanic eruptions from both ends, eating in public, dinner was almost ready, what if the injection had worked and she *couldn't* eat?

'Go put some make-up on your eye. Imagine walkin' into the door like that.'

Gaslighting was a thing he did, but she was starting to recognise it for what it was. The internet had taught her that. She trudged slowly up the stairs, still feeling depleted after her bathroom adventures. She pulled on jeans, the most enormous size she had been able to buy. They were tight. They weren't meant to be tight. An oversized, baggy men's XXXL jumper followed.

She crashed into the mirror as he slapped the back of her head. What had she done?

'I told you ... make-up.'

'Give me a chance.'

'We are in a hurry,' he snapped. 'Look, we will just, or rather *you* will say you walked into a door,' he smirked, 'just like you did.'

She didn't dare sigh outwardly.

The evening was as much hell as she thought it would be. Several bathroom visits and picking at food. He kept glaring at her. She raised her hand a little as if to ask what she'd done wrong.

They got outside when he suddenly pushed her, she fell on her face, then couldn't get up. She struggled to her knees and was stuck. He walked on. Embarrassed, she accepted help from strangers to stand up, not standing tall, never that, but standing upright.

'Thank you, I'm so sorry.' She didn't know what to say, so she told the truth. 'Sorry, I'm too fat to help myself up.'

She got a taxi home.

'Cleo!' she shouted. Cleo limped in and stopped in front of her. There was a cut above her eye. She understood instantly what had happened. That was unforgivable. She cleaned up Cleo as best she could and gave her some of her favourite chicken treats.

The next day dawned, and she was up early, making his breakfast, a full fry-up, orange juice and tea. Hoping to sweeten *his* mood, if not hers. He didn't complain. Today was going to be a good day.

'This orange juice is sweet, not the normal shit you serve up.'

She didn't reply.

No trips to the bathroom, no hunger pangs. No pointless internet, just reading a book, an Agatha Christie book. She prepped for dinner. Steak pie and all the trimmings. Roly-poly and custard for seconds and a large glass of his favourite cola because that was sweet. He was sure to be happy.

She couldn't tell what kinda mood he was in when he came in.

'I've made dinner, all your favourites. Cola instead of beer. Just as a treat.'

'Not feelin' great, a bit of a dodgy tummy. And why the hell would I want cola instead of beer?'

'Must be what I had yesterday. You will be fine. I'll get you a beer after dinner.' She dodged the question about the cola. 'Do you still want dinner?'

'Yeah, I'll force it down. If I'm going to be sick, I'd rather be sick with somethin' in my stomach.'

'Go sit down, and I'll bring it to you.'

He smacked his lips and grunted.

She brought their plates through, picked at hers, watching him as he ate and drank. Grateful that he finished it all, especially the cola.

'I want a baby. Can a fat pig like you get pregnant?' He slurred and asked as he slouched in front of the television. 'I want a piss.' He stood up and went to the bathroom, staggering as he went.

She decided to never answer that question. There was no way she would have his baby even if she could.

'I'm going to bed,' he shouted from the top of the stairs.

'OK, I'll be up soon.' She shouted back.

She sat all night in her chair, daydreaming about what it would be like to be thin. So many things running through her mind. What if she ended up being a strong, *thin,* independent woman? What a thought.

It was 7 a.m. when she went upstairs. She slowly pushed open the door to their bedroom. He was lying on top of the bedclothes, still fully dressed. His breathing seemed shallow. He was mumbling in his sleep. She shook him awake, or tried to, but he whispered that he was too tired. She watched a vein throb in his forehead.

She went back downstairs and shook herself. She decided another 24 hours should do it. She phoned his work, calling in because he was sick. He would be angry at her taking the initiative, but he wasn't in a fit state. She flicked through magazines and turned the morning television on. They had an article about the weight loss injections. Someone had died. Knowing my luck, she thought.

By early afternoon, she was bored waiting. She went back upstairs to check on him. Still there, still with the fluttery breathing and the pulsing temple.

She lifted a pillow and held it over his face. She could smother him. He wouldn't fight back. She put the pillow down. Killing him that way was altogether too physical. There were other means.

He hiccupped in his sleep and tried to move but failed. She supposed she had loved him once. She doubted he had ever loved *her*. The first time he had hit her was before they got married. And she still married him; someone should have questioned her sanity. He had lovely eyes. She gave him that. She struggled to think of any other good points. It was time. She pulled on a jacket and called for a taxi.

'Take me to the police station.'

The police office had 'Welcome' etched on the door in eight languages. She wondered if she'd be welcome. She pushed the stiff door open.

The woman at the front counter wasn't a police officer but wore a uniform.

'Can I help you?'

'Yes, I fed my husband antifreeze. Luckily, it's sweet, so he didn't taste it in the drinks I gave him ... He shouldn't have been so quick to suggest we needed the stuff; I mean, it's not even winter. Poisoning is such a girlie way to kill someone, and he'd hate that, so why the bloody hell not? He should be dead any time now, or he will be soon. He shouldn't have hurt my dog.'

This Is Where We Are Now
by Michele Hinchliffe

Rohan Kulkarni combs his silver-flecked black hair away from his face. He is a handsome, fine-featured man (though too self-effacing to ever think of himself in this way). He washes his hands in the bathroom sink, carefully avoiding his reflection in the mirror. He does not wish to be reminded of the many sleepless nights he has endured over the past few weeks. From across the hallway in the kitchen, the sounds of his wife Ana encouraging their five-year-old son Nish to hurry and eat breakfast drift. They have an important appointment this morning. Rohan straightens his tie and exhales. Even on the most life-defining of days we still must dress, eat, tend to the ordinary, as absurd as it feels in the moment.

His phone vibrates on the window ledge, startling him slightly. He picks it up and opens the message. It's Yumna from Right to Remain:

'Good luck this morning. Just remember everything we went over. I'll call you later, see how it went.'

He replies, 'Thanks, I appreciate it.'

He opens the Uber app and books a car to Lunar House in Croydon for 10 a.m. That should give them enough time to get from their Airbnb in Orpington to their 11 a.m. asylum screening interview, allowing for the London traffic. He pays the fare in advance, as Yumna advised, to reduce the risk of not securing a driver because of the combination of his name and destination.

Nish appears at the bathroom door followed closely by Ana. Rohan moves aside to let them get to the sink. She hands Nish a toothbrush and squeezes some paste on his brush then her own.

'Hey, no sucking on that toothbrush, *mijo*!' Ana says, and Nish beams a smile at her, pink and white toothpaste stuck to his lips and teeth, then diligently starts to brush. Rohan smiles at Ana and gently squeezes her free hand.

'The taxi will be here in about ten minutes.'

She nods at him while continuing to brush, he can't read her face with the toothbrush in her mouth, but he thinks he sees fear in her eyes and the sight of it cleaves him.

Rohan met Ana six years earlier at a fundraiser hosted by the hospital Rohan worked in as an obstetrician and gynecologist. Ana was a research scientist ten years his junior, they bonded over chicken kebabs and a shared love of economics and dogs. At 48 years old, Rohan had long considered himself married to his job and had begun to come to terms with the fact, by turns shaming and regretful, that a family life would not be his path. If finding Ana was a surprise, then the arrival of their son Nish one year later felt miraculous. A father at 49. People could hardly believe it, least of all him. Ana moved into Rohan's small two-storey rental house near the University, and they got a Labrador called Nala. Life was sweet. Even when the pandemic hit in the following months, they seemed somehow insulated in their own little bubble. They loved their work, they loved their son, they loved each other. But alongside their love story, a counter-narrative was emerging. Their country was changing. The seeds of hatred, injustice and control, quietly sown years before, were germinating and would quickly grow roots and take hold.

Rohan's phone pings, the Uber is outside. He runs through a collection of paperwork one final time, places it inside a folder and into his small rucksack. The family head down the stairs to the waiting car.

'Lunar House then, is it?' The driver glances at them in his rear-view mirror. He does not smile.

'Yes, thank you.' *Another brown family here to suck up resources and dilute the culture*, Rohan reads the driver's mind. Like this is what he wants for himself and his family. Like this is a choice. He would like to say all this out loud, but it would do him no good so instead he just smiles weakly, nods and sits back in his seat.

Streets slip by, the buildings and cars familiar only from films and TV shows. Nish sits on Ana's knee, and she talks to him about the things they see on the way. He presses his little hand on the window. Rohan's heart hurts. The decision to leave—if you can call it a decision—felt both a long time in the making and altogether too fast when it finally happened. Rohan's work, the residency programme he had set up in one of the most deprived areas of his country, was falling apart. Rohan was no stranger to working in challenging circumstances. He had run clinics where patients came to appointments on horseback, or where he and his nurses would drive down dirt roads to provide the health care that he firmly believed was every human's right. But the regime change in his country meant he could not do his job anymore. The rule of law itself was collapsing. There was a time he lived and died by his patients. But that changed the day Ana arrived home from work only a few weeks ago, eyes swollen, sobbing.

'They've cut all my funding. The lab shuts next week. It's over.'

As Rohan held her, something inside him turned. The nebulous fears that had been building over the past few years seemed in that moment to crystallise into the knowledge that this was not going to get better. That this was the moment to get out.

The Uber arrives at Lunar House in Croydon. Rohan thanks the driver, the driver says nothing, and they alight onto the pavement. It is a bright morning, and the sky is covered in high white cloud. Rohan and Ana squint as they look up at the twenty-storey Brutalist behemoth before them, both foreboding and banal. Nish hops around at their feet. Ana takes one hand, Rohan takes the other and he squeals with excitement as they swing him back and forth on their way over to the tinted, mirrored glass double doors of the Home Office Immigration Centre. A burly security man in a black beanie hat, wearing a stab vest, adorned with walkie talkie and security pass opens the door to them.

'Letter?'

Rohan hands over the Home Office letter with the appointment details on it.

The security man reads it, hands the letter back and opens the door wide signalling for them to come inside. There is a queue of around 20 people snaking around a series of stanchions and belts. The foyer has floor to ceiling windows on three sides, tinted on the inside, mirrored on the out. There is a glass cubicle at the front of the queue. Inside a woman takes paperwork from people and communicates with them through a rectangular slot. Beside the cubicle there is a turnstile which flashes green when the woman allows entry. There is also a bag check. Nish, observing the scene, asks excitedly, 'Are we going on a plane again?'

Rohan and Ana look at each other, then Ana says gently, 'no, *mijo*, but you're right, this really looks like an airport.'

'Aw,' Nish says, and looks down, shoulders drooping.

Rohan recalls the day, two short weeks ago but now belonging to another world, when they sat Nish down to explain they were leaving to go on a big adventure somewhere where they might decide to live. At five years old, this proposition was exciting. But there was the issue of Nala.

'But I don't *want* to leave Nala,' Nish howled.

Nala lay in her bed, eyebrows dancing back and forth, watching the drama of her fate unfolding between the three of them.

'But Nala can't come, *mijo*, we told you she isn't allowed to come on the airplane.'

'I don't want a big adventure if Nala can't come!'

They went around and around like this until Nish, red-eyed and defeated, fell asleep. They decided it was best to take Nala to the re-homing centre while Nish slept. Ana wept as she gave Nala a final cuddle, inhaling her toasted popcorn scent one last time.

'You're such a good girl.'

Nala's liquid chestnut eyes bore a look of betrayal; it is a look they will never forget.

After around twenty minutes they arrive at the front of the queue, are checked in and make their way to the Screening Unit waiting area.

Eventually, a porcine man, sweating in a polyester shirt, appears from behind a door. 'Kulkarni?'

Rohan stands up. 'Yes, that's us.'

The man holds the door open and motions to them to go into the room with a tilt of his meaty head.

Rohan leads Ana and Nish towards the door. Nish is shy of this man, picking up something unwelcoming about his energy. He hides behind Ana's leg.

The man looks at Nish and says, 'there's a family room available, if you want it.'

'No, thanks. We don't have anyone else to look after him. I want him here.' Ana replies firmly.

The man raises his eyebrows and holds up his hands and says, 'up to you. This shouldn't take too long.'

Rohan and Ana sit on two plastic chairs; Nish sits on Ana's knee. The man sits opposite them behind a small desk with a laptop and a few files on top of it. There is a stained coffee cup with a faded floral pattern. The room smells of stale body odour. There is a window with closed vertical blinds and a strip of fluorescent lighting on the ceiling. The walls are creamy tobacco-stain yellow, peeling in places.

'So, Mr Kulkarni—'

'It's Doctor—Doctor Kulkarni.'

The interviewer raises his eyes from his laptop briefly and without looking at Rohan sighs and says, '*Doctor* Kulkarni. Your papers please?'

Rohan hands over the required documents.

The man absently glances at them, then does a double take. 'Oh-ho, well. This should be interesting. Mr Kulkarni, can you explain to me why you feel you need the protection of His Majesty's government?'

Rohan is a gentle man but there is a heat spreading out from his belly and his hands, resting on his lap, grow tense, stiffening into claw shapes. Ana, sensing this, discreetly pushes her knee against his. His hands relax again.

Rohan sits up in his seat and starts to explain how the obstetrics and gynecology residency programme he established collapsed after the law changed in 2022, allowing his state to ban abortions. How it is now illegal to perform procedures which are the standard of care the world over. How medics have been financially incentivised by the government to report on colleagues breaking the law, even when it is to save a mother's life. How the law has been made so opaque that his work is now a field of uncertainty. How he and his colleagues live in fear that the next patient will be the one they must decide to either save and face prosecution or allow to die in trying to abide by the law.

'These are human rights violations of the most abhorrent nature, and they are sanctioned by my country's government,' Rohan says, 'it has become intolerable.'

Then Ana speaks up. 'I am a research scientist, originally from El Salvador. My field is biomedical science, in particular reproductive health. The government has cut my funding because my research concerns women. They have taken away my job, my life's work. I have worked at University Hospital San Antonio in Texas since I graduated 22 years ago. But now my name, the colour of my skin, the country I am from mean I am under threat of deportation, even though I have a valid Green Card.'

Her throat catches and she lowers her eyes. She tilts her head down slightly, inhaling the scent of Nish's hair, lifts her head, then continues:

'It is no longer safe for us in the United States. We speak English, we can be assets to the UK. We just want to live our lives and raise our son in a free, democratic country, like ours used to be.

Hope
by Charity Reed

The waves crash around the piles and cleats. Spray stings my face, and I lick the salt from my lips. I watch as a lone surfer takes her life in her hands, rising on a swell that takes my stomach with it. She looks so fearless, the cold ocean tugging at her legs as they swing from her board. It might as well be a matchstick she's riding out there, silhouetted against the greying sky, wind whipping around her. I lose sight of her for a few seconds, and I think she's gone forever, taken into the deep water. My gut lurches again and I'm getting ready to call the coastguard when she reappears, triumphant and soaring on a crest. She heads toward land as smoothly as the birds who whirl and dive above her, a part of the same fierce element. I wrap my scarf a little tighter against the stiff wind and turn to look back up the pier. I wish I'd had her spirit, her tenacity. When I was her age, I would never have dared to rock the boat at home, let alone surf in a storm. Maybe if I had, I wouldn't be here today.

I still remember the conversation in the back kitchen. We lived in the back kitchen, the front room always kept for best, plastic covers on furniture that never saw visitors. I always wondered why guests that never came were more important than the family that lived there. That was the day it became apparent I would be leaving home for the first time. Dad stayed silent. Mum did not. She went biblical, with all manner of wailing and gnashing of teeth. My protestations, unheard. She ended with her usual plea, 'why can't you be more like Paula Purvis? Why do you always have to be so—so—*you*?'

I said, 'You don't even know what Paula Purvis gets up to.'

Mum folded her arms and sneered. 'Exactly. Her mother never has to worry about what the neighbours will say.'

I gave up as usual. 'I'm *so* sorry,' I spat as I slammed the door.

I remember playing *Love's Just a Broken Heart,* the gramophone at top volume, tinny and rattling on the dressing table. I remember the mascara marks on my pillow, wet with snot. And I remember how lonely I felt, lonely and scared. Dad brought me a cup of tea soon after and I only noticed when he tapped at the door, quiet in case I was sleeping, that the record was still spinning, clicking on the turntable.

'She'll come round,' he said to me. 'Everything will be alright.'

'Thanks Dad.'

And he was right. Everything was all right, for a while. I tried to tell Mum before I left that Paula Purvis was no saint. 'She smokes behind the chapel, Mum.' I felt like a right grass, but I said it anyway, desperate for any kind of approval. I knew it was true, I'd bummed a ciggy off her behind the chapel more than once.

'I've never heard about it.' Her lips were tight as she attempted to take the glaze off a plate with her tea-towel.If she hadn't heard about it, it hadn't happened.

'I even smelled wacky baccy on her once.'

'And how do you know what wacky baccy smells like, young lady? Are you taking drugs now as well as—*everything else*?' I couldn't win. I sometimes wondered if Paula's mum wished Paula could be more like me. I didn't expect so.

I moved down here not long after that and took a temping job as a secretary. Most of the other girls that shared the house were fun. I felt free living here, away from the nagging and the judgement.

This was where I met Margorie. She was my best friend, and we laughed a lot in those few months, over everything and nothing. We played Beatles records together in our rooms, she was in love with George Harrison, I with John Lennon, and we shared our dreams for the future, with no idea that we'd lose touch a few short months later. It was Margorie who first took me to Jean's Café. 'Hey Gracie,' she called out to me one day as I returned from work.

'Wotcha, Marge?'

'I found a great caf'. Wanna get out of the house for a bit?'

I laughed. 'I've just got back.'

'Yeah, well I've been stuck 'ere all bloody day, c'mon.'

'No work today?' I asked.

'Off sick.' Marjorie mimed heaving and spewing and laughed.

We linked arms and headed down the road together, crossing over onto Middle Street. I remember we got whistled at by some boys on bikes, Margorie thrust two fingers skywards.

'Piss off you dirty buggers,' she shouted after them, and she cackled with glee at their disappointed faces. 'He was a bit of alright actually,' she said as they cycled off, her face full of regret as though she'd just thrown back a prize goldfish at the fair.

'You didn't have to be rude; he'd have probably stopped and paid for your tea and cake if you'd have given 'im the come on.' I didn't understand Margorie sometimes.

'Oh yeah, one look at me up close and 'ed have run a bleedin' mile.' She was right, but we had each other, and we weren't really interested in boys just then. We'd both sworn off them. We'd 'had our fill' as Margorie put it.

'Ooh Marge—look at them cakes.' I couldn't believe I hadn't been here before. We discovered Jean's scones that day, warm, crumbly, and smothered in raspberry jam.

After that we'd go there and spend our wages every Saturday, and sometimes after work in the week. It wasn't fancy, but it was clean, quaint, Gingham-clad, and cheap. And the cakes were delicious. Sometimes we'd buy bread and dripping, sometimes a slice of fruit cake, or a scone. Occasionally we'd treat ourselves to milkshakes, they cost more but it was nicer when the weather got too hot.

Jean's was just a five-minute walk from Fitzpatrick's Boarding House. That's what it was called, a respectable-sounding home for disreputable girls. An unmarried mother's home. People think those places are terrible, all doom and gloom—and of course it was depressing in some ways, none of us wanted to be there, but I have fond memories of the girls. We were just unfortunate. In some cases, it was our own fault of course; I'd been stupid enough to think I was in love. Margorie just loved sex. One girl, Susan, had been attacked on her way home from the cinema. Poor love, she was under the doctor for her nerves. Lynette's parents said she could have kept her baby if the father had been white. Ironic: she married him a year later, eloped to Gretna Green, and they had two kids—but they'll never get that first one back. I bumped into her in the Arndale Centre of all places, about a month ago—totally out of the blue. We did a double-take but recognised each other immediately, and, as we caught up, she showed me photos. She was buying books for her youngest who'd been accepted into Durham University. I'm glad times have changed. There were two Margarets there as well. We never got their stories because they didn't really mix. Margorie always said she didn't understand how either of them ended up in that condition anyway.

'*Lesbians*, Gracie,' she told me in hushed tones.

I wasn't quite sure what lesbians did, so I asked her and got a guffaw in return. Then she opened her two fingers and started wiggling her tongue through them. I still didn't understand.

'Like my old Aunt Mary and her 'special friend' Belinda. Land girls they was, in the war. Been living together since 1943.' She guffawed again. 'The 'ole family knows but not one of us ever lets on. 'Cept once, at a family do, Aunt Mary announces that she prefers fish to sausages and me old nan spat out 'er false teeth laughing.'

I still didn't understand at the time, but I laughed anyway.

'Nice really,' she said. ''Ain't hurting no one and a damn sight 'appier than most married couples I know. It's a funny old world.'

That year was a long sweltering summer when the days still went on for hours after work. And it was an adventure, free of parental authority. And it was a tragedy, when innocence was lost.

It was the sixth of August when it happened. Margorie had been manic for days. Her moods were always up and down but she was crazy happy that week. We'd gone to the penny arcades on the Friday after work and her laughter was louder than ever. The children on their school holidays were rude and annoying, mothers and grandmothers soaked up the sun, sipping tea on the pier outside, waiting for them to come running back whining for more change or an ice cream.

'You know Gracie, I just don't feel pregnant today,' she told me.

I laughed. 'You still look it Marge.' I dropped a copper into the penny falls, despondent as it landed, useless on the copper heap.

'I know—I'm an elephant,' followed by her trademark shriek. 'But—I just feel lighter somehow, like I did before.' She gazed out at the sea, and she looked so serene.

Margorie didn't want her baby. Barely seventeen and due to give birth in two months, her carefree outlook on life didn't seem naturally maternal. She had told me that she had no problem giving the baby to some poor souls who couldn't have their own children. 'Not everyone's blessed with the ability to get up the duff from a two-minute knee trembler Gracie,' she had once told me with the wisdom of Solomon.

'You look pinker in the cheeks somehow Marge, maybe you're finally 'glowing.'' We both fell about laughing—poor Margorie had been so sick during her confinement. Her skin had erupted in spots, her hair was lank, and she'd been what the doctors called 'hysterical.'

'Well, it's about bloody time Gracie. Remind me never to do this again. I think I'll be a career woman.'

'I'm not sure girls like us, from council estates, get to be career women Marge.' Another penny chinked into the machine, lost again in the pile. 'Damnit.'

'It's awright for you Gracie, you're a Catholic grammar-school girl. Clever like. You could be a career woman; you've got three O levels.'

'I hated grammar-school, I'd much rather have gone to your secondary mod. Sounds like much more fun.'

She squealed in delight, nodding at my belly. 'You've had enough fun. You posh girls get plenty.'

'I'm not posh!' I punctuated my indignation with a 'fuck off' and instantly looked around feeling awful in case I'd been overheard. Margorie just laughed and waddled over to the one-armed bandit. I heard the clunking of the arm as she pulled it down, and the clinking of the coppers cascading into the tray.

'Must be my lucky day,' she shrieked, face crinkled with joy.

That night I heard her shriek again, but there was no joy. The doctor came out, and I heard the hushed voices of the landlady and the doctor, and I heard the screams. The next day I was told that Marge had lost the baby. The baby. The unwanted. The soon-to-be gifted to another. Nobody could have known how much she really wanted him though. Not until after. If the doctors thought there was hysteria before she lost that baby, they should have seen the state she was in after he was gone. I never heard her laugh after that. They let her stay in the room for a week and then just threw her out. Nobody wanted a tainted thing like her around the other girls.

I wrote to her for a while, but the letters that came back were sad. She told me in one of them that her baby was fully formed when he was born. Dead and blue but a proper baby.

'I could see his little toes and his little willy, and his little face Gracie, his poor little dead face.'

Back then, if a foetus was under seven months, they didn't call it a stillbirth like they do now, she wasn't allowed to hold him or say goodbye. It was 'just a miscarriage', like you'd dropped a bag of shopping. Mis-carry. Nobody spoke much about it. And then the letters stopped coming. I hung around with the new girl for a while, Kath, who lived on the same landing as me. Nice enough. Daft enough to believe that she couldn't get pregnant if she did it standing up. It was never the same, never so much fun as with Marge. Kath left at the beginning of September; her parents hurrying her away from the shame, her dad muttering 'at least you're respectable again.' They'd told friends and family she'd been 'working up in London' for the last six months. God help us. And then it was my turn.

I awoke around five-thirty on the morning of the twenty-eighth of September. The dog days were beginning to fade, but it was still warm, and the sun was appearing in the eastern sky. I still remember lying there, scared to call out, watching the dust motes floating like mayflies in the beam that came through the gap in the curtains as I bit my pillow. The candlewick bedspread twisted between my fingers as I tried to deny the pain shuddering through me. Mrs Fitzpatrick, the landlady, either heard me or had a sixth sense for such things because I heard her slip through the door and felt her plump down beside me on the bed.

'It's time Grace, dear,' she said. And I knew that it was.

The midwife came and you were born at half past seven. They praised me for being so quick. Imagine that. As if I had anything to do with it. I hadn't had much to do with any of it. I hadn't wanted to sleep with Will. That was his idea, I just felt guilty saying no. I hadn't wanted to come here, none of us did. That was Mum's idea, I just felt guilty saying no. I hadn't even wanted a baby until I held you. And I never knew real guilt, or grief until they took you from me. I thought of Margorie, not being allowed to hold her little blue boy. Never having the chance to tell her baby how much he was loved before they parted.

I went down to the pier after I said goodbye to you, waiting for my train, and I wept. The salt tang of the ocean still takes me back to that day. When I got back home, I learned that I too had been 'working up in London'. Good grief! You have to laugh.

And here I am again. You're twenty-one today. They used to say that meant 'the key of the door.' So, I've brought you a key. It's not much but it's all I have left from those days. The key of the door behind which you were born. A small key, to a small room that gave me freedom, and laughter, and tears. I don't know why I kept it, but now I give it to you. Well, I can't give it to you. I can't see you, can't even look for you, I signed away that right on a cold day in November when they made me give you up. Six weeks, that's all we had. It wasn't enough.

I throw the key as far out to sea as I can. 'Happy birthday,' I whisper into the wind. I spy the woman on the surfboard again. She's with another girl now, they're flying on top of those waves like tiny angels out there. I hope you've found that kind of freedom in your life, a freedom I didn't dare to find until so much later. I don't even know what they called you, your new family. I called you Hope.

What We Remember
by Aimee McGowan

'It's not a good day, Allie. Been in and out mostly. She's had a wee nap and is sitting by the window.' Liam looked pained, as he did every other day when I came to visit Nan. She had been diagnosed with Alzheimer's when she was in her eighties, and now, at ninety-six, she had far surpassed everyone's expectations. Everyone commented, 'she's a tough one, your Nan,' or, 'don't worry, Allie, she'll have another good day soon. We'll phone if she happens on one.'

The phone never rang, so I made sure I was there every other day, just in case.

'Thanks, Liam, I'll just sit with her a while,' I replied, trying hard to put a contented smile on my face. Being there was never easy, especially when she had no clue who I was or why I was talking to her, but she raised me, so it was the least I could do.

He nodded and smiled back as I pulled out the tray of Turkish Delight. The care home had long since given up arguing with me about her little treats. On Tuesdays, I brought home-made mince and tatties. On Thursdays, I brought a fish supper. On Sundays, I brought Turkish Delight. It was our thing. I could never stand Turkish Delight, so she always had the box to herself, and it only made her enjoy it more, not worrying about having to share. I hung my jacket up on the peg on the back of the door and walked over to the window where she was sitting. Her room wasn't much, but it was nice; a blue feature wall was behind her bed, and just past that was the 'living room'. In reality, it was a small coffee table, two armchairs and a pull-out sofa bed in case someone wanted to stay over with her, but it was cosy enough. We'd rearranged it when she moved in with her insistence to see the ocean out the window. How she could see it past the grey clouds and haze that never seemed to leave was beyond me, but she wouldn't compromise on her view.

I made a little noise with my feet and cleared my throat, so I didn't scare her as I walked behind her chair. I learned the hard way that scaring her was a great way to get yourself a black eye and a million questions from your primary four class for a week and a half.

'Hi Nan, how are you today?' I said, as I did every other day I visited.

She turned her head to the side, as if she were expecting my kiss. My heart skipped a beat and my stomach clenched with the hope with would turn out to be a good day. They were becoming fewer and farther between this past year. I dropped my head and kissed her before settling down on the armchair beside hers. She followed me with her eyes; her forehead crinkled just a little as she tried to place me in her memories. This was progress. Sometimes, she became upset, and I'd have to sit outside for half an hour while the nurses tried to calm her down.

'Hello. I know you, don't I?' she asked, her head tilted slightly to the side the way puppies do.

'Yes, I'm your granddaughter, Allie,' I said, leaning forward in the chair. I felt like I needed to move, to do something, excitement and hope building rapidly.

'Hm,' was her only reply. I searched her face for something, but I couldn't find any indication in her milky eyes that she recognised me. I sat back in the chair as my stomach returned to normal, though it felt like it had picked up some stones somehow, leaving me heavy. We stared out the window, happy to sit in silence for a time.

'You remind me of Bessie.' She said, the croak of her barely used voice making me jump.

'Bessie?' I asked. I'd never heard her talk about a Bessie before. She rarely discussed her past except for small titbits when I was growing up; *back in my day* or *when I was wee* were her favourites, but sometimes you'd catch her smiling to herself, lost in a memory of some long ago time, but she'd never elaborate more than; 'uck, just a silly old woman remembering silly old times,' and that would be end of it.

'Mm-hm.' She said as she nodded slightly, her white hair so full of hairspray that it stayed in place as she continued to stare out the window.

'She had a set of lungs on her, you know. Best wee piper I'd ever seen.' Her voice grew stronger with each word, like it was finding itself again. She seemed surer too, like the more she spoke, the more memories she uncovered for herself. Her milky eyes became the slightest bit clearer, and her head rose just a little.

'Piped outside our jail, so she did.' She said, and I felt like I'd been punched, the air swiftly knocked from my lungs.

'Jail, Nan? You were in jail?' I spat the words. Nan knitted, mended, fundraised, cleaned, and fed everyone, whether they wanted it or not. How could she think she'd ever been to jail?

'Jail. I was twenty, I think. Can't remember now. Terrible place. What's her name now? Cannae mind.' She stared out into the distance for a while; her eyes focused on something I couldn't see. I was sure she was wrong. *Did she read this somewhere*? But this was the clearest I've seen her in a long time. But she still didn't recognise me, not really. She knew that she knew me, which was great, but didn't fully know me. I doubt she'd have begun discussing her past if she had. She had never opened up about her life. I knew she was born in 1902 and that she'd had a brief fling with a soldier who'd stopped in Edinburgh after the war. Mum had come in '46. It had never been discussed beyond that. I think her family refused to help her in her situation, and she had to bring her daughter up alone. I was born in '75, and after mum passed, she took care of me. It was about the total of what I knew about her life. The nurses were right about her being strong.

'Jennie.' She announced, as if she'd spent the whole time pondering.

'Who's Jennie, Nan?' I asked, after she'd gone silent again. I didn't want her to lose her memory again, no matter how fractured or wrong it seemed. She was remembering something, at least.

'Jennie. She got taken away, sent back. I remember, I think. Where was—she had to go—it wasn't here—America? No. I—I.

I can't. Hm.' I searched her face for signs she was going to become upset or angry, it happened sometimes, when she couldn't grasp the memory. She'd never had a temper until this horrible disease stole her away. Sometimes, she forgot she was ninety-five and was convinced she was in her forties again.

'Nan, it's ok if you don't remember.' I said, reaching out to hold her hand. Her bones stuck out beneath freezing, wafer-thin skin. I got up and got the throw from the bed and wrapped it around her.

'Thank you, Bessie. You always were a good girl.' She said, smiling up at me.

'You're welcome. Would you like a cup of tea?' I asked. In truth, I needed a moment to myself to figure out what she was talking about, each question answered only raised a hundred more.

'That would be nice. Thank you.' She replied, seeming miles away again.

I closed the door as softly as I could manage behind me, as I made my way to the tea cart in the reception room. It was filled with elderly people in wheelchairs, some on chairs with walking sticks in front of them, leaning their chins on the handles. There were a couple of women at a table shuffling cards. I recognised one that used to visit with Nan as she noticed me and waved me over.

'Hiya lass, how are you? How's Rosie doing today?' she asked, it was odd hearing her called Rosie, anyone who knew her when we were young strictly referred to her as Rose, or Miss Young.

'I'm ok, thank you. Nan's just the same, has her good days and bad,' I said, not sure how much they knew about her.

'What's today? I've not seen her out of her room in a long, long time. I worry, you know? But they tell me that she wouldn't recognise me anymore, since I only came to know her here, you know? They say the older memories are the ones they remember; anything new gets lost in there. Good or bad today?' She asked, still shuffling the cards. The other lady stared at her hands, mesmerised by the movement.

'Em. I'm actually not sure, she's talking about people I've never heard of: Bessie and Jennie. She's never talked about her past much before, so I'm not sure what she means.' I didn't tell her that she'd said she had been in jail. Whether it was true or not, it seemed to me like a betrayal of trust, and something she wouldn't ever have wanted made public.

'Oh, does she mean Bessie Watson? She was famous, before my time, of course, but I'm sure your Nan mentioned that she knew her. I might be wrong, but my old mind's a steel trap for nonsense information.' She tapped her head, then resumed shuffling. The cards had probably been shuffled so much that they were back in their original order.

'Bessie Watson?' I asked, shaking my head a little. I didn't know the name. Not that I could recall, anyway.

'Her that played the pipes.' She said, as if this would make a memory pop into my head. It didn't, unfortunately.

'I'm sorry, I don't know who that is,' I replied, my eyebrows pulling down as I tried to search my own memories. Nothing.

'Was, lass. Was. She passed away a few years back. She was amazing. A real person to look up to, you know?'

'Why? What did she do?' I asked. She'd piqued my interest, apart from needing to know why Nan had mentioned her, I was suddenly invested in knowing this woman who was a role model.

'She was the youngest suffragist. Well, North of the border, anyhow. She played the pipes at marches, piped for the women locked up, hunger striking and the like. She went to London with them, won awards or something for her contributions. She was fierce. A woman to be reckoned with. She wasn't violent, mind you. Was too young at the time, I think. But she helped whoever she could, however she could.'

She stopped moving the cards around, and the other lady must've become bored waiting and left. I took her chair, my interest compelling me to know more.

'How would Nan have known her, though? Nan wasn't a suffragist.' Not that I knew, anyway. Though the Nan I'd known and loved had led a different life from the one I knew.

'She didn't. Well, she did. They were friends. Your Nan wasn't a suffragist, but her mum was. She'd been in jail a few times, the cat and mouse act caused havoc on the family. In and out she was. Hunger strikes - your Nan nursing her back to health, then back in, so she said. Didn't she tell you any of this? It was in the news, and my own mammy kept papers for years. Took us forever to clear out her house when she passed, God rest her soul.'

She continued after that, but I couldn't keep up, my mind was whirling at this revelation. I had to go back to Nan. I stood, quicker than I'd meant to, knocking the table a bit. She fell silent and looked up at me, her eyebrows raised.

'Sorry, Violet. I need to take Nan her tea. Thanks for telling me this, I didn't know any of it. And thanks for the time you've spent with her over the years, I know she appreciated it.' I appreciated her. It seemed Nan opened to her more than she had to me in my entire life.

I made her tea and added two sugar cubes, my hands shaking slightly with the weight of the cup. I opened the door and found her still in her chair.

'Nan? I've brought your tea.' I said, hoping she wouldn't startle with my voice, and hoping against all odds that she was still in the mood to share. I put the cup on the table in front of her and sat down.

'Thank you, Bessie. You've done more for me than I could ever repay. I wish I could have gone to your funeral. When I saw it in the paper, I couldn't believe my eyes. But they wouldn't let me go. You saved me. And her. She was great, wasn't she? What they did to her, she'd scream through the night. Wake up choking on invisible tubes. She wasn't the same after that. How could she be? But your playing kept her spirits up. I will always be thankful for that.' She managed, though painfully slow. It was the most I'd heard her say in years. I couldn't reply; the emotion she had infused in each word had my throat closing and my eyes stinging. I leaned forward and gave her the cup of tea. She nodded thanks and took a sip, her hands struggling to hold the cup level.

'Bessie? I missed her.' Her voice became small again, distant and frail. She stared at the cup for a moment before looking back up at me.

'Mum, I'm tired, can I go to bed?' She said, staring at me, pleading with me, like one of my school children.

'Of course, Na—I mean, of course, Rosie. Come and I'll help you.'

I put the cup on the table and took the throw from her shoulders, carefully as I could, lifting her arm and guiding her to her bed. I pulled back the covers and didn't bother changing her out of her black joggers. They'd keep her warm and were comfortable enough, anyway. I tucked her in and gave a kiss on her forehead.

'I love you Mum, thank you.' She whispered before closing her eyes.

'I love you, too.' I said, closing the door behind me.

I went straight home and pulled out her old boxes. I hadn't been through them, not once. She'd told me we would look together at some point, but we'd never gotten around to it. There were some old records, some knick-knacks, like the stones I'd painted after our visit to Ayr beach, and the ticket she'd bought to my graduation ceremony. Right at the bottom was a medal, some newspaper clippings and an old, musty teddy bear. I held the medal up, trying to make out the engraving on the front. It was hung on a purple, yellowed white and green ribbon, with a metal bar along the bottom. The date was too worn to make out, but the words 'FED BY FORCE' were inscribed along the top. There was a small note tucked into the back where the pin was. 'Awarded posthumously in recognition of a gallant act' was all I could make out, but I'd seen this before.

My mind whirled as I tidied up and got ready for bed. I turned the lamp off and lay down when the phone rang. It was the care home. They'd checked on Nan after I left and found that she'd passed between my leaving and their check. Tears ran down my face as I listened to their condolences and details of what would happen the next day. I hung up and let myself cry, for the first time since her diagnosis. It wasn't just about her death. It was about her life. She'd gone through so much, and I didn't know half of it. One thing was for sure, though; I came from a line of strong, courageous women. I would find out their stories, then tell them.

A Moment of Grief

by Laura Scott

The spirited scent of vintage rose floats around me as I recollect my gran sitting on her velvet wing-back armchair, cradling her great-grandson for the first time. Her feathery white hair was set to perfection, her nude-pink lipstick enhanced her smile, and her skin glowed through her delicate foundation when she gazed down at him. His untainted face peered back at her through the pale-blue mountains of the fleecy blanket he was wrapped in as he soaked up her soft-spoken words.

I wish I could tell her what has happened to me, to us. I long to confide in her. Tell her, I know how it feels. No one else could know what this is like, to feel this pain. The loss, the emptiness. But my gran, she would know, she would understand. Like a geyser erupting, my tears flow, releasing the exhaustion and tension that has been building over the weeks. My body jerks forward and I fall onto my hands and knees, the pain pumping through my blood vessels—grating like razors. My wails resonate around the empty room.

I was only three years old when my grandad died of an embolism in his lung. I know this because my gran told me, more than once. I remember her telling me how she found out that day, how she was working as a nurse at the hospital, and how she was escorted down the hallway by the head nurse of the ward. She knew something was wrong when she walked past one of her good friends—a nurse who would always have a smile for you and always did her job with energy and enthusiasm—her eyes were down; she didn't look up. When Gran was taken into a waiting room, usually used for relatives of patients, she was told the news, and she crumbled to the floor.

I was so young when my grandad died, my memories are vague, but I remember my mum taking me to go and pick Gran up from work. She was sitting in an empty room, in a wooden chair, sobbing, the sound echoing. For some reason, I remember the green vinyl floor and the room feeling cold. I couldn't understand what was going on. I thought she would be happy that Grandad had gone to heaven. I remember a nurse coming in with a glass of water and a pill for my gran to swallow. I don't know if it helped much.

Gran kept my grandad's memory alive by talking about him so often, telling me stories and showing me photographs. I was told how much he adored me when she showed me a photograph of the first time he held me in his arms as a newborn baby. I am glad he got to meet me, but I wish he had met my son.

I was told the story of how they would meet up at their local dancehall. She had to sneak out of her bedroom window to go; her parents were strict and didn't like that he was Protestant and she was Catholic. When the music played for the first dance of the night, he would never actually say the words; *Do you want to dance?* But instead, he would stand on the dance floor in front of her, as she sat in the chair waiting, and he would nod his head to the side a few times. That was his signal; he didn't need to say a word. Gran would tell me how she loved to dance and how you knew you were in love with someone when you could gaze into their eyes and everyone else around you seemed to disappear. It was as though nothing else in the world mattered.

Now, as I stare at the empty chair, I gather myself in my moment of grief. I manage to crawl over to a box of tissues and dab my face. The tissue, once white, now a mish-mash of ivory beige, pink and black—the guise that conceals my worries from the world, sliding off. I recall the words my gran would say to me time and time again, 'Life is terrible without your man … terrible.' I touch my ring finger, soothing the indent left by the precious metal that was once there. I think back to how happy I was when I first met my husband and how, over the years, I would get caught up in the mundane tasks of life, not making or spending enough time with him. How naïve and unappreciative I could be at times. Death, the harsh lesson of how precious life is. While I sit on the floor and look up at Gran's empty chair, who would have known that I would be in the same position as she had been? When I used to watch her grieve over my grandad, sob over his photographs, I wondered if she would ever get better. I would think, she has me now; her other grandchildren, are we not enough? But it wasn't about that, it wasn't about us not being enough. Now I get it. Now, I understand. And I realise how terrible life is, without your man.

The Witch That Never Burnt
by Rose Campbell-Smith

"We are the granddaughters of the witches you couldn't burn."

–Silvia Federici

Scotland, 1662. The wind carried peat smoke and fear in equal measure. In these hills a woman could be a saint at dawn and a witch by dusk, and the snow kept no record of the difference. Winter pressed hard against the thatch, cold and sharp as a drawn blade. Even the fire seemed afraid to burn too brightly, as if it too might be accused.

I traced my fingertips across the rough wooden table, my touch ghostlike. The pain had dulled to an ache, but the absence is what truly haunted me. Where once my nails had been, there were only raw, uneven stubs—souvenirs of my suffering.

Because they needed someone to blame.

The flickering candlelight cast wavering shadows on the damp stone walls of my hut. I curled my hands into fists, pressing them against my lap, willing myself to forget. But memories are insidious things, creeping in no matter how hard I try to shut them out.

My mother had been the village midwife, the one they trusted with their pains and their secrets. She had delivered every squalling bairn, comforted every labouring mother. But when she took ill and died, there was no one left to care for Lady MacDonald when her time came. Ma's grave had barely settled when they summoned me to the big house late in the evening, the air thick with the scent of burning tallow and fear. Lady MacDonald was in trouble: her pains too strong, the blood too much. I did what little I could, but it was not enough: the first tiny babe was born still;

the second gasped only once before falling silent; by morning the Lady herself was gone.

I knew some things about childbirth—what herbs could ease the pain, which ones could slow the bleeding. I had watched my mother work, seen how she calmed the frightened, how her hands moved with certainty when the time came. But I was not my mother. I could not make sleeping bairns wake when the God Almighty had already called them back home. I could not breathe life into tiny lungs that would never draw air. And there is only so much blood a body can lose before there is nothing left. I was powerless. And for that, they hated me.

They turned on me almost at once. Whispers spread like fire in dry grass.

'If yer Ma had been alive, Lady MacDonald would have lived.'

'If yer Ma had been alive, the bairns would have thrived.'

But Ma was dead, and I was all that remained of her craft. Lord MacDonald did not whisper—he roared: his grief curdled into fury, his face red with wine and wrath as he pointed a trembling finger at me.

'Witch!' he bellowed. *'She took my gifts from God and gave them to the Devil!'*

Spittle flew from his lips as he advanced, his hands clenched into fists. The room had been silent before, heavy with the weight of death, but now the others stirred. Their lord had spoken, and so it must be true. The midwife's daughter had failed. The midwife's daughter had murdered. The midwife's daughter was a witch. They believe a woman can summon storms or steal life with a glance. All it took was one word—and blood would follow.

I never had a chance.

I had screamed when they took me, dragged from my home in the dead of the following night by rough hands and snarling voices. They tore me from the only life I had known and called me a witch. I had begged when they chained me, my cries swallowed by the cold, unforgiving stone of the dungeon. But mercy was not something my captors, or in this case my torturers, possessed. The first, Lord MacDonald, the master of these lands.

The second, Father McColligan, the parish priest and the third, Rab Turner, the local trapper and butcher.

All three had known me since I was a wee lass. They had known my mother—had taken her medicines when sickness swept through the village. They had known my father—had shared a drink with him more than once at the harvest feast. And yet, when the talk started, when the fear took hold, they did not hesitate.

Not even for a moment.

Father McColligan had murmured prayers as he pressed the branding iron to my thigh, burning the Devil out of me, he claimed. Rab Turner, the butcher, had done worse with his knife—also in the name of God Almighty. But the worst was the pricking; it went on for weeks. They stripped me bare, my skin exposed to the cold, and drove pins into my arms, legs, even the tender flesh beneath my ribs—watching, waiting for the place I would not feel. When I screamed, they pressed harder. When I bled, they said the Devil's mark was still hidden. They were not satisfied with pins. They sent for a bodkin from a village three day's travel to the south—a wicked thing of iron; what followed was no quieter. It was slower. It was worse. My cries filled the cold stone chamber, mingling with the scent of sweat and scorched flesh. They held my arms tight as they worked, shoving the iron deeper, turning it, waiting.

'I'll find the mark,' Rab Turner had said, his breath hot against my ear, his excitement barely contained. He jabbed and scraped with his knife, driving the metal deep into my flesh, waiting for the telltale spot that would not bleed, that would not feel. I had no Devil's mark, but it matters not. They would have torn me to pieces searching for one. That was only the beginning. They wanted a confession. It did not matter if it was true. When the needles and the bodkins failed to find the Devil's mark, they turned to cruder methods. They held me down, my wrists pinned against the rough wooden table, and pried my fingers apart.

'Confess,' Rab Turner had murmured, his breath warm against my cheek, his knife glinting in the candlelight. I clenched my jaw, refusing to give them satisfaction. The first nail came away with a sickening pop, the pain so sharp, so white-hot, that for a

moment, I could not even scream. The second came slower, peeled from the flesh with deliberate cruelty.

'Confess,' he said again, voice calm, as if he were asking me to pass the bread at supper.

By the time they reached the last, my fingers were slick with blood, my breath ragged. My body trembled, but still, I said nothing. I would not give them what they wanted. I would not lie. And so, they moved on to worse things.

Lord MacDonald watched; he watched it all, his lip curled in disgust, sipping his fine wine as I writhed in pain. He never dirtied his hands, never touched the iron or the blade, but his presence alone was enough. He was the master of this place, and they all took their cue from him. Sometimes, in the flickering candlelight, Lord MacDonald looked like the Devil himself. The shadows stretched his face, deepened the hollows of his cheeks, made his eyes gleam like embers in the dark. And though he sneered as if repulsed, I saw it—that wild glint of pleasure that slipped through when he thought no one was looking. He enjoyed this.

Not the way Rab Turner did, with his knives and his sweat-slicked hands. Not the way Father McColligan did, chanting his prayers between my screams. No, Lord MacDonald relished the suffering from a distance, savouring it like his fine wine, slow and rich on his tongue. He thought himself above it all. But he would suffer just the same.

As I lay chained on the cold floor, alone and powerless, they came on different nights again and again—Rab the butcher, and the Lord. Each took from me what could never be returned. They thought it a secret, each believing the other knew nothing. But I knew. And if Father McColligan had ever found out, he'd have had us all burnt for it.

They had broken me, starved me, bled me dry, all without any evidence being presented against me. Yet I had endured for months, waiting and praying for the justice of peace to come and settle the matter; either way, I needed it to end. And when the trial came, it was little more than a spectacle—no search for truth, only a stage for old grudges and wounded pride. The Justice of the Peace had no love for Lord MacDonald, and the trial became his chance to wound the Lord, not to save me—so in the end, it was spite, not mercy, that set me free. They stripped me of dignity, not life—and hatred is all they left me to wear. There was no apology. No recompense. Only the bitter wind against my bruised skin as they cast me back into the world, they had ripped me from. Luck was on my side, though justice was not. I was innocent, but only because two powerful men chose to wound each other, and I was their weapon—a choice they would live to regret.

I was young, unmarried, with my whole life ahead of me. But after what they had done, who would have me now? Once, they called me bonnie. My hair shone like rippling water in the sun, and my cheeks flushed with the warmth of youth. Men used to steal glances when I passed, and the village women would sigh, saying I would have no trouble finding a husband. But they stripped that from me. Now, look at me. Even though I had been declared innocent, I bear the scars of their cruelty. My skin marked with burns and bruises. And inside, something was broken—shattered and rearranged. Would I ever have children? Even if my body could endure it, my soul may not. I was not the same girl who had been dragged into the dark. I had been reborn in agony, reforged in hatred. And now—it was time.

The moon hangs heavy in the sky as I move through the village, a wraith in the night. The air is thick with the scent of damp earth and lingering smoke from hearth fires now reduced to embers. My bare feet make no sound on the dirt path, but I feel every stone, every sharp twig biting into my soles—a reminder that I am still flesh, still alive, though I should not be. The houses huddle together, dark and silent, their thatched roofs glistening with frost. A dog whimpers somewhere in the distance, sensing the storm that walks among them. The wind breathes softly through the narrow streets, carrying the mingled smells of cold ash, alcohol, and unwashed bodies. The scent of blood will soon join them.

The butcher's hut is first in my path. The reek of blood clings to the walls, thick and metallic, seeping into the wooden beams. Soon, it will not be only from animals. On the right, a freshly cut side of veal hangs beside a sheep carcass, their exposed flesh pale in the dim light. To the left, a butcher block sits stained and well-worn, a neat row of knives resting atop it, their edges gleaming. Rab Turner had always been so fond of his knives—I shall let him see how sharp they truly are. I pick up two of the largest blades, their weight unfamiliar in my hands. The curtain—a thin sheet strung across the room—sways gently in the night breeze. I pull it back. He is sprawled on his back, the heavy rise and fall of his chest betraying deep sleep. I kneel beside him, so close I can hear the slow, wet rasp of his breath.

Leaning in, I hiss, 'I'm here to confess.' His eyes flutter open, unfocused at first. Then they lock onto mine. Recognition dawns—too late. The first knife sinks into his throat, silencing him before he can cry out. The second drives into his belly, using both hands and all my might—hard, deep, and twisting. His body jerks, a gurgling wet sound escaping his lips as blood spills over my hands, hot and thick. His wet screams die as swiftly as his heartbeat.

Father McColligan prays for salvation in the church, but none comes. His voice rises inside as I strike the flint. Sparks fall onto the rush matting, which smoulders, then flares—flames crawling along the dried reeds toward the tapestries. The fire climbs eagerly, devouring the fabric, the pulpit. It rises, winding like a serpent along the rafters, feeding on the beams that once sheltered his sermons. I stand outside, rope in hand, ready to seal his fate. Through the growing inferno, our eyes meet. His lips stop moving. For a moment, his prayers falter as realisation dawns. I pull the rope tight, lashing the doors shut. Instantly, his fists pound against the wood.

'In God's holy name—open this door! I beg you—let me out!' But there is no mercy left in me. His pleas dissolve into screams, rising with the fire—then silenced by its roar. I watch as the flames engulf the church, the holy man still inside, his faith reduced to cinders. His God does not come.

Lord MacDonald's manor is last. He wakes to the sensation of cold steel pressing against his throat. His breath hitches, his body tensing beneath me. I sit astride his chest, his own dagger clasped in my hands, its tip poised just above the place where his pulse thrums wildly. For the first time, he begs.

'Please… stop.' I smile. He had never listened when I begged. When I had cried for them to stop. I put all my weight behind the blade and push. A wet gasp escapes his lips as the steel sinks in, tearing through skin, muscle, life itself. The red of his blood seeps from him, spreading across the white pillows like spilt wine. It flows, rich and dark, pooling around his head like a twisted crown. As I stand, I let my fingers brush carelessly against the oil lamp on the bedside table. It tips, tumbles, and shatters against the floor. The flames leap instantly, licking hungrily at the heavy drapes that frame the bed. They spread with terrifying ease, climbing, consuming, devouring. I do not run. Down the stairs, my feet carry me with steady purpose. I cross the grand entryway, past gilded portraits and tapestries that will soon turn to ash. At the massive front door, I pause only to pull it closed.

Ahead of me, the night is dark, the air crisp, the road open. Behind me the village burns, smoke curling into the heavens as I walk away. I do not look back. There is nothing left for me there. No more pain. No more fear. No more monsters. Only the road ahead, bathed in silver moonlight, and the promise of freedom. Each breath I take is heavy with the lives I have ended. Behind every strong woman is a story that gave her no choice. I carry the weight of what I've done like a second skin—never far, never forgotten. Strength was never what I wanted. It was what was left to me.

If you look for me in the history books, you will not find me. There will be no record of my torture, no mention of my freedom, nor a whisper of my vengeance. Because it is 'His-story,' remember! And men do not write about the things they got deadly wrong. I have walked out of fire and shadow into my own story. I am Ava McGregor, the witch they never burnt. I lived—and in my daughters, I will live forever.

A Grandmother's Love Is Forever and Always

by Rose Campbell-Smith

Life before Granny was complicated—let's just say it was not a life for children. But that all changed when she became my world, my anchor. My brother was seven and I was five, old enough to know—she would say something once and expect it to be done. Granny wasn't one for repeating herself, and she certainly wasn't one for nonsense.

She had a way of making the world feel steady, like the ground beneath our feet wasn't going to shift anymore. Mornings smelled of porridge and milky tea, evenings of lavender soap and the faint scent of coal dust from the fireplace.

When she tucked us in at night, she'd always say, 'You're safe now, and that's that.' No arguments, no doubts—just the solid truth of her voice wrapping around us like a warm woolly blanket.

My brother and I travelled through the Scottish Highlands and Lowlands with my grandmother many times as children. My Granny was a masterful storyteller; we were captivated by the stories she would weave—of kelpies in the lochs, of warriors and poets, of great feasts in grand halls. Summers were spent at the loch, the sun beating down, sparkling on the dark water. Winters brought snow-filled glens, towering drifts I could lose myself in, white-capped trees, and frozen waters perfect for monsters to hide beneath.

At home in the hush of night, as the moon cast its silvery glow through the window, nestled beside her, I would listen to her soft murmurs, as she would unfold entire worlds, painting vivid landscapes filled with vibrant characters and rich folklore. Her voice, a gentle melody, would conjure images of mythical creatures and brave heroes, transporting me to realms where the impossible felt within reach. These tales, laced with lessons and wisdom, became the very foundation of my imagination. The cadence of her voice, the fascinating images she painted with words—I hung on every sentence. Without realising it, I was learning the power of storytelling—how words could transport, comfort, and even shape the way we saw the world.

As I grew older, the rush of daily life and the blaring cacophony of the digital age dulled those stories to mere whispers. Books still lined my shelves, but Granny's voice—her stories—became a distant hum. I didn't know it then, but I was letting go of something precious. The magic of my childhood, once joyful and boundless, became buried beneath responsibilities and the relentless passage of time.

It wasn't until I became a parent, delving back into the enchanting stories that had once captured my imagination as a child, that I felt a flicker of the lost wonder and magic resurface within me. Those tales, filled with adventures and lessons, ignited a spark I thought long extinguished. Reading aloud to my daughter, I heard echoes of Granny in my own voice, felt the magic stir again. It was different, though—now I wasn't just a listener; I was shaping stories myself, passing them down. However, as my daughter entered her teenage years, that flicker began to fade, replaced by the all-too-familiar challenges of adolescence—where innocence gave way to cynicism, and the allure of storytelling lost its glow amid the chaos of growing up. I watched her drift away from bedtime tales, just as I once had. It was a bittersweet realisation, watching the enchantment vanish as she navigated the complexities of her teenage world, and I went back to my rush of daily life.

Then bam—COVID-19 hit like a tsunami. The Coronavirus (SARS-CoV-2) outbreak was sudden and terrifying. No one saw it coming. One day, life was normal—work, routine, plans for the future—and the next, the world seemed to shut down overnight. At first, I didn't know how far it would go or what it would mean for my life. I remember sitting at home, watching the news, feeling a growing sense of unease. Reports of millions infected, hospitals overflowing, and rising death tolls made me realise just how fragile human life is.

Like many families, we feared the virus and its potential to snatch away our loved ones. It was during the final years of my grandmother's life that the world grappled with lockdowns and isolation. Faced with uncertainty, I made the difficult choice to leave my job and become her full-time caregiver. The days stretched into weeks, then months, each moment shadowed by the weight of the unknown. But those long, quiet days weren't just about routine; they became a journey back in time.

Together, Granny and I unearthed old photographs, revisited memories, and she told her stories again, and this time, I wrote them down. In the stillness of lockdown, I found myself reaching for the stories that had once felt like home—not just her tales of sea monsters and warriors, but the real stories—the tales of her youth, her resilience, her love.

I found myself writing more, not just for her, but for myself. The act of putting words to paper felt like reaching back through time, reconnecting with something I had almost lost. Granny had given me more than just stories—she had given me a way to understand the world, to make sense of grief, love, and time itself. In a world that seemed to be unravelling, we stitched together the threads of our past, holding onto them as an anchor.

Outside, the streets weren't just quiet—they were still in a strange, frightening way. Panic buying emptied shelves, and essential workers became the backbone of a fragile society. But inside our little world, I found something unexpected: connection, understanding, and a kind of peace amidst the storm, a gift amidst the crisis. The global pandemic, as devastating as it was, gifted many of us with something unexpected: time. Time to reflect, to reconsider, to reconnect.

It changed our lives in ways I never imagined. It brought fear and loss, but also moments of reflection and rediscovery. And though those days were heavy with uncertainty, they left me with something I will always cherish—the time I spent with my grandmother, the stories we shared, and the love that carried us through.

I have always perceived time as a slow and conscious force, moving with its own rhythm, like a dance that deepens our connection to the moments and experiences that shape us. Unlike the fast-paced contemporary world, time, to me, is not merely a march from one moment to the next but a series of deliberate, meaningful steps. This perspective offers a richer existence, reminding us that life is fleeting and must be savoured—and we did. Little did I know that it would be our last chapter together.

On the summer solstice, the longest day of 2021, as the sun stretched into the evening, our journey together reached its end. As the sun dipped below the horizon, I lost not just my grandmother, but my best friend, my mentor, and my guiding light. She was not alone. My daughter and I—her "two special girls"—held her hands until the very end, whispering words of love, gratitude, and quiet goodbyes. It broke my heart to see her go, to watch the final moments of the woman who had shaped so much of who I am. In that still, sacred moment, we clung to her just as she had always held us—with warmth, with strength, with an unbreakable bond. The longest day became the hardest, one in which our family said goodbye to its most cherished storyteller, our timeless legend, and though the world felt emptier without her, the stories she gifted us would live on, forever woven into the fabric of our hearts and minds.

I recall the warmth of Granny's embrace—the safety, the love, the forever. The way she'd pull me close when we cooried in, asking, 'how much do I love you?' And I, in innocent uncertainty, would respond, 'I don't know.' Her answer always came with a gentle squeeze: 'As much as I can cuddle you.'

She regaled me with tales of Fairy Queens, and brave warriors, and her songs—oh, her songs were like soothing lullabies, that filled the air on stormy nights and dreary afternoons. Her melodies and stories were the balm for my tears, the comfort during times of sickness and sadness.

Now she's gone, but love remains—constant, like time itself. And so do the stories.

Granny made me a storyteller before I even knew I wanted to write. She showed me how words could hold a life together, how they could carry love across generations. Even now, when I sit down to write, I hear her voice, steady and sure. And I know—just as she promised—some things never truly die. I have come to realise that much like time itself, love is a dance that never really stops. It lingers in the echoes of laughter, the warmth of old stories—and she, my hero, my Granny, is still twirling within it.

Sneezing In the Clouds
by Robin Montgomery-Smith

Arkansas, USA, 1977

I winced as I sat in my seat on the school bus. The scrape, which was just starting to bleed through my tights, was not as bad as I thought. I rubbed it with the end of my scarf, my nose crinkling with the discomfort.

Beads of sweat sat unmoving on my forehead from the run to the bus stop. My alarm had failed to wake me on time, and I was lucky to have caught the bus just as the doors were closing. Mrs Dutch, always smiling, noticed me limping towards the bus stop and hesitated just long enough for me to make it.

'Why you limpin'?' she asked as I clambered up the steep steps.

'Fell—on—the way.'

'You okay, sweetheart?'

'Yes, ma'am.'

I pushed my way through long legs, stretched out to trip me to my usual seat, throwing myself down, thankful I had made it. Our school bus was always loud, but Mrs Dutch never seemed to be worried about it. A few stops later, I was waiting for everyone else to get off before limping down the step last, as usual.

'You have a good day, sweetheart, ya hear?'

'Thank you, Mrs Dutch.'

The day at school competed with that morning for which was worse. At recess, I was sitting on a bench reading a book and a group of girls approached me. Kaylee was standing in front, her wiry hair pushing out of the elastic band she wore to pull it back. Her arms crossed, she spoke down her nose at me.

'I heard you called me a bitch.'

Without looking up from my book, but no longer reading, my heart was beating in my throat, and I felt the heat spread all over my face.

'Kaylee, I didn't call you anything.'

'Stephanie said she heard you talking about me.'

'I don't talk about anybody.'

'I believe Stephanie.'

'Okay.'

'So you did call me a bitch, then.'

I sighed. I knew what was coming and I braced myself. I closed my book and slid it into my backpack. I raised my head to face her just as her hand slapped me so hard that I lost my breath. I sat still. I dared not move. She slapped me again. I didn't fall over, but it took me a little longer to sit up straight again. Lava-tears streamed down my face. There were no sounds other than the thump of my heart, now in my ears, and Kaylee's laughter as she threw strike after strike, unmatched by my refusal to fight back.

Her cackles were broken when another girl pushed through the crowd and pulled Kaylee away from me. Terry was bigger and most of the mean girls in my school feared her. I drew in a deep breath, hoping my punishment for being small, shy, and withdrawn, was over. A teacher ran into the melee and pulled Kaylee out of the crowd by her collar, screaming at her. I felt a tug on my hair as one of the girls who had been standing behind me reminded me who was in charge before she walked away.

'You okay?' Terry stayed behind as the crowd dispersed.

'Yeah.'

She sat next to me on the bench and lifted my chin, assessing the damage.

'It hurt?'

'Nah, it's fine. Happens all the time.'

'Whatcha readin'?'

'The Count of Monte Cristo.'

'Ain't heard o' that one. Is it any good?'

'I like it.'

'It's thick, though, huh?'

'Yeah.'

'Why do they pick on you?'

'Dunno.' I shrugged my shoulders.

'I'll keep an eye out, 'K?'

'For what?'

'Them,' she pointed at a clutch of girls, whispering to themselves, their eyes cutting towards the two of us on the bench. 'They'll leave you alone. Trust me.'

'Why?'

'Why will they leave you alone? Because I'll fuckin' make them, that's why.'

'No, I mean, why—me?'

'You ain't like them. You're nice to everybody. I reckon you're pretty smart, too, 'cos you're readin' all the time.'

'I guess.'

The bell rang and we all fell into lines to file back into our classrooms. The principal was standing just inside the door and pulled me aside. He lifted my face in his meaty hand, turning my head from one side to the other.

'You bleedin' anywhere, girl?

'I don't think so.'

'What started it?'

I shrugged.

'Speak up. Then who started it?'

I shrugged again.

'Kaylee said you hit her first. That true?'

'No, sir.'

'So, she hit you first?'

I shrugged. My eyes grew blurry with tears threatening to fall onto my still stinging cheeks.

'Get to class. Stay out of trouble.'

I pulled my backpack close to me as I walked into the classroom. I paid little attention to anything my teachers said in any of my lessons. I was glad when I heard at lunch that Kaylee had been sent home for the rest of the day. At least I knew I could get home without another incident.

I took my time walking back from the bus stop that afternoon. I walked the long way home and when I arrived, my mother was waiting for me. She sat in her chair, legs crossed, the one on top swinging. A lit cigarette dangled from her lips. She held it and took a long draw, then blew the smoke out before speaking.

'Where have you been?'

'At school.'

'You know what I mean. Why did it take you so long to get home after the bus?'

'It was late.' I hated lying to my mother, but the words just tumbled out of my mouth before I could stop them.

'You need to get the dishes done.'

I looked over my shoulder, out of the window. The daylight was shorter this time of year and I knew if I didn't get outside soon, it would be too dark.

'You can go outside when you do the dishes.'

Without a word, I put my backpack in my room, changed out of my school clothes, and while standing on a stool because my small frame wasn't tall enough to reach the sink, I washed the dishes from dinner the night before and my mother's dishes from breakfast and lunch that day. I rinsed them, dried them, and put them away, dragging the stool over to the built-in kitchen cabinet.

'Momma, I'm done with the dishes. Can I go outside?'

'Are they dry?'

'Yes, ma'am.'

'Put away?'

'Yes, ma'am.'

'Did you clean the sink? And the counters?'

'Yes, ma'am.'

'All right. I guess you can go outside for a bit. Be back in here before dark, ya hear me?'

'I will, Momma.'

I made a break for the door and stepped down onto the brown grass which spotted the ground in front of the house. Trees lined the space between the street and the yard. Everything was dusty. There was never any green grass. I walked around the yard before I noticed Grandma sitting on her front porch next door. The whir of the pea sheller Grandpa had made for her from an old washing machine, droned into the open spaces between our yard and hers. I walked towards her and when she saw me, she pulled her foot off the pedal and grinned. I did not return her smile.

'Aww, my girl. Come here. Come to Grandma.'

I walked in zigzags, kicking rocks and clumps of grass on the way.

My shoulders slumped, my head down, hair in my face, I climbed up the concrete steps to the front porch and leant into Grandma's open arms. She kissed my forehead and pushed me back so she could see my face.

'What's the matter? Tell Grandma what's wrong.'

'Nuthin', Grandma.'

'Somethin's the matter. You never have this sour look on your face.'

'Just a bad day.'

'A bad day, huh? Tell me all about it.'

I leaned my head on her soft shoulder, breathed in the vanilla she always used as perfume, and told her everything.

'That is a bad day,' she whispered as she pulled me in close, tightening her arms around me, as if to squeeze the bad day away—'You know what? If I could, I'd lift you up so high that you'd sneeze in the clouds.'

I pulled back and looked at her face. 'Grandma! You can't reach that high.'

'But if I could, I would. Then you wouldn't fall on your way to the bus, deal with mean girls at school, or ever have to do dishes on a stool again. You'd be too busy sneezin' to worry about all that other stuff.'

I have no idea if it was Grandma's firm, loving hug, or her words about lifting me up, but I felt somehow lighter. After helping her finish shelling the peas from Grandpa's farm, I walked back home, just next door, but I stood taller, my head higher, and my long hair flowing behind me. I imagined Grandma picking me up and stretching so far to put me in the clouds. I kept that image with me.

Over the years, whenever I see someone I care about feeling unsure about themselves or notice their self-esteem has had a kick, I repeat Grandma's words.

'If I could, I'd lift you so high, you'd sneeze in the clouds.'

The effect still works. Every single time.

MEET THE SISTERS

Author Biographies

Rose Campbell-Smith

A GRANDMOTHER'S LOVE IS FOREVER AND ALWAYS
A CHAT WITH PAT ⌘ PHOENIX RISING
UNTANGLING TIME ⌘ WAVES OF SISTERHOOD
MY BRIDGE TO NOWHERE
THE WITCH THAT NEVER BURNT
WAVES OF SISTERHOOD

Rose Campbell-Smith lives beside the sea in East Lothian, Scotland, with her long suffering husband and her big, lazy dog. Rose is the mother of a 25-year-old daughter, a community volunteer and a regular surfer. Currently studying for an Open University degree, Rose has a wide variety of interests, including environmental science and Latin, as well as her true love, writing.

A huge thank you to my husband, John, my daughter, Lauryn, and all my family and friends for their amazing love and support. To those who've left footprints on my heart—your love and guidance will stay with me forever.

Scotland, my beautiful home, thank you for your stories and spirit that inspire me every day.

And to the teachers, mentors, and friends who've helped me grow—your wisdom means the world. I'm so grateful to have shared this journey with you all.

Heather Grossart

CUCKOO ⌘ LIFE IS SWEET

Heather hates writing bios and she's old enough to put her foot down and not do it. She also hates photos.

She would like to thank everyone who tolerates her.

Michele Hinchliffe

MARY MARY ✕ MOTHER'S DAY
THIS IS WHERE WE ARE NOW

Michele Hinchliffe grew up on the West Coast of Scotland. When she isn't at her laptop she can usually be found on an Ayrshire beach with her dog or in the Atlantic hanging out with the seals.

My thanks to Bob for his encouragement, tolerance and sheer endurance. And to Margaret and Walter for always showing up and leading with love.

Aimee McGowan

20lb. 13s. 4d. ✤ *BEETROOT* ✤ *IT ONLY TOOK ONE*
WHAT WE REMEMBER

Growing up in Scotland gave Aimee a deep love of nature and family bonds. She uses these loves in her writing, creating emotional and meaningful stories. Aimee is a health and safety consultant by day, pet lover and baker by night. When she's not writing, Aimee spends her time completing her degree at The Open University, volunteering for her local school and taking care of her two little boys.

Aimee values family, and would like to thank her Nanny Ann, Mum Sandra, Karen, and sister Abbie: Thanks for being so strong and kind, I couldn't do it without you. A huge thank you to her two boys, who show her that life doesn't need to be full of adventure to appreciate its beauty.

Robin Montgomery-Smith

I WAITED FOR YOU ✤ *JOSIE'S SECRET*
THE DANCE ✤ *THE GLISTENING MAN*
SNEEZING IN THE CLOUDS

A storyteller and lover of language with one foot in fiction and the other in real life (and occasionally tripping over both), Robin Montgomery-Smith writes short tales and is currently wrangling a historical fiction novel into submission. She's been published in online magazines, trade journals, and once self-published a book inspired by her own life events—proof that questionable decisions make excellent plot twists. Armed with a first-class honours degree in English Literature & Creative Writing, she lives in Scotland, where she's been long enough to call drizzle a personality trait.

I want to thank my husband, Peter for his love and unwavering support, my children and grandchildren for keeping my feet on the ground, my friends and extended family for always cheering me on, and of course these amazing women who have allowed me to join them in the wonderful journey to finishing this epic project. But I have to give special thanks to my grandparents, Harold and Jessie, because without them, I would not be the me I am today.

Charity Reed

FIVE FIND A BODY ⁂ REFLECTIONS ⁂ HOPE
A PERFECT ARRANGEMENT
IN SEARCH OF STRAWBERRIES

Originally from Cumbria, Charity's love of nature and awful weather has seen her move further north to rural Scotland. A writer of short stories and poetry, she tends to focus on whatever pops into her head at the time – usually around the themes of love and family, nature, sci-fi, and murder. Having graduated from the Open University with a first class BA (Honours) in English and Creative Writing, she loved it so much she's now embarked on a master's.

Charity would like to thank her incredibly talented parents, Helen and Trevor, for passing on a little of their genetics, Debs, Ruth and Jesse for being there throughout everything, Declan for being the most discerning reader ever, Jude, Amis, Aggie and Ada for giving her some small sense of responsibility, Irene Hossack for being an inspirational tutor, and Dr Sharon Goodman for all her support.

Laura Scott

A MOMENT OF GRIEF ꕤ *A RARE NIGHT IN*
CLOSE TO THE EDGE ꕤ *LAUNCH DAY*
RED SUEDE HEELS

Laura Scott lives in Central Scotland and began journaling and writing poetry to help cope with her grief when she was widowed in 2018. She has an artistic background — previously working as a make-up and lash artist within her own beauty salon. She enjoys drawing, painting and reading in her spare time and is currently in her final year of a BA (Honours) Arts & Humanities Degree (Creative Writing). You can read more of her writing on Substack: https://open.substack.com/pub/laurascott

Laura would like to thank her family for all their motivation and support. A special thanks to her son, they have been one another's rock, establishing a stronger relationship in the past seven years as they navigate their grief together.

And to all the inspiring women she has met through this process, she wouldn't be here without them.

Gaynor Adkins

COVER ILLUSTRATOR

Gaynor is an illustrator and the founder of Quirky Queen Illustrations. Her work is bold, blending curiosity, provocation and humour, to explore themes of social justice, inclusion, and identity.

With a First Class BA (Hons) from The Open University and an upcoming MA in Illustration at Falmouth University, Gaynor blends punk aesthetics, visual symbols and patterns with layered meaning, and joyful defiance. The cover for *Cloud Sneezing* stitches together themes of female empowerment, elevation, sisterhood, matriarchy, into a patchwork of resilience. Gaynor's illustrations are designed to provoke thought, spark curiosity, and deliver messages that matter.

Lee A. Jackson

EDITORIAL DIRECTOR

Author, editor, and story evangelist.

Stories are how we make sense of the world, share our knowledge, and build connections. I took on the editing and organizing of this anthology project to help a new batch of emerging authors do just that. I am honored to be a part of their efforts.

I've been a writer and editor in various industries for forty years. I have degrees, honours, certifications, and whatnot—some from the days just before the internet became a thing—but now I impart my knowledge of story craft to engineers, researchers, and administrators at NASA.

In my free time, I write speculative fiction, study everything writing, and coach writers and editors. I live in Cleveland, Ohio with my family of humans and cats, more books than shelves, and cabinets full of collectable curiosities.

A note for our readers: *Most of the writing in this anthology uses British spelling and punctuation. There are also 'Britishisms' and Scots dialect. These are not errors. These and some other words, phrases, and creative choices were made by the authors themselves and intentionally preserved for artistic purposes.*

AFTERWORD: The View from the Clouds

To hold this book in your hands is to stand with us at the summit of a journey that began, rather fittingly, in a digital common room. What started as individual pursuits—students of the Open University, each quietly honing her craft—blossomed into a collective, vibrant force. We became 'the sisters', bound not by blood, but by ink, critiques, mutual encouragement, and an unwavering commitment to telling women's stories.

The title, *Cloud Sneezing*, perfectly captures the spirit of this project. It is the joy and sheer exuberance of aspiring so high, of lifting one another up past the treeline and into the atmosphere, until we are collectively achieving something that, individually, might have felt too distant to attempt. It's the delightful, slightly ridiculous feeling of having achieved a dream through shared effort and laughter.

Within these pages, you have read portraits of courage, resilience, and the quiet, often fierce, ways women navigate the world. These stories, penned by women for women, reflect the diverse experiences and voices of our collective—a testament to the fact that when we support one another, there is no limit to the heights we can reach.

This anthology is the product of passion, certainly. It is the result of countless hours of peer editing, late-night chats, and the kind of honest feedback only true friends can give.

Our deepest hope is that the bonds forged in the writing of this book—the sisterhood that powered its creation—are felt in the reading of it. Thank you for joining us on this elevated journey.

Keep reaching high, and don't forget to look up.

— The Sisters of the Melius Scripto Common Room

WAVES OF SISTERHOOD
by Rose Campbell-Smith

In the rhythm of water, I find calm in the tide.
Let go of chaos, with sisters beside.
The tide's sweet embrace, a whisper, a guide,
uncovering strength, no longer must hide.

With each wave that breaks, my worries recede.
The surf sings of hope, of love, of need.
Sun-kissed horizons and salt in our hair,
we dive into healing, releasing our cares.

Ice-cold waters crash, a jolt to the skin.
Excitement like thunder, surges within.
Another bolt, I paddle through fears.
Laughter and frolic give way to my tears.

Bound by the water, by laughter, by grace,
in every swell, we reclaim our space.
In each splash, in each swell, stories unfold:
of healing, of sisterhood, of courage bold.

So here's to the waters, the tides that we ride,
with each wave we conquer, we stand side by side.
In the depths of the surf, we are wild, we are free.
Finding peace in the currents, together, you and me.

Scottish Women's Aid

One last thing, The Sisters are proud to support Scottish Women's Aid with a portion of the proceeds from this book, ensuring that the strength found in these narratives extends into real-world action. Ten percent of all royalties from *Cloud Sneezing* will support their vital work in protecting and empowering women.

Scottish Women's Aid is the leading organisation in Scotland working towards the prevention of domestic abuse. Since 1976, they have been at the forefront of shaping responses to domestic abuse in Scotland. They are proud of the work they do, with a wide range of partners, to achieve change in Scotland, across the UK, and internationally, striving toward a shared vision of a world where domestic abuse is not tolerated.

If you need advice or support, please call.
Helpline: 0800 027 1234

If you feel you can donate more, please use the Scottish Women's Aid QR code below.

scottish women's aid
#SC001099

Acknowledgements

The sisters would like to thank the Open University for bringing us together, the tutors who taught us how to get better at our craft, and Ed Swithenby who set up the common room in which we began this journey.

There are so many people who've supported us personally though this, and we've thanked them on our bio pages—but we would also like to thank Melius Scripto Press International for taking a chance on the book. We've learned so much from them and they've been wonderful putting up with all our questions, inexperience, and a democratic process.

Lastly, because it has been a democratic process, we'd like to thank each other for all the hard work that's gone into it. Through all the highs and lows of this journey, we really have lifted each other high enough to sneeze in the clouds—achoo!!

Finis

MELIUS SCRIPTO
PRESS INTERNATIONAL

http://www.meliusscriptopress.com

Printed in Dunstable, United Kingdom

77449347R00137